# PRAISE FOR
# JULIA BRYAN THOMAS

"Julia Bryan Thomas has ensured that readers of *For Those Who Are Lost* will never forget the children of Guernsey displaced during World War II. This is a captivating and complex story about family, about deception, about flawed characters in inconceivable circumstances, and about the power of love to both damage and heal."

—Kelly Mustian, author of *The Girls in the Stilt House*

"This richly layered story about losing, finding, and forgiving unfolds when a Nazi threat to an innocent island off the coast of France is imminent. Desperate action is taken and children are sent into the unknown where destinies are altered. Then the isolation and pressures of a tedious war beget heartaches and heroes. *For Those Who Are Lost* is riddled with secrets and sins for the sake of survival. Kudos to Thomas for a poignant and compelling read."

—Leah Weiss, bestselling author of
*If the Creek Don't Rise* and *All the Little Hopes*

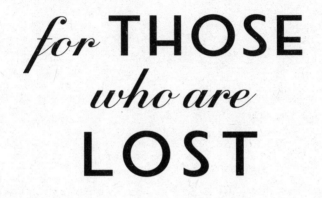

*for* THOSE *who are* LOST

# for THOSE who are LOST

### A NOVEL

## JULIA BRYAN THOMAS

Published by Sourcebooks Landmark, an imprint of Sourcebooks
P.O. Box 4410, Naperville, Illinois 60567–4410
(630) 961-3900
sourcebooks.com

Library of Congress Cataloging-in-Publication Data

Names: Thomas, Julia, author.
Title: For those who are lost : a novel / Julia Thomas.
Description: Naperville, Illinois : Sourcebooks Landmark, [2022]
Identifiers: LCCN 2022002456 (print) | LCCN 2022002457 (ebook) |
  (trade paperback) | (epub)
Subjects: LCGFT: Novels.
Classification: LCC PS3620.H6286 F67 2022  (print) | LCC PS3620.H6286
  (ebook) | DDC 813/.6--dc23
LC record available at https://lccn.loc.gov/2022002456
LC ebook record available at https://lccn.loc.gov/2022002457

Printed and bound in the United States of America.
VP 10 9 8 7 6 5 4 3 2 1

*To Sherry, for the time when we were lost*

# PART ONE

# 1

---

*Lily*

It doesn't make for sanity, does it, living with
the devil.

—DAPHNE DU MAURIER, *REBECCA*

He told her she could not go; therefore, she would go. Lily Carré
stood in her bedroom, inspecting her image in the tall, oval mirror
that had belonged to her grandmother. She wore her best frock, and
over it, she slipped on her emerald-green coat, buttoning the cloth
buttons and tying the sash about her narrow waist. She adjusted
the beret on her head, smoothing the auburn locks back from her
face. Giving herself a critical last look, she opened her handbag to
make certain everything was in order. Her papers, her shiny gold
compact mirror, her favorite lip rouge—a few letters tied with blue

ribbon. Snapping it shut, she turned to inspect the valise on the bed to see if she had forgotten anything, because she wasn't coming back. Inside, she had packed a few dresses, her best nightgown and wrap, a new pair of stockings, her mother's gold charm bracelet, and an umbrella. Britain would be as wet as Guernsey, perhaps wetter. Lily started to close the case and then opened it again, reaching for a book on the dresser, *Rebecca* by Daphne du Maurier. It was a new copy. She had worn out the last one, and it had only been published two years earlier.

For a moment, she twisted the diamond ring on her finger, wondering if she should remove it, deciding not to. She could sell it if she needed money. Closing the case, she went downstairs and set it by the front door.

The house was silent. Lily turned and walked through each of the rooms slowly, as if to seal them in her memory. She had lived there since the day she married Ian. Though it was even grander than she imagined, she had loved it from the first moment she had seen it. Her parents had been delighted at her good fortune. They were innocents, of course, who believed having money was the key to happiness and a good life. Lily had been disabused of that notion almost from the start. What was a home without love, she wondered, but an empty shell? It had become an unbearable situation.

Glancing at her watch, she went into Ian's study to give it a final look. She loved that room in particular: the marble fireplace with the clock over the mantel, the leather-bound books lining the shelves along the wall, the sturdy leather chair where Ian sat in the evenings, smoking his pipe and reading the newspaper, the settee upholstered in pearl-white roses where she would sit near him while doing needlepoint. They lived like kings compared with many of the other islanders. It would be hard to let it all go. Hard, but not impossible. She went over to the bookshelf where Ian kept a large French *tabac* jar and opened the lid. Although it still smelled of tobacco, it hadn't been used for that purpose in more than a year, perhaps longer. Most of Ian's money was in the bank, of course, but he was a suspicious, stubborn man who always kept a large reserve of funds hidden in case he ever needed it. Lily reached inside and pulled out a faded velvet bag, opening it only long enough to make certain every pound note was there. She wasn't supposed to know of its existence, but she had once spied him sliding something inside and had looked in it the following day after he had left the house. He was unaware he had given her the means to leave him.

Lily gathered her things and pulled the door closed behind her, not bothering to lock it. She picked up her case and went down the path to the gate, steeling herself for the walk down the steep road to the school. Her heart thumped harder than usual with the velvet bag in her possession, its heft making her handbag sway against her arm with every step.

For five years, she had been a dutiful wife. She had honored and obeyed her husband and kept her vows, overlooking Ian's flaming temper. She had hidden black eyes and deep, painful bruises, careful never to let anyone see the havoc he wreaked on her life. It had been particularly difficult to conceal it from her parents. She was forced to tell them she kept catching colds in order to keep them away from the house. She had endured the pain of childlessness and the hopeless feeling that she could never change her life. Each day became more difficult than the one before until finally, she couldn't stay.

Sweat began to form on her brow now, and she unbuttoned her coat and removed her beret, putting it into the case before trudging forward. She had wanted to leave him for years but hadn't known how. But with the ever-looming threat of war, she knew if she didn't leave now, she might never be able to escape.

It was the twentieth of June. The Allies had retreated from Dunkirk sixteen days earlier, spreading fear across the Channel Islands that German occupation was imminent. France had fallen. There was no longer a buffer between the Germans and Guernsey, a self-governing dependency of the British Crown, which was situated a mere thirty miles off the coast of Normandy. The English soldiers who protected them had shipped out, leaving the islanders to their fate. Everyone knew it was only a matter of time before the island was invaded and their land used as a stepping-stone for Hitler to push his forces into England.

The previous day, the government suddenly announced that it would begin evacuations, starting with the schoolchildren and as many teachers as possible to accompany them. These women and their charges would be taken to England and then sent by train to various cities across the country and perhaps into Scotland as well. The islanders were told parents would be allowed to follow later and meet their children there. Lily's sister, Helen, younger by five years, was a teacher at Saint Martins Primary School, and she knew for a fact that Helen did not want to leave the island. She was the youngest teacher at her school, having taught for only a year, and terrified about the prospect of accompanying her pupils to an unfamiliar country. Speculation was rampant that teachers would be stranded with students in drafty barns and warehouses across England, hidden around the country with no food or beds or even water to drink. Nevertheless, they were expected to go if at all possible and take responsibility for their pupils for, if necessary, the duration of the war.

Lily hadn't told Helen she was coming. There was little time to make the decision as it was, and she had heard on the radio an hour earlier that the harbor already bustled with ships and mail boats and barges, some ready to set sail for Weymouth within the hour. Lily planned to be on one of those vessels. Fate had given her a way of escape, and she had to take the only opportunity she was given.

Struggling with her valise, she made her way to the schoolyard. People milled about everywhere, noisy children and frantic parents preparing to part for an unknown length of time.

She searched for her sister among the throng, finally catching a glimpse of her standing with a small group near the entrance of the school. Lily made her way through the crowd and walked up to her sister, setting her case on the ground at her feet.

Helen turned to look at her, surprise registering on her face. "Lily! What are you doing here?"

"I need to talk to you," she replied.

"But we spoke last night," Helen said, frowning. There wasn't time for complications.

Lily looked at the woman standing next to her sister. She was nearing thirty, with a slight figure, her blond hair pulled back in a knot. Two children clutched at her arms, and the youngest, a girl, hid her face in her mother's skirt.

"Mrs. Simon," Helen said, turning back to the woman. "This is my sister, Mrs. Carré."

The woman nodded in Lily's direction but turned her attention back to the matter at hand. "Will you stay with them until I can come and meet you in England, Miss Matthews?" she demanded. "Will you hold on to their hands? Promise never to let them out of your sight?"

Dozens of similar conversations were taking place all around them. Reality began to set in as Lily realized what these families were giving up. The future, which had stretched before them with a comforting sameness, was suddenly bleak and uncertain.

"Of course I will," Helen said, assuring her. She bent low to reassure the children. "We'll be fine, won't we?"

Not far from where they stood, a dusty bus pulled up in front of the school and a man alighted, holding a clipboard in front of him. His presence stilled the entire crowd. There is a terrible moment before one has to do a difficult thing, that moment when one knows that the inevitable is about to happen. Lily could feel the apprehension of the crowd, and gooseflesh came up on her arm.

"A through D!" the driver called. "If your last name begins with an A through a D, please board the bus at this time."

The woman in front of Lily wrung her hands. "I wish I could come with you, but my husband says we have to make arrangements for the farm."

"Parents will follow us shortly." Helen replied, looking about for help. "Look, there's the headmaster. Ask him, just to be certain."

Mrs. Simon took hold of her children and put the boy's hand in Helen's and the girl's into Lily's. For a moment, Lily was shocked. Although she had been married for five years, there had never been any children. After the first few painful years, she had tried not to allow herself to think of what might have been. The small girl looked up at her, tears in her eyes, her nose running. Lily took a handkerchief from her handbag and bent down to wipe the tiny face. She was a beautiful child, blond and blue eyed like her mother, and in spite of herself, Lily felt a sharp pang of longing.

"I'll speak to the headmaster," Mrs. Simon said, turning away.

"What are you doing here?" Helen said, turning to face Lily, still holding on to the boy. "And why on earth do you have a suitcase?"

"I'm going with you," Lily replied. Some of life's most important decisions are made in a single day, and this was one of them. There was no going back. It took a moment for the words to register, and her sister stared at her, trying to understand.

"But you can't," Helen protested when she could speak. "For one thing, you aren't a teacher. And for another, you're supposed to take care of Mother and Dad. They're counting on you. Besides, we can't *both* leave them. They'd never manage on their own."

Lily took a deep breath. "Would you rather stay instead?"

"I, I can't," Helen stammered. She pulled her cardigan closer around her shoulders. "These children are my responsibility."

"Do you want to go?" Lily asked in a low voice, searching her sister's eyes for the answer. "Is this what you want to do, Helen?"

"Of course not," her sister replied, leaning closer. "I'd rather go with the family later, if Mother and Dad will leave the farm."

"Then stay," Lily replied. "This is something I need to do. I have to."

"What about Ian?" Helen asked.

"If he asks after me, tell him you don't know where I am. That'll be true enough."

"What is he going to think?"

Lily shrugged. "I asked if I could go with you to make sure you're all right. He told me no. To be honest, I've already heard the word no more than enough times in my life. He doesn't get to tell me what to do anymore."

Her sister shook her head, grappling with this new complication.

She stared for a moment at the toes of her shoes. "I don't know what to do."

Lily put her hand on Helen's arm. "Yes, you do. I'll tell them you've sprained your ankle or something. Just get out of here at once."

Helen's face creased into a frown. "Am I being an awful coward?"

"I don't think staying behind makes you a coward," Lily said. "When your heart tells you to do something, you have to listen."

For a moment, neither spoke. Then Helen nodded, releasing the boy's hand. She bent forward and kissed Lily on the cheek.

"Godspeed," she said. "Write to us when you can."

Lily nodded. After her sister went into the building, she looked down at the boy, who was watching her with a curious expression on his face.

"What's your name?" she asked.

"Henry Simon," he replied. His hair had been slicked back, and he was wearing clean clothes and sturdy shoes for a farm boy. He was slim and blond like his sister.

"How old are you, Henry?" she asked.

"Nine, miss," he replied.

"And your sister?" she said, squeezing the small hand she held in her own. "What is her name?"

"Catherine," he answered in a measured, monosyllabic way.

"And how old is Catherine?" Lily persisted.

"Four," he said before clapping his hand over his mouth. "I mean, almost five. She'll be five on her next birthday."

Which meant, Lily realized, that the girl wasn't old enough to go without a parent in attendance. Mrs. Simon was smuggling her daughter off the island in order to protect her from the invasion. Lily had read that women were allowed to evacuate with the schoolteachers and children if they had infants and toddlers, but with fewer than twenty-four hours to make a decision, no one knew exactly what to do. A sense of panic had overtaken them all. They waited for a few minutes, and Lily turned to try to find their mother, but she was nowhere to be seen.

"Where are your things?" she asked the boy.

He pointed at a couple of rucksacks on the ground. They were pathetically thin. Like her, they had brought only the bare necessities.

"Can you carry them?" she asked.

He nodded and Lily lifted her case.

"Follow me," she said.

Still holding the girl's hand, Lily led the children to the bus, where they joined the queue.

She watched as a dozen others boarded the bus before it was their turn.

"Name?" the driver asked when they stepped toward him.

"Carré," she said. "Do you need to see my papers?"

"That won't be necessary," he replied, obviously in a rush. He was no doubt a busy man. He would transport several busloads to the vessels waiting to get them to England before nightfall. "And the children?"

"They're with me."

"Climb aboard, then, miss," he said.

She led the children to seats as close as possible to the front of the bus. Lily put Henry next to the window and pulled Catherine onto her lap, squeezing her own case under the seat. Every second would count when they got down to the harbor, where people from some of the other schools were likely already queueing to get onto ships. The bus filled quickly, and the driver climbed aboard and closed the door behind them.

"What about Mummy?" Henry asked, kneeling on his seat to better see out the window. "We didn't get to say goodbye."

"She knows you're safe and she'll be coming for you soon," Lily answered. She could feel the girl begin to tremble in her arms. It was unexpected yet pleasant. She had the urge to smooth the girl's hair. Instead, she pulled her closer as the bus lurched into motion.

A scream rippled through the air, and Lily looked out the window in time to see Mrs. Simon waving her arms, trying to get the bus to stop. Lily caught her breath. The driver, however, neither saw nor heard her cries, and the bus began to rumble down the road, heading for the harbor.


Guernsey was an island of particular beauty, Lily always felt, a gem sparkling in the sea, secreted away and known only to a few due to its remote location in the English Channel between England and

France. As the bus trundled down the quiet lanes, she clutched the child on her lap and took in the beauty of an island summer for the final time. Wildflowers were abloom all around them. Giant echiums and wild orchids, which had reared their heads in May, still swayed in the breeze along with the bluebells of June. Her favorites, however, were the bog pimpernels that flowered in the middle of summer. A few of the bright pink blossoms could already be seen peeping through the fields as they passed. It gave Lily a feeling of comfort in this uncertain time.

She would never come back, she knew. As much as she loved Guernsey, she would never live with Ian again in his house on the hill or have the chance to say goodbye to her parents or friends. She would miss her family and the island, but the rest of her life was ahead of her, and her breath caught in anticipation. The few times she had ventured abroad were infrequent trips to Jersey, which was situated between Guernsey and the coast of France, and a honeymoon trip to Paris five years earlier, a time when life held more promise than had proven to be true.

She came from a small family on the north side of her island, and her childhood had been perfect, as far as she was concerned. Along with her younger brother and sister, she had grown up on a farm and enjoyed a good life: indulgent parents, the freedom to explore fields and streams, afternoons spent on empty beaches collecting shells and the odd treasures that washed onto the shore. She fed apples to small donkeys and voraciously devoured books, often under the shade of the trees on the far side of the barn. Her love of reading made her a good student, and she always did well in school.

The island was small enough to be insular but large enough for anonymity should one wish it—twenty-five square miles of hills and fields and beaches, divided into ten parishes. One could walk it end to end in a day. Though the population exceeded forty thousand, people tended to congregate in groups dictated by their church, schools, class, and occupations. Lily had been one of those people who had enjoyed a quiet rural life in Torteval on the western coast until she had married Ian, when they had moved to Saint Peter Port on the eastern coast, elevating her not only from rural to city life but to a different class and station as well.

Although her childhood had been idyllic, adulthood had been less so: a broken heart followed by a whirlwind courtship with Ian; losing her brother, Tom, in the war; an unhappy, violent marriage. Her mind was set on escape. But she wouldn't allow herself to dwell on the past.

The only thing that mattered was getting to England safely. Then she could start over. The women and children on the bus were all as anxious as she; to a person, each was lost in their thoughts, wondering where this long and difficult day would end.

# 2

---

*Lily*

Saint Peter Port had never been more crowded than it was that afternoon. Ships and boats of all sizes filled the harbor, but it was clear that many of the people waiting to get aboard one of the vessels would have to wait another day. Lily was determined not to be one of those people. She kept a close eye on Henry, telling him to stay near, as she pulled her suitcase behind her and kept Catherine clutched to her side. She had always been a rule-abiding person in the past, but if she hesitated, all hope of getting aboard one of the ships would be lost. Pushing through the crowd, she ignored looks and complaints from some of the others who said they were in line. As far as she could see, there was nowhere to queue, only a sea of women and children clustered on the quay and piers.

"Good boy," she told Henry, relieved that he had the strength to keep up with her, although she knew that even if he didn't want to follow her, he wouldn't abandon his sister. They were in a helpless position.

Elbowing her way through countless others, she finally stopped when they were close to the pier. She couldn't see who was in charge or what was being done, but they daren't sit or try to rest or someone would push past them. No one appeared to be in charge as hundreds of young women and children waited for a chance to board. Once on the pier, her hopes began to surge. There were at least seventy people in front of her but still hundreds behind. She set her sights on one of the larger ships, where there would be seats and a more comfortable means of travel, but as they made their way to the front of the line, a cattle barge pulled up, and they were forced to climb aboard.

Lily stood with the children on the deck, willing the journey to begin. Neither Henry nor Catherine cried, and Lily was certain it was due to shock. Even she didn't know what to expect. Every familiar thing that had made up their lives would soon be a speck on the horizon, the unknown looming ahead of them across a seemingly endless channel.

Henry took hold of her sleeve to get her attention.

"I'm hungry," he said.

Lily looked down at Catherine, who nodded solemnly in agreement.

"Did you bring anything to eat?" Lily asked.

There was certainly nothing to feed them on the barge, and she hadn't even thought of food in her haste to leave home.

When he shrugged, she lifted one of the children's bags and found an apple inside. She found one in the other as well. Shining them on the cuff of her sleeve, she gave one to each of them. Then she dragged their bags to a cargo area and lifted Henry and Catherine onto one of the large wooden crates. She took off her coat and laid it on the crate next to them and sat down, still clutching her handbag.

The wind whipped around them, gulls squawking overhead. The barge was unsteady, captive to the battering waves, making it difficult to stand. It was hot on the water, and Lily fanned herself with a handkerchief as the sun beat down on their heads. She looked about at the women and children who climbed aboard, some with suitcases and bags and others who hadn't taken the time to pack in their desperation to secure passage on one of the boats. It was a relief when one of the crew members untied the rope and they began to float away from the dock. Henry leaned forward, watching as the barge began to move. Catherine, clearly frightened, leaned into her instinctively for comfort.

Everyone turned when they heard a shout and watched someone jump off the pier into the water, swimming toward them. He tried to pull himself up the side but couldn't quite make it. Two of the crew members went over and hauled him up onto the barge, and he stood there, drenched but smiling, a boy of no more than fifteen. He turned to wave to his friends who had been left behind.

"I made it!" he shouted. "We're bound for Jolly Olde England, mates!"

"How far is it?" Henry asked, looking at Lily with concern.

"I'm afraid I don't know," she answered. "Let's try to get comfortable."

They spent more than two interminable hours at sea. Occasionally, infants or toddlers let out a cry, but the majority of the two hundred passengers squeezed onto the barge were silent, huddling against one another to buffer against the wind and waiting and wondering what would happen next. A few times, a child got sick over the edge of the boat. Henry and Catherine clung to each other, and eventually the girl fell asleep with her head on Lily's lap.

Lily took out her umbrella to shade the child from the harsh midday sun, thinking about what she had done. In a few short hours, Ian would come home to an empty house, unaware that she had left him. She had drawn into her shell after their last major row and had been quiet in recent weeks as she mulled her options. She couldn't go home to her parents. Ian wouldn't allow it. He was poised to take a role in the government, and a divorce would damage his political ambitions. Her parents wouldn't take her in anyway. Her mother had made it clear that once a woman became a wife, it was her duty to obey her husband and accept her responsibilities to care for her family and her house, regardless of domestic struggles. In any case, they couldn't take on an additional burden. Both of her parents had become shadows of their former selves after her brother died and were having difficulty running the farm on their own. Helen still lived at home and contributed her income to keeping up the household and her energy to taking care of the chores the best she could, but Lily knew it was a losing proposition. They would be forced to sell the farm and move into a smaller house in Saint Peter Port before long, a move that would demoralize them even further. They had anticipated marrying off their pretty daughters to wealthy young men and leaving the farm to Tom. Lily knew she would be giving them another disappointment, but she couldn't stay in her marriage for another day, not even for her parents.

She would miss her beautiful white house with its red tile roof and matching red front door, which, to a girl who had grown up on a farm, was the most marvelous home she had ever seen. Even five years after moving in, she hadn't gotten used to its size and comforts. It wasn't as grand as some in Saint Peter Port, like Hauteville House, the enormous white mansion where Victor Hugo penned *Les Misérables* during his exile from France after calling Napoleon a traitor, but it was grand nonetheless. She and Ian employed a cook and gardeners and a maid to manage its upkeep, allowing Lily the singular role of mistress of the house. It was a role she had managed to keep up for years.

The funds hidden in the velvet bag were sizable but not enough to last forever. She would eventually have to find work and a place to live, depending on her wits and abilities to see her through. At first, she thought of going to London, but the crowded city of millions would be intimidating for a woman used to life on a quiet island. However, she had a plan in mind, a destination more suited to her personality and situation.

At long last, Weymouth came into view. She folded the umbrella, staring out at the activity on the pier and the vessels crowded around it as they drew closer to the bustling port. Another ship ahead of them was debarking passengers, and they had to wait their turn.

"Wake up, Catherine," Lily said, gently lifting the child off her lap.

Lily's legs were stiff from sitting for too long. She had begun to think they would never go ashore. Although she had not been to England, the port had a reassuring familiarity about it. She knew little of Dorset or anywhere on the southern coast of England other than what she had read in Thomas Hardy books, but Weymouth, teeming with hundreds of newly arrived passengers, looked much the same as the port at home.

She rose to get a better look, watching the boats jockey for position near the pier. It was a good half hour before the barge eventually docked. This time, Lily held back to avoid the anxious crush of bodies struggling to make their way to solid ground. Her objective had been reached: making it safely to England. When the crowd thinned out, she gave the children's bags to Henry and took Catherine by the hand.

"Stay with me," she told him.

They joined the line of people waiting to disembark. She spotted policemen on the pier below, directing tired women and children to join lines of others walking in the direction of town. With no other idea of what to do, they followed behind. Lily maintained some distance between them and the others so the children wouldn't be jostled any more than she could help. They were led down a half dozen roads until they reached a large building and were ushered inside. She felt a moment's trepidation at the entrance, but there was nowhere else to go.

Inside, a large common room was filled with tables set up all around, stations for various services to be performed. They stepped closer to get a better look.

"Look!" she said to Henry. "They have food for us."

Volunteers handed out fat sandwiches of bread and jam, along with cups of water and milk.

The sea air had made them hungry, and they each took a sandwich and ate it in a few bites. Henry finished his first, and Lily broke off part of hers and gave it to him. She had no idea when they might eat again.

After the sandwiches, which left her desperately wishing for a mug of tea, they were directed to another room. The children were put into lines to be inspected for lice and other medical issues. Lily held their belongings and waited with them, keeping an eye on Catherine in particular.

"Child's name, please," the woman instructed when they finally reached the table, nodding at the boy.

"Henry Simon," Lily stated, watching as his name was written on the card.

"Parents' names?" the woman continued.

Lily looked at Henry. "What is your mother's name?"

"Ave," he replied, shrugging.

"Better make that Mrs. Simon of Guernsey," Lily supplied, having no idea what name he was trying to say. "He went to Saint Martins School near Saint Peter Port if that helps."

"And the girl?" the woman asked. "Is she his sibling?"

"Yes," answered Lily. "Her name is Catherine."

The children were asked to remove their clothing down to their undergarments, and Lily waited as they underwent the requisite inspection. She watched the doctor look into their ears and noses, running his fingers through their scalps with cotton gloves, inspecting them for lice, listening for the possibility of mucus in their lungs. It would have been an indignity for anyone to be so exposed, but certainly for hungry, tired children. After they were given back their clothing, Lily helped them get dressed, buttoning buttons and tying Henry's belt around his narrow waist.

"Go on through to the next room," the nurse instructed.

They gathered their things and went through the doorway, where a policeman had stepped up to speak to the small crowd.

"Gather 'round!" he shouted, stepping onto a crate to address them all. "We're taking groups of ten or so at a time to get you onto trains this evening. You'll be brought to places where people can take care of you."

Henry moved closer to Lily, obviously frightened. There had

been too many changes in a single day for such a young boy. All the children looked about nervously. People gathered their belongings and began to file through the door where another policeman stood, directing them to the station.

They trudged through the town, Lily's case becoming heavier with every step. Catherine began to cry and wanted to be carried, but Lily couldn't manage it. Instead, she gripped the child's hand tighter.

"Come on, Catherine," she said, trying to soothe her. "It won't be much longer now."

It was nearly four o'clock, and they were already getting hungry again. Lily hoped there would be something more substantial provided to them soon. Eventually, they made it to the station.

Inside, they were surrounded by a sea of bodies, children crying and screaming to make themselves heard over the din of the trains. Teachers were frustrated and tired, barely managing their tired charges. Catherine clung to her, afraid of the commotion. Lily put her arms around the child, trying to shield her from the pushing and shoving of the crowd. It was too much for any of them to deal with after what they had already been through. Lily felt lost. She could only imagine how a four-year-old was feeling after such a miserable day.

A short woman with spectacles approached them when they entered the station. "Are you one of the teachers from Guernsey?"

"Yes," she replied. It was easier than trying to explain her situation.

"You'll be on that train there," the woman said, holding out an envelope. "Give these tickets to the porter."

"Where is this train headed?" Lily asked.

"This is the line to Manchester, ma'am," she answered before briskly moving along.

Lily clutched her handbag to her chest, considering her options. She had been good at geography in school, and Manchester, she knew, was in the north of England. That was not where she wanted to go. It was a dark, dirty industrial town by all accounts. Some of the children who were sent there would probably be moved to smaller villages in the countryside, where they could get fresh air and have a wholesome place to shelter during the occupation. But others might not be so lucky, leaving an island paradise for a smoke-filled, grimy city.

They inched their way forward toward the train, which would carry its passengers through the night and where they would once again be without food or a comfortable place to rest after a long journey. Lily thought for a moment about Helen, glad her sister hadn't decided to come. It was too much of an emotional toll, dealing with so many crying, hungry children with nothing to sustain them but jam and a few crusts of bread. Heaven knew what was waiting for them in Manchester. Some might even be put on another train at dawn, headed toward the unknown.

Taking a step forward, Lily's heart began to pound. She couldn't get on that train. It would mean her escape had been for nothing. Looking down at Henry and Catherine, she tried to work out what to do. All she wanted was to leave the station and find a hotel where she could get her thoughts together after the tumultuous day. She had left her husband, her family, and the only life she had ever known. She hadn't thought far enough ahead to realize that it would mean accompanying small children to their eventual destinations and waiting out the war.

She turned to look at one of the teachers behind her, who was standing with a group of young boys.

"What will happen when the train arrives in Manchester?" she asked.

"Your guess is as good as mine," the woman answered, shifting her suitcase. She glanced down at Catherine and then gave her a sympathetic smile. "But I suppose they'll put the young ones like her in one place, and the older ones will go to some sort of school."

Stunned, Lily turned around to think it all through. Another thing she had not considered; Henry might be sent away to attend school somewhere, and he was just old enough to handle it. His situation was out of her hands. But her heart ached for Catherine, who would be one of hundreds of small children relegated to a makeshift orphanage ill-equipped to meet their needs, either physically or emotionally. Her mother, who had been terrified to let them go, wouldn't want a life like that for her beautiful young daughter. Looking down at Catherine, who clung to her, Lily realized she couldn't let it happen. Although she had planned solely for her own escape, it was suddenly clear that she couldn't abandon this vulnerable child to an uncertain, bleak future.

At last, it was time for them to board. Lily's heart pounded as she made a sudden decision. She reached into her handbag, extracted a ten-pound note, and slipped it into Henry's rucksack. Then she patted him on the back and smiled at him.

"There's a good boy," she said. "Everything will be fine."

He gave her a nervous look and then stepped up onto the train, expecting her to follow.

However, she took Catherine's hand and moved out of line to allow the people behind her to board after Henry. Quickly, Lily led the girl away from the platform and back into the station, searching until she found a porter.

"Is there a hotel nearby?" she asked.

"A few streets that way, miss," he said, pointing.

She nodded and trudged forward, her case and Catherine's knapsack in one hand and the child's hand in her other. Catherine had started to cry again, but she pulled her along, desperate to get out of the station and away from the crowds.

It was an impulsive decision, and Lily was stricken with guilt. She tried to tell herself the children would be separated anyway, whether she came with them or stayed behind. Henry was a bright child, and he was older. He could manage on his own. But Catherine was too young to be left with a nine-year-old brother who had neither the means nor the ability to care for a tiny child, and she shuddered to think where she would end up if Lily didn't take responsibility for Catherine herself.

"I want Mummy," Catherine whined.

"I know," Lily murmured. "It won't be long now."

Her shoes pinched with every step, and she stumbled as Catherine pulled at her arm. Miserably, she put one foot in front of the other, the suitcase in one hand and the girl's hand in the other. She could have cried with relief when the hotel came into view. Inside, she set down her case and went over to the desk where the clerk looked up from her blotter.

"Do you have a room, please?" Lily asked.

The woman looked at her and then at the child, finally nodding. Lily asked the price and, when it was given, set the money on the counter.

"Is there any chance we could get some tea and something to eat?" she asked. "We've had a very long journey."

"It's not our usual custom," the woman admitted. "But you look done in. I'll bring up a tray in a few minutes."

"You're most kind," Lily answered.

She took the key and then led Catherine up the steps, unlocking the door and letting them into the room. Inside, there was a bed, a table, and two chairs tucked under a window in the corner. Lily was particularly interested in the bed, which would be the first she had slept in without Ian in five years. She felt a surge of pleasure at the thought.

Opening Catherine's bag, she lifted out two dresses and a nightshirt, smoothing out the wrinkles with her hand.

"Come here, darling," she said. "Let's get you into something comfortable."

She unlaced Catherine's shoes and pulled them off, setting them neatly under the bed. Then she gently rubbed her feet.

"Stand up and I'll unbutton your dress."

The weary child did as she was told. Lily removed the dress, lifting it over her head. She folded it and set it on a chair and then reached for the nightshirt, helping Catherine put it on. It tied in the front, and Lily made a small bow.

"We'll have a bath tomorrow," she promised. "Tonight we need to rest."

The tea arrived a few minutes later with a plate of scones, and they ate one each. Lily wrapped the third in a serviette to save for tomorrow. It was an unfamiliar yet pleasant experience to tuck the child into bed. When Catherine was asleep, Lily changed into her nightgown and crawled in beside her. Turning off the lamp, she pulled up the quilt, moved closer to the warm, sleeping child, and quickly fell asleep to the rhythmic sound of Catherine's breathing.

The following morning, Lily wasn't certain what woke her: the sliver of sunlight filtering through the curtains or her growing hunger. She stretched, disoriented for a moment, and then sat up.

Catherine was still asleep, and Lily pulled the quilt over her shoulder. The child's face was pink and flushed, her hair damp against the pillow. Lily felt protective of the girl already. She had been right to keep her safe from the crushing crowds and the unknown dangers of Manchester. A four-year-old was far too young to handle such turmoil.

She stood and began to sort out their things, dressing quickly in the quiet room. Catherine only had two dresses, and she wasn't going to put her in the one she had traveled in the day before, which was rumpled and soiled from the long trip. She poured water from the pitcher into the basin to wet a cloth and went back over to wake her.

"Hello, sleepyhead," she murmured, waiting as the child began to move. "Are you hungry this morning?"

The child sat up and looked about the room. "Where's Mummy? Can we go and see her today?"

"We're on an adventure, Catherine," Lily said. "So, no, we won't see Mummy today. But we will go downstairs and get something to eat."

She washed the child's face and hands and helped her dress. After combing her hair, she repacked her suitcase and filled Catherine's small bag, carrying them with her down the stairs and tucking them behind a chair in the front room. Then, she took the girl by the hand and walked into the dining room, where the proprietress was serving breakfast.

Lily led Catherine to a table and pulled out a chair for her. "Here we are. Let's get something to eat. I'm hungry, are you?"

Catherine nodded, looking around the room.

"How are you feeling?" Lily asked. "Are your feet sore from walking so much yesterday?"

The child nodded again.

"You can talk to me, you know," she said. "You don't have to be afraid. I won't let anything happen to you."

"Where is Henry?" Catherine asked.

"Henry had to go to a place for boys," Lily said matter-of-factly. "You're a girl, and so you get to stay with me."

"I want to go home."

"I'm afraid we can't go home now," she replied. "But soon, we'll get on a train and take it to a nice place. Then we'll find somewhere we can stay for a while."

Catherine looked at her, trying to absorb the information. "And then Mummy will come?"

"Sooner or later," she replied.

The proprietress arrived a minute later, hefting a teapot and setting it on the table.

"You're not one of them teachers, I see," the woman said.

Lily gave her a questioning look.

"You're wearing a wedding ring, aren't you?"

Lily twisted the ring on her finger.

"That's right," she said. "Although, actually, I'm a widow."

The lie came readily enough. How easy it was to dispose of an unwanted husband with a few mere words.

"I'll be right back with some milk for your little girl."

When she returned, Lily thanked her and turned her attention to Catherine, handing her the glass of milk. The child took a long drink and then looked up at her before taking another sip.

Lily smiled and poured herself a cup of tea, lifting the hot, comforting drink to her lips.

"What do you like to eat for breakfast?" she asked.

"Porridge," Catherine said.

"Well then, we shall ask for porridge," Lily replied. She folded the napkin on her lap and waited for the woman to return.

As they waited for the meal to arrive, they sat quietly together. Lily wondered if Catherine was a naturally reticent child or if she was merely subdued by the strangeness of their situation and being parted from her brother. For a fleeting moment, she wondered how Henry was doing and if the train had made it to Manchester. She hoped that a teacher or parent on the train had taken responsibility for him. Like his sister, he was a good child, and she felt guilty leaving him behind. She wouldn't have minded having him along if it weren't for the difficulty of caring for two children. One was certainly easier, especially one like Catherine. She couldn't help wondering what the child's mother was thinking, to send them so ill prepared for a lengthy stay away from home. Lily had gone through the child's meager things and realized there wasn't a doll or toy for her to play with, a situation that must be rectified at once. When the woman returned, she turned to her and smiled.

"Is there somewhere close by where I could get a couple of things for a child?" she asked. "A toy and some clothes perhaps?"

The woman studied her for a moment. "There's a shop in Blackburn Street, about two roads over."

"Thank you," Lily replied. "We'll be leaving after breakfast."

"Yes, missus."

Lily placed the bowl of porridge in front of Catherine, picking up a spoon and handing it to the girl. They ate their meal in silence. Lily wrapped the leftover sausages in the same napkin with the scones in case the child got hungry later on the train. After wiping Catherine's face, she shepherded her to the reception area. There, she paid the bill, gathered their things, and then led the child outside, where she hailed a cab.

Rosewood's in Blackburn Street had just opened their doors when Lily and Catherine arrived. The display in the window was full of things to tempt a child, and they stepped inside to look around. Lily had rarely allowed herself to go into children's shops at home. It had been too painful, since she did not have a son or daughter of her own to buy things for. She let go of Catherine's hand and followed the girl as she wandered over to a shelf full of toys.

"Do you see something you would like?" she asked.

Catherine looked at her and then back at the extravagant

display before her, then walked up and touched a finger to a doll. It was a pretty thing, like Catherine herself, with a porcelain face and curly hair and a cloth body dressed in a satiny gown. Lily picked it up and handed it to her.

"There," she said, smiling. "A present for a good girl. Now, let's find you a couple of things to wear."

She searched through racks of clothing, finally choosing two dresses, one pink with smocking on the bib and another in cornflower blue with a piped collar. Then she found a white cardigan to go with them. At the moment, Catherine wore a dingy brown sweater, as unappealing a garment as Lily could imagine. It had probably belonged to her brother and been handed down when he had outgrown it. She took the items to the counter and paid for them and then folded them into Catherine's bag.

The sun was hotter than it had been the day before, and Lily led Catherine back to the station, relieved they would spend a few hours on a train, out of the sun's glare. She led her up to a ticket booth and studied the schedule.

"I want to go to Cornwall," she told the ticket master.

"Where to in Cornwall, ma'am?" he asked, raising his cap to see her better.

"Do you have a map?"

He gave her a curious look and then passed one through the small glass window. She looked it over for a minute and then handed it back.

"Will there be a dining car on the train to Saint Austell?" she asked.

"Of course."

"Then two tickets for Saint Austell, please."

She couldn't tell much from the map, but Saint Austell was a good distance from Weymouth as well as a coastal village, which would be more familiar for both Catherine and herself. Tucking the tickets in her bag, she led the girl to a bench where they could wait until the train's departure at nine thirty.

The crowd at the station was lighter than it had been the night before, when thousands of Guernsey children and teachers had been packed off for parts unknown. Everything had been desperate and rushed. Catherine clasped her doll to her chest, whispering to it softly, and Lily was glad she had gotten it for her. The child needed comfort and distraction at a time like this.

When they were allowed to board the train, they chose a seat in an empty carriage. Lily rolled her coat into a pillow when Catherine got tired, and the child napped for almost two hours as they trundled through Dorset and eventually into eastern Cornwall.

Lily stared at the view, thinking how fortunate she was to be on this train at this very moment. She took her book from her suitcase and held it on her lap, running her finger over the cover. Du Maurier's tale of a woman who, like herself, had married a wealthy man—a marriage that was not destined for happiness— had appealed to her own sense of loneliness and hurt. Lily hadn't been locked in a room like the author's second Mrs. de Winter, but she was a prisoner all the same. A prisoner of conventionality, of public opinion, and of poverty if she had chosen to divorce him. But Fate had intervened, and she resolved not to think of Ian any more than she could help. She would put him out of her mind, and he would never control her again.

Eventually, she reached for her handbag and extracted the parcel of letters. She held them in her hands for a moment, toying with the blue ribbon. They were letters from Andrew. In one, he even asked for her hand in marriage, a proposal he would later whisper into her ear. When he was killed in a motoring accident a month later, she knew she would never find love again. She married Ian six months later for financial security and to try to stop the flood of memories, which threatened to devour her soul. The most she had hoped for was children to love and to whom she could devote herself. But that hadn't happened. Instead, she'd endured five miserable years with a difficult and cruel man.

Those days, fortunately, were over, and her future stretched in front of her, full of possibility. She leaned back against the seat and gazed at Catherine, who slept across from her as the train rumbled farther and farther from their old life, one Lily wasn't sorry to leave behind forever.

# 3

---

*Ava*

I suppose sooner or later in the life of everyone comes a moment of trial. We all of us have our particular devil who rides us and torments us, and we must give battle in the end.

—DAPHNE DU MAURIER, *REBECCA*

Ava Simon, née Bertrand, dropped her arms to her sides and watched the bus pulling out of sight, knowing she couldn't run fast enough to catch it. She turned away from the crowd to hide her pain. All she wanted was one more chance to see her children before they left the island. She wanted to smell the tops of their heads as she had on the day they were born. They belonged to her, Henry and Catherine; her family was all she held dear in the world. She and her husband, Joseph, had been torn about whether or not to send the children away, and she had tried to object. Surely, even if the Germans invaded Guernsey, they wouldn't separate families, would they? They wouldn't abuse women and children. It seemed unimaginable that such horrors could come so close to home. She hurried from the school in the direction of their farm, still haunted by the looks on her children's faces. They had been woken early in the morning and told they were being sent away with little time to explain why. Ava, who hadn't slept all night, had risen before dawn and cooked a huge breakfast for them with sausages and hotcakes and eggs instead of their usual porridge. Still, they barely touched their food. Catherine cried through most of the meal. Henry had begged not to go, telling them how he would be more useful to them on the farm. Their pleas had been a dagger in her heart and, she was certain, in Joseph's as well. All they had was the farm and each other. That was all they'd ever wanted out of life.

*You can't see the future*, she thought. *This must be the right thing to do.* If she allowed herself to think otherwise, she would go mad, not to mention she would begin to hate her husband, who had insisted that their children couldn't live on an island during an occupation. He hoped to find a buyer for the livestock so the two of them could follow within a few days. It was true, he couldn't leave the animals to starve, but there was no promise that someone would buy them or would even be able to take them on for the duration of their absence, however long that might be.

She dried her tears as she walked, steeling herself to face facts.

Normally, facing reality was easy for her to do. She was a stoic woman. One had to be, running a farm. She had little in the way of vulnerability apart from her children. Life would be impossible without them, wondering where they would sleep and what they would eat, who would care for them, if they were being treated kindly or cruelly without a mother to protect them. Miss Matthews from the school was gentle, but she was very young to be solely responsible for frightened children who didn't understand what was happening. Ava knew *a mother* was the only one who could protect them properly. Joseph was a good father, but men weren't sentimental in the way women were. From the first moment she had looked into Henry's eyes, she had found the meaning of her existence. She was equally smitten with Catherine, who had been even more delicate and in need of protection. Their daughter wasn't even old enough to go to school yet, but Joseph insisted that Henry would take care of her until they could be reunited. And he would, she knew it. It was the only alternative. Ava had to be practical. Thousands had been killed in France, and now Hitler had his eye on England. Yes, she thought, rubbing her arms against a sudden chill, they did the right thing. She didn't even want to imagine what terrors lay ahead in the coming days.

Ava stopped running after she was away from the schoolyard and the pitying gazes of the other parents and tried to calm down.

It was a beautiful late-spring day with a warm breeze and Saint Peter Port daisies sprouting all across the island. It certainly didn't feel like the end of her life as she knew it. If she was honest with herself, she was angry with Joseph for not letting her go with the children, although she knew it would take both of them to manage everything that had to be done to leave the island. Their farmhand, seventeen-year-old Colin, who had been with them for three years, had left to join the war weeks ago, and Joseph would need her help to make the rest of the arrangements.

Their farm, which had belonged to her parents and her grandparents before them, was a few miles down the southern coast from Saint Peter Port, reached by a long, winding road. It was close enough to get to town when they needed to and far enough away to have privacy on the island. The parishes, like Saint Martin, where the Simons lived, tended to keep to themselves. The village was dotted with farms and cottages, shops and pubs, and a long, curving, rocky coastline that spanned four miles. From the cliffs, they had incomparable views of the English Channel facing France. The Simons' white stone house was small and compact, sitting on the top of a hill overlooking the sea, with a barn housing a few animals and a large garden where she spent many hours growing as much of their own food as they could. They didn't have a great deal of money but had wanted for little, being both frugal and realistic about their expectations. And the islanders were a generous people, sharing baby clothes and prams, passing things from one family to another when the need arose. Ava was proud to share with others when it had been her turn. Over the years, she had become adept at sewing clothes for the children, and Joseph was handy with tools, carving rocking horses and building swings for them under the trees. Until the threat of war, they had been more than happy.

Joseph Simon was a good man, which was why she had agreed to marry him. He was the quiet sort, never asking much but giving whatever was required and more. When they were courting, her favorite thing was to sit next to him in church, feeling the warmth of him by her side. She often thought that God had brought them together. His presence comforted her when she was worried or afraid, and when he reassured her, she believed him because he was trustworthy and good. She'd lived long enough to see there were plenty of men walking this earth who had no goodness in them whatsoever, and she remained grateful every day that Joseph wasn't one of them. But letting go of her children, allowing them to be taken away on faith without knowing when she would ever see them again, brought Ava the first doubts she had experienced in years.

She walked up the path to the house, opening the door. The first thing she did was to go into the kitchen, marking the date on the calendar: the twentieth of June, the day her children left the land of their birth and were shipped with thousands of others across the sea. She had no way to know for certain, but she felt deep down that things would never be the same. Even if they were to be reunited in a few days, as she desperately hoped, the sense of abandonment they must be feeling would take years to get over. Never had she expected to have to break their hearts in such a manner.

It was strangely empty inside the house. Mothers all over the island were feeling the same bitter sensation at that precise moment, she knew. Ava leaned against the kitchen table, straining to listen, as if Henry and Catherine would come running down the stairs in search of something to eat. Instead, the only sound was the occasional squawk of the gulls overhead and the slap of the sea against the rocks. She sank into a chair, thinking how silent the house would be without Henry bringing in frogs from the pond or Catherine carting her doll around in its miniature pram that they had saved for months to buy for her last birthday. A wave of regret washed over her when she realized that just the day before, she had scolded her daughter for banging it against a doorframe, as if the paint on the wall was more important than her child's happiness.

When Joseph came in from the fields, he found her sitting in the same spot. She hadn't moved to cook supper or even turn on a light. Though he no doubt felt the same searing pain, he pulled out a chair and sat beside her, taking hold of her hand.

"What have we done?" Ava asked, tears threatening once again.

Joseph's strong fingers squeezed her own. "We saved their lives, Ave. It's what we had to do. Think how you'd feel if everyone else's children were safe and ours were here in harm's way. We couldn't do that to them."

She lifted her face, studying the serious expression on his face. "But when will we see them again?" she murmured. "When will we know that everything will be all right?"

"Only God knows the answer to that," he replied.

She tried to agree, but her faith was being tested to its outer limits. So many Guernsey children were facing an uncertain future. Some among them would surely be lost. Catherine, in particular, was so small. She wasn't even old enough to go. Why had she sent them? What good could possibly come of it?

Nevertheless, she held her tongue. Even though her husband wouldn't complain, she knew he was suffering as well. She couldn't be a burden to him on top of what they were already facing. They had to be practical. There was a great deal to sort out in order to follow the children as soon as possible.

"What do we do now?" she asked. "Who will take the cows?"

"We've got to try to get money for them," he answered. "We can't afford to simply give them away."

"But that will take time," she replied, her anger rising.

"I'll go into town in the morning and see what we can do."

It was no use arguing. They had done all they could for one day. Tomorrow, she hoped, would be a day of promise, bringing them one step closer to seeing the children again. Joseph wanted it, too, she knew.

Ava stood. "I'll make supper."

"Would you like me to do it?" he asked.

He was good to offer, but even his most valiant attempts were inedible. Any other time, she would have teased him about it, but her heart was too heavy just now.

"No," she answered. "I can manage."

Cooking was the one thing she knew she could do no matter what was happening in her life. Through tragedies and joys, she, like her mother before her, resolutely chopped and stirred and prepared meal after meal. Even in the midst of her pain, she slipped the apron over her head and tied it about her waist. Feeding her family was the thing she did best. She paused for a moment, thinking of the scones she made in the afternoons, with aromas so tempting the smell brought the children from wherever they had been playing to sit at the stools in the kitchen, asking for a treat. She could almost set a clock by it. But tonight, she wouldn't make scones. She couldn't.

She fried eggs for supper. She didn't really care what she ate, but she had to face facts: food was simply fuel to keep one going. They ate in silence, which wasn't unusual unless Henry had an eventful day at school. When he finished, Joseph cleared the table and would have stayed to help, but Ava didn't feel like company. She sent him into the other room and began to sort the kitchen.

After the last dish was dry, she walked up the stairs, bone tired. She stopped in Henry's room, where she found his rubber boots tossed in a corner. She picked them up and stood them neatly next to his dresser. He wore those boots in every weather, generally whenever he accompanied his father around the farm. They were always filthy from jumping in puddles or stepping in muck, and now was no exception. She didn't have the heart to clean them. *Let them stay the way he left them until he returns*, she thought. Everything needed to be the same for the children when they returned home: meals at the usual hour and church on Sunday and a family walk on Saturday evenings down to the sea, where they collected rocks and stones at the water's edge. The sill in Henry's room was cluttered with them, gray and white, like soldiers lined up in a row. His schoolbooks were stacked on a small table, and she opened the reader, looking at the first story inside. He'd read it to her the day before, practicing before he read it to his teacher. She closed the book almost reverently, thankful to have memories to get her through.

She wandered into Catherine's room and went up to the hooks where her daughter's small dresses hung. The pink gingham was still there. It was Ava's favorite. She hadn't sent it because she knew it wasn't a practical garment for a child who had to travel so far. Reaching up, she took it down from the hook and held it to her face, inhaling the sweetness of the summer air from flapping on the clothesline and the unmistakable perfume of her daughter's scent.

Catherine slept in a small bed that Joseph had built and carved from the wood of a fallen tree. The foot and the head were of equal height, and it had been painted pale gray. She would outgrow it one day, probably within the next year or two, though Ava planned to keep it forever. In the silence of the room, she knelt in front of it and folded her hands in prayer. If God was real and listened to the groanings of the human heart, she prayed, may he be merciful enough to bring them all together again. When she heard Joseph's foot on the stair, she stood, laying the dress across the bed. She would pray there again tomorrow. And God would listen. He had to. The scripture most prominent in her mind was about the millstone; if anyone harmed a little child, it would be better for him to have a millstone hung around his neck and drowned in the depths of the sea. And if anyone harmed a hair on one of her children's heads, Ava knew, she would gut them like a fish. That was the moment she realized that hate was an even more powerful motivator than love.

# 4

---

*Ava*

Several days passed without successfully finding a buyer for the livestock. Ava tried to control her impatience, but she was ready to go after the children. Joseph was concerned with the practical aspects, like having the money to look for them once they were on English soil.

"I'm going to try to get work on the docks," he said one morning. He had hardly touched his breakfast—the only sign Ava had that he was as troubled by events as she was. "We'll need to pay for our passage on one of those ships and have something to last us for a while in England."

There was always work on the docks, Ava knew. Everything was imported from England or France unless it could be grown on the island itself.

"Do you think you can find something?" she asked.

They were both aware that there was little time to earn enough to escape. Any day now, soldiers would step foot on their shore.

"I have to try," he answered.

Day after day, they scoured the newspapers for information. News of the evacuated children was scarce, merely acknowledgment that they had been received into the port at Weymouth and many of them put on trains, sending them all over the country. They had no way of knowing which part of England Henry and Catherine were in. Ava resolved to go to the Matthews's farm so that she could ask Helen's parents to let her know if they heard anything from their daughter. Any letter from her that got through would surely contain news of her children as well.

The Red Cross announced it would establish communication between parents and children at some undesignated point in the future. Communiqués would be brief, fewer than twenty-five words, and might only be sent every year or two at the most. The thought was disheartening. How were parents expected to cope with so little information about the condition and whereabouts of their sons and daughters? Yet cope they must. There was no other alternative if they ever wanted to see their children again.

Ava rode her bicycle down to the village the next day. If one didn't know any better, it would seem an ordinary morning in Saint Peter Port. The crowds had dispersed, and people were going about their business. She headed for the library in Market Square, a favorite place to lose herself whenever she felt troubled. Henry and Catherine loved going there as well. Even though her daughter was too young to read, she loved books, and as often as not, Henry took her on his lap and read her stories. His tenderness was one of the reasons Ava trusted him to look after his sister. He was a good brother and a good son.

Ava chose a couple of books to borrow and slipped them into the basket of her bike.

She'd promised herself she wouldn't go down to the docks, but she couldn't resist. She had shuddered when she had seen photographs in the newspaper of the crowds during the evacuation. How frightening it must have been for all those children to be driven like cattle onto ships and sent off to the unknown.

As she pedaled down the cobbled streets, she froze when she saw a familiar figure walking nearby, basket in hand, on her way to the market. A strangled feeling rose in her throat. Ava jumped from the bicycle, dropping it on the street, and ran after her.

"Miss Matthews!" she shouted, reaching out and taking hold of her arm.

Helen Matthews, Henry's teacher from school, turned around and stared at Ava, her face growing pale.

"It is you!" Ava cried. "How… Why… How can you possibly be here? You're supposed to be with my children!"

Helen was young, twenty-one, she believed, but the only comfort she'd had was knowing that Henry and Catherine were with someone Henry knew. The girl stood before her, dumbstruck, while Ava's hopes were dashed into pieces.

"What are you doing here?" she demanded again, trying not to raise her voice. "Why aren't you in England?"

"I twisted my ankle," Helen said, looking uncomfortable. "So my sister went in my place."

Ava stared at the young woman, dressed in a pretty blue frock. In spite of herself, she looked down at her drab shoes and dress. Everything about Ava's life was plain. Her children were the only color and light in her world.

"You left my children alone at the worst time of their lives," Ava snapped. "How dare you?"

Helen took a few steps back, recoiling as if she had been hit.

Ava turned and walked away.

The situation was worse than she feared. Her children had been evacuated in the company of a total stranger. She didn't care that it was the teacher's sister. It was someone unfamiliar to them, someone they didn't know if they could trust. She felt as if she might be sick.

"Please, Mrs. Simon, can I do anything for you?" Helen called after her.

Ava didn't answer. Instead, she went over and got onto her bicycle, her grief renewed to an unbearable level. She cycled home, tears stinging the corners of her eyes, never once looking behind her.

The following day, at 6:45 p.m. on the twenty-eighth of June, Saint Peter Port was bombed by three German planes. The attack lasted nearly an hour, leaving the entire island shaken. Ava and Joseph took shelter in the cellar during the attack. When the bombing stopped, they got into their car and drove toward the village in shock. The sky was filled with smoke and the town was burning. As they got closer, they could see flames from the taller buildings and hear the shouts of the terrified crowds.

"Even the ambulances were hit," someone shouted as they approached.

They later learned that crates of tomatoes, Guernsey's chief export, had been thought by the Germans to be munitions to fight against them. Panic and grief overtook the island. Two days later, on the thirtieth, the Germans arrived. The news spread around the island in a matter of hours. Everyone stayed inside, reluctant to venture out until they knew it was safe.

Ava knew then her fate was sealed. A new, horrible reality was waiting to be faced. It was too late for them to evacuate and go after Henry and Catherine. For a few days, no one knew what to do or where to turn, relying on newspaper accounts for information. They were ordered to cooperate with the Germans and do whatever they were asked. At first, the soldiers had been polite, and the islanders in turn attempted civility in an effort to prevent violence from escalating, but they didn't trust them.

Joseph went into town for more information. Ava wondered if the English would come to their rescue. And if not the English, perhaps the Americans could be convinced to get involved and liberate the islands. There was a slim chance, she knew, but one had to hope.

"What's happening?" Ava asked when Joseph came through the door. She could see from his face that the situation was grim.

"They're going to let us keep the government for now," he replied, setting his hat on the table.

She came over to sit next to him. "What does that mean?"

"Not much, I'm afraid," he answered. "The Germans have said that any new laws would be subject to their approval. Which means we're not really self-governing at the moment. We're expected to cooperate with them as much as possible."

"Anything else?"

"I went to the bank, but the funds were frozen," he continued. "All the assets are in England, and the banks don't have access to them as long as we're an occupied land."

"But we have so little money here, Joseph," she protested. "I think I have a few pound notes in the dresser upstairs. Not enough to last for long."

"We didn't think we'd need it," he said, sighing. "We were always able to go the bank when we needed something before. You don't appreciate something until you no longer have it."

"How will we get food?" she asked.

"I've been told bartering is illegal, but I think we can supply some of our nearest neighbors with milk and eggs and they can give us some things in return. Maybe not the Masons. We don't know them well enough. And of course, we've got the vegetable garden, too. There won't be much else for a while, I'm afraid. I can fish, perhaps."

Ava stood and began to pace. "We were right to send the children away. We would barely be able to feed them. It's going to be difficult enough with two."

He went over and took her by the hand, turning her to face him. "We did the right thing, you know we did. They're safer there than they would be here."

"If only we knew where they are," Ava said, turning away.

"We may not hear anything for quite a while."

"How long do you think this will go on?" she asked.

"Until the English beat the Germans and win the bloody war," he answered. "God only knows when that will be."

"What if they don't?" Ava asked, taking off her apron and laying it over a chair. "What if the English don't win the war?"

Joseph didn't answer. The alternative was unimaginable.

Bus service was discontinued a few days later, leaving residents to make their own way around the island. Slowly, they stopped doing their usual things. Joseph found work unloading cargo from the ships and barges, backbreaking work that left him unable to care for the livestock, too. Ava took over everything herself. She worked from morning until night, feeding chickens, milking cows, working in the garden, keeping house, and cooking meals. With everything on her mind, she was glad for the distraction. After their evening meal, they both went to bed, falling asleep immediately. It was easier that way. Easier not to think about the children. Easier being too exhausted to care about the changes happening around them.

Her world shrunk. She talked to the chickens and cows. She walked down to the beach, looking for rocks and stones to give to Henry when he came home. She put away her best dress so she could save the fabric to make one for Catherine when she came home, wondering if it would be in months or even years.

They went to town on Saturday to go to the market, and Ava got her first look at the port during occupation. She was shocked at the number of soldiers walking about and wondered why Joseph hadn't mentioned it. Perhaps he was trying not to frighten her. They were stopped three times and questioned, each time becoming more concerned than the time before. Shops had rationing signs in their windows. People hurried about, keeping to themselves. They were struggling just as she was, she could see it in their faces. But there was something else, something she couldn't quite put her finger on.

"Joseph," she said, grabbing his sleeve when she realized what was wrong.

"What is it?" he asked.

"Look around," she murmured. "There are no children."

They turned and glanced at the other villagers. He turned and nodded to her, uncertain what to say. They knew some people had refused to send their children away, but they weren't allowing them to wander freely about the town, either. The occupation had changed everything.

After making their purchases, they were given flyers by a forbidding-looking soldier, telling them that all radios must be turned in to the German headquarters by the following Friday. Homes would be searched to make certain everyone complied. Ava read the notice over Joseph's shoulder, and he caught her eye, shaking his head. She knew what he meant, but they couldn't speak freely with the eyes and ears of the Third Reich among them.

Naively, she had imagined life wouldn't change a great deal. Losing their children seemed punishment enough. But now the war, with all its trials and heartaches, had become so much more real. They were prisoners, barely able to walk about freely. Inquisitive eyes followed them at every turn. Soldiers began to visit every home, making certain that everyone complied with the rules and expectations of the German government.

Ava was glad her parents weren't alive to see this. They had lived happy, simple lives on their island home, just as she and Joseph did. She could imagine her father, who had served in World War I, telling off the Germans in no uncertain terms. This was his land and not theirs, no matter what they might say. It gave her comfort to think of it.

That afternoon, Joseph took the radio from the kitchen where they listened to the evening news and broke it into a dozen pieces.

"If we can't have it, the Germans can't have it, either," he'd said. "Let them take this if it means so much to them."

"What about—"

He lifted a hand and shook his head. She knew instinctively that some things must never be spoken. However, she was aware later that day that her husband had removed the other radio from their bedroom, the one that had belonged to her parents. He took it out to the barn and buried it under the hay in the loft. They would be severely punished if they disobeyed orders, but Joseph took care to conceal it in the farthest corner under a sheet of tarpaulin.

He would comply with the laws the best he could, but he wouldn't capitulate entirely to the Germans. Anger surged in her chest at the thought. She knew that she wouldn't be able to give them everything, either.

They stopped going to church, afraid to venture too far from home. Joseph sometimes read to her from the Book of Common Prayer over breakfast, but the words washed over her without penetrating her soul. If faith was the substance of things not seen, she hadn't a single ounce of it left. Too much had been asked of them already.

Even God couldn't expect any more.

# 5

---

*Henry*

From the moment he stepped foot on the train, Henry Simon knew something was wrong. He turned around to speak to the woman who was looking after him and Catherine, but someone else had inexplicably taken her place. He was prodded farther and farther down the narrow aisle until at last he found an empty seat and stood on it, turning around to watch for his sister and the woman to step into the carriage, but he couldn't find them anywhere.

It was the most dreadful day of his life. He could still see the looks on his parents' faces when they told him that morning that he and Catherine were being sent away. It would haunt him as long as he lived.

"I have something important to tell you, Henry," his father had said at breakfast. "You're going to England with your sister today."

He remembered staring at the fat, round sausages on his plate, but he couldn't begin to swallow.

"Why are we going away?" he asked. "Are you coming, too?"

Henry saw the glance that passed between his parents.

"No, Son," his father replied. "Just you and Catherine. All the students from your school and your teachers are going to England today."

"It will only be for a short while," his mother added. "Your father and I will come to get you soon."

"Are we in trouble?" he asked.

He tried to be a good boy, but he was always forgetting things, like leaving his penknife in the barn instead of bringing it back into the house where it belonged. It was ever so hard to keep track of things.

"No, you're not in trouble," his mother assured him, but still, he looked to his father for the answer.

"Do you know the job that soldiers do, Henry?" his father asked.

"They protect people and keep them safe, like the English soldiers who were here," he answered. "They're mostly good, except for the bad ones who fight the English. They are bullies who hurt people."

"That's right," his father said, nodding. "Good lad. And that's why we're sending you away for a little while. There will be an awful lot of soldiers coming here, and we don't want all the children to get scared."

"But we can't go away on our own," Henry protested, setting down his fork. "Where will we stay?"

His mother ruffled his hair. "We don't know yet, but we don't want you to worry, Henry. There will be teachers from your school looking after you. And you'll have a job to keep you busy, too: looking after Catherine."

He looked at his younger sister, aghast. They played together, but she was small and hard to manage sometimes. He couldn't possibly take care of her. Besides, it wasn't his job. That's what mothers were for.

"Let me stay," he begged. "I'll do more to help out, I promise."

"We know you would," his mother answered. "But we can't let you. We need you to look after Catherine and wait for us until we can come for you."

He got a heavy feeling in his chest as he thought of his parents now. He wished his sister would get on the train so he could put his arms about her and keep her safe. His mother would want him to do that. Catherine wasn't used to being with strangers. He knew she must be scared, and the thought of it made him feel sick.

Henry clutched his duffel to his chest, staring at the ears of the older boy in front of him. Catherine and Miss Matthews's sister were nowhere to be seen. Henry wasn't even certain he could describe the woman to anyone, apart from the fact that she was pretty and she had reddish hair. He turned around and looked at those who had boarded before him. At the back of the train car, he saw another teacher from his school, although he couldn't remember her name. A lump came into his throat and he tried not to cry.

He was going to be in so much trouble. It had been his responsibility to take care of Catherine, and he had already let them all down.

The train, impossibly, began to move with a shriek of the whistle and a jolt of the carriage. He tried to get hold of himself. He would have to be tougher than this in order to find his sister and keep her safe. He had to be the man of the family until they made it back home to their parents.

When it was clear that they had left the station and Catherine was nowhere to be seen, he put his pack over his shoulder and walked down the length of the carriage to speak to the teacher he recognized from his school.

"Miss, can you help me?" he asked.

She looked up at him in surprise. She was young—not as young as Miss Matthews, but young all the same. Her face had a tired, pinched expression, and he knew that all of them, even every single grown-up on the train, wished they were back in their beds at home in Guernsey, far from this England place with its noisy, rumbly trains.

"What's the problem, young man?" she asked.

"My sister's missing."

A worried look came over her face.

"What's your name?" she asked.

"Henry Simon," he replied. "I'm in Miss Matthews's class."

"Where is Miss Matthews, dear?"

He shrugged. "She didn't come. She gave us to a lady to bring us here."

"Is the lady a teacher, too?"

"I don't think so," he answered. "She's Miss Matthews's sister. She told Miss Matthews to pretend she hurt her leg and she would go on the boat with us instead."

"That must have been terribly scary for you, Henry," the woman said, obviously taken aback. "I'm Miss Fairley. Who is your sister's teacher, then?"

Henry got a sheepish look on his face. "She's too little for school. She's only four."

"And your mother had to send her anyway, is that right?"

Her voice held no reproach, so Henry felt safe telling her the truth. "They need me to look after her, but she's not here, miss. I think they didn't get on the train. They were right behind me when I got on, I promise."

"We'll sort it out, all right?" She gave a faint smile. "Do you have your things? I think you should come and sit by me."

Henry nodded and took the seat next to her, relieved to have unburdened himself to someone trustworthy. He wedged himself into the seat where he could look out the window. He couldn't look at the ground below because it made him feel ill. Instead, he stared at the English countryside as the sky began to grow dark. Over the next hour, he found the rocking of the train carriage soothing, and using his duffel as a pillow, he leaned against the window and fell asleep.

He woke two or three times in the middle of the night. It was black as pitch outside, and there were barely any stars in the sky. Yet still the train lumbered along the track. He had no idea how long they had been traveling. He looked at Miss Fairley, who was sleeping with her arms around two of her students, wishing he too could be taken into her comforting embrace. He had to remember that no matter how upset he was, Catherine was even more so. He hoped he was wrong and they would find her at the station when they arrived in Manchester, but even a nine-year-old is no fool. He was being punished for some infraction he had committed in the recent past, perhaps when his father had told him to bring in wood for the stove and he had made Catherine do it, or for the time he had gone down to look for toads in the creek instead of taking a saw back to Mr. Brouard down the road. When he remembered he was to have taken it, he hid it in the barn to prevent his crime from being revealed. He was always forgetting things, and now he'd done the worst and forgotten, just for a second, to keep his eye on his sister. Miss Matthews's sister had seemed nice, but his mother had told him not to trust strangers, and he'd neglected to do the one thing she'd told him he must do.

The train was still barreling down the tracks in the hours before dawn, and people around him woke one by one, stretching sore and tired limbs by walking up and down the narrow aisle of the carriage. It was at least another hour before the train finally pulled into the station. Henry stayed near Miss Fairley, who was overseeing a half dozen charges. He followed her off the train and remained at her side as they were herded into more lines leading to yet another anonymous building. Once again, volunteers manned tables with bread and jam, and while he devoured three of the sandwiches, grateful for any food at all, he wondered if they would ever have anything else to eat again.

The children were divided into groups with one or two adults, and he managed to get assigned to Miss Fairley. Then they were loaded onto a bus and driven an hour away to an abandoned school building that had been refitted as a dormitory. The children were assigned bunks, measured for clothing and shoes, and given basic instructions about meals and exercise, in which they were all expected to take part.

"How long will we be here?" he murmured to Miss Fairley after they were dismissed.

She shook her head. "I'm afraid I don't know."

Later, he heard some of the older children talking about being divided once again and possibly sent to farms in the area. Farms he knew, but being separated from everyone he'd ever known sounded like a punishment he couldn't endure.

After they were given a bowl of thin soup, Miss Fairley ushered her charges back to the dormitory.

"I think you should all have a short nap," she said.

Ordinarily, Henry would have protested, but like the others, he was exhausted. He opened his duffel to look for a clean shirt, but when he put his hand in, he drew out a ten-pound note. Folding it quickly, lest anyone should see, he hid it in the toe of his shoe. Perhaps his father had put it there in case he ever needed anything, although he had never seen his parents with so large a sum. Retying his shoe, he climbed into bed, holding the duffel to his chest for comfort.

He slept long and hard, and when he awoke, he saw that the others were still sleeping. Instead of getting up, he lay there wondering what to do. After a while, he rose from the bunk and quietly left the room, determined to discover what he could about where they were. He slipped outside and began to look around.

The main building was old and not terribly large. Henry peered in windows and saw classrooms not unlike his own at school: desks, chairs, and blackboards at the front of the room. He missed school, if he was honest. Some children might not, but he certainly did. The building where the bunks were located was found a few hundred yards away from the school building, but beyond that, there were no other signs of life. A wooded area was behind them, an empty road in front with no traffic whatsoever.

He wandered back toward the woods and explored for a while. He found a creek, which he decided he would visit every day. At least he could look for tadpoles and frogs.

When he returned to the dormitory, the children were taken into the main building for a speech, which he couldn't quite grasp in his eagerness to devour the lamb stew that was set in front of him. All the children did the same. The next morning, however, they were spoken to again before breakfast, and Henry realized there would be a schedule to which they would have to conform. Breakfast at seven thirty, lessons from eight until eleven, lunch, nap, afternoon exercise, dinner, bed at seven. It was comforting to get into a routine. He looked forward to the meals and lessons, and he was going to learn how to play cricket, although he didn't think he would be any good at it. Still, the nights were hard. He thought of his family and wondered if they missed him. He wondered where his sister was or if she was even in England anymore. He thought of his parents and how much explaining he would have to do when he saw them. Would they come to get him? he wondered. And if so, when? But more troubling was the thought that even if they did take a ship across the Channel to England, how in the world would they find one small boy and his little lost sister?

One hot afternoon, he decided to skip the nap and spend the time exploring the creek. He found a few sturdy sticks and built a small enclosure where he could go and sit when he felt unhappy. He hadn't really made friends. It didn't seem as though any of them had. They were still numb from all the changes in their lives. There was a pecking order, but Henry wasn't one to jockey for a position in it. He preferred to think and to read, wishing there were books that he could borrow from the school. So far, most of the lessons had been writing and math. There was no *Treasure Island* on the shelf, no copies of *The Call of the Wild*, which he had read earlier that year. Sometimes he would tell himself stories so he could remember them. He didn't want to forget everything.

There were few adults in charge, and even they seemed unsure what to do with the large number of lonely young boys. They fed them, gave them instructions, and taught them, but he didn't feel any sense of belonging no matter what they said.

One afternoon, he sat on the bank, digging with one of the sticks in the mud, listening for the sound of birds and small creatures. He wondered, for the hundredth time, when he would see his beloved creek and when he would be reunited with his family. He wanted to write them a letter, but it wasn't allowed. Henry lingered in the shade of the trees, trying to make sense of what had happened and what in the world he was going to do. When he returned to the dormitory, he realized he had been gone longer than he thought, for Miss Fairley looked upset when she saw him.

"Henry!" she said. "Where have you been? I've been looking for you for a couple of hours. Are you all right?"

"I'm fine, miss," he replied.

But Henry wasn't fine at all. He didn't want to worry her further, but most nights after everyone was asleep, he put his face into his pillow and cried. Judging from the look on her face, it seemed as though she might be doing the same thing, too.

# PART TWO

# 6

---

*Peter*

It was a typical June morning in Saint Austell parish. Peter Ashby, at thirty-four the youngest vicar in the history of Holy Trinity Church, had finished a satisfying hour of work on his next sermon, the Fruits of the Spirit. It was a sermon his parishioners had no doubt heard on numerous occasions and one that was difficult to make fresh after so many readings, as simple as the concept may be. The fruits of the spirit, it seemed to Peter, were fairly obvious upon even a brief encounter with a fellow human being. One's countenance supplied immediate recognition, he often felt, of the spirit within. Some people radiated love, joy, and kindness. Patience and gentleness were a little less common in his experience. Even more rare were faithfulness and self-control. Many people, even some he knew well, struggled with those attributes. He himself did on occasion. It was part of the dilemma of being human. As he meditated on the passage in Paul's letter to the Galatians, he kept stopping at one phrase: "against such there is no law." What law, he pondered, would try to prevent any of these qualities from being shown? It was absurd to even think about.

He decided the Apostle Paul was contrasting the freedom of salvation with the problem of adhering to the strict tenets of the law. Law in general, he found, was a harsh concept. He far preferred mercy and love to rules meant to prohibit behavior. It seemed an idea that belonged to the Dark Ages. How much better life would be if humanity was governed by a peaceful heart rather than by merely following societal laws, if the way we treated one another stemmed from thankfulness and goodness rather than obligation. How much better, indeed.

Peter wrote the last sentence of the sermon with a flourish of his pen and set it down on his desk, standing to stretch. Looking out the window, he saw that it was a fine morning. The previous day's rain had abated, and the sun was shining in a nearly cloudless sky. The church bells began to chime the hour—eleven o'clock—and Peter smiled to himself, taking his coat from the hook and stepping outside.

The daffodils along the side of the building were in full bloom, thanks to the prodigious attention of their gardener, Mr. Wharton. The church was at its best on a sunny morning. Peter headed in the direction of Queens Head for a quick pint before lunch, hoping to find his friend Gavin there. He always rewarded himself when he finished the week's sermon. He crossed the road, hands in his pockets, in an excellent mood.

"Hello, Vicar!" a woman called from behind him.

He turned to see two of his parishioners, Mary Hamblin and Hannah Byers, waving at him.

They were clearly delighted at their good fortune of seeing their bachelor vicar in the middle of the week.

Peter waved back, smiling. "Good morning, ladies! I hope you have a pleasant day."

He was aware that he was the object of attention from the women in the village, but he had escaped the snare of marriage thus far and hoped his luck would hold for some time to come. He was in no hurry to do anything apart from writing sermons to give on Sundays and meeting the relatively light workload of Holy Trinity Church.

It was the church he had grown up in, and he loved it. Even though he'd wandered farther afield for a time, studying at Oxford and living in London for a few years, he'd been delighted to come back to the village he'd known his whole life. A hundred years earlier, Saint Austell had been a tin mining town, but its favorable location on the southern coast of Cornwall, known as the Cornish Riviera, was a highly attractive place to live. Sheltered coves, calm waters, and sand beaches were a draw for people from all over the country. He'd spent his childhood digging in the sand on those very beaches, and it was satisfying to enjoy it all these years later. His friends were here, too, the people he had grown up with and respected and for whom he cared.

His childhood home, where his parents still lived, was a two-story stone cottage, situated under the viaduct that had been built only forty years before for the train service that connected Saint Austell to the outer world. As a boy, he'd loved listening to the steam engines as they rumbled overhead, marveling at the engineering that made such a thing possible. The entire time he had lived away from Cornwall, he had missed it all: the trains, the slower pace of village life, the sharp tang of sea air.

He walked into the pub and ordered a pint, counting out eleven pence onto the bar. Peter watched as the barman poured the glass with a fine head of foam on top.

"Over here!" a voice called out.

Peter lifted his pint and headed over to a table, sitting across from his friend Gavin Brooks.

"How's the haberdashery business this fine morning, Gav?" he asked.

"As long as people got heads, we'll sell hats," Gavin said, holding up his glass.

Peter saluted with his own. "Cheers."

They slurped the foam off the top of their beer as Peter looked around.

"It's pretty quiet here today," he remarked.

"I like when we have it all to ourselves." Gavin took another gulp and set the mug down. "Is Charles back yet?"

"Not yet," Peter answered. His curate was attending to his

mother in Portsmouth while she recovered from heart surgery. "I told him not to rush things. He needs to make certain she can manage on her own before he comes back."

"Good man."

"How's Susie?" Peter asked.

Gavin had been his best friend at school, and Peter had married Gavin and Susie when he returned from London five years ago. They were as happy a pair as any he had seen, and Susie was pregnant with their second child.

"Her back hurts a bit these days," Gavin answered. "I think that means this one will be a boy."

"You know you'd love another girl," Peter remarked, leaning back in his seat. "You got so lucky with the first one."

Gavin tapped his chest and smiled. "That one's got me heart, God bless her."

"To Alice's health," Peter replied. "And her saint of a mother."

"Hear, hear."

They lifted their glasses once more, wiping away the foam before setting them down again.

"What's the sermon to be about this week, then, Vicar?" Gavin asked.

Peter laughed. "You'll have to wait until Sunday. You know I don't give my sermons twice."

"Fair enough." Gavin folded his hands on the table. "So what do you make of the news this week?"

"It's grim, isn't it?" Peter replied, sobering. "I don't know if you heard the Simpsons lost their son in the fighting a couple of weeks ago."

"Not Ben?"

"I'm afraid so. And he was only nineteen."

Gavin grunted. "We're going to see a great deal more suffering before it's over."

"And it seems the Channel Islands are facing occupation any day," Peter remarked. "Did you read about the evacuations?"

"It's devastating," his friend replied. "Can you imagine if we had to put Alice on a boat and send her to the other side of the country, without any idea where she was? It would kill us. I don't know what we'd do."

Peter nodded. "Jersey missed their chance. They only got a small fraction of their children out compared to Guernsey. I can't imagine which is worse, evacuating your children to a foreign land or trying to protect them during an occupation. The enemy is coming. The islands are vulnerable to all sorts of madness."

Gavin nodded solemnly. "We'll be hearing the roar of German engines before we know it."

"I hope not," Peter said.

"I don't think hope has much to do with it." Gavin sighed. "In any case, we're hours from London. Maybe we'll be spared if it comes to that."

"Something to pray for."

The two men sat in silence for a while, then Peter finished the last of his pint.

"Well, I promised Mrs. Heaton I wouldn't be late for lunch again," he said, patting his friend on the back. "Give my love to the family."

"I will," Gavin said. "Susie wants you to come for dinner soon."

"I look forward to it."

Peter went back out into the sunshine and walked to the vicarage, an old redbrick house that the previous tenant's wife had surrounded with rose bushes. The housekeeper, Clara Heaton, did the cooking, the wash, and the cleaning and in general kept his life sorted out as she had the vicar before him. It was one of the reasons he didn't need a wife. He couldn't possibly see two women operating out of the same kitchen. On the other hand, neither did he need two women telling him what to do.

"What have we today, Mrs. Heaton?" he called as he walked through the front door.

The house had been equipped decades before and featured rooms full of dark Victorian furniture. The only contributions he had made during his tenure were a cricket bat, a framed photo of all-rounder Frank Woolley, and a bookcase filled with some of his favorites from university. In fact, he might just pull one from the shelf and eat his reheated roast beef sandwich on the good sofa, in spite of the fact that it would outrage Mrs. Heaton, who believed all meals should be eaten at the table.

"Someone to see you, Vicar," the housekeeper said, coming out of the kitchen. She wiped her hands on a towel and raised a brow, cocking her head toward the living room.

He gave her a questioning look and then went into the front room where a beautiful young woman and her child were seated on the stuffy, hard-as-a-rock settee, waiting for him.

"How do you do?" he said, almost tongue-tied in the presence of such a lovely pair. "I'm Peter Ashby, the vicar of Holy Trinity Church. How may I help you?"

The woman rose from her seat, and he shook her hand.

"My name is Lily Carré," she said. "And this is Catherine. I'm sorry to impose on you, but I didn't know where else to turn."

"Please, have a seat," he said, sitting in the nearest chair across from her. "How can I help?"

He couldn't help but wonder why she would come to him for assistance. Most of his dealings with the public were to do with health issues of the older population, and nearly all those were members of the church.

"I've lost everything," she said, sitting up to face him squarely. "I've had to leave my home, and I need to start over. I don't know where to begin. At the moment, we don't even have a roof over our heads."

Peter scratched his chin, thinking. He glanced at her hand and saw that she was wearing a ring, but before he could ask about her husband, she looked down at her hand as well.

"I'm a widow," she stated.

"And you don't have family in the area?" he asked.

"I'm afraid not."

There were a thousand questions he wanted to ask. How long

had she been a widow? Was her husband a soldier who had been killed in one of the skirmishes in France? Had she been evicted from her home? Was she living in Cornwall when everything had fallen apart? However, he could see from the look on her face that her composure would begin to crack if he got too personal. And there was the child to consider. The girl, who looked to be around four, sat next to the woman, watching him intently.

Peter did a quick mental calculation. There was a benevolence fund at the church, but it was sorely depleted. He'd thought they would have a bake sale or perhaps a craft fair later in the summer to raise additional funds, but with the war looming, they were unlikely to get to do it for the foreseeable future.

"Is there anything else you could tell me about your situation?" he asked in an attempt at delicacy.

An idea began to form in the back of his mind as he awaited her reply. She looked down at her hands. They were lovely and delicate, as exquisite as the young woman herself.

"I feel terrible troubling you about it," she said, reaching out and touching the top of her daughter's head in an affectionate gesture. "I didn't know where else to go."

"Not at all," he replied.

"My husband was killed a few months ago in a motoring accident. We'd been living in Kent and we were left without any means to pay the rent. You see, I couldn't find a job, and there was no one to look after Catherine. Then something moved me to get on a train and come here. Perhaps this will be a place where I can finally find a new start in life."

He nodded. "Could you excuse me for a moment, please? I'll ask Mrs. Heaton to bring in some tea for us. I have to make a telephone call."

The look on her face nearly crushed his spirit. What bad luck to have lived through such a wrenching ordeal and to lose one's husband and home in the process.

Peter strode into the kitchen. "Mrs. Heaton, would you be so good as to take in some tea and sandwiches to our guests? I have to place a call, and I'll join them afterward."

"Of course," she answered.

One of his oldest parishioners, Albert Duncan, had passed away a few months earlier. Peter had long been friends with Duncan's daughter, Emily, and he recalled her saying that she wasn't prepared to sell Duncan's small one-bedroom cottage on the southern edge of the village for sentimental reasons. They hadn't discussed it in more than a month, and she may have changed her mind, but if not, perhaps he could persuade her to lend it temporarily to someone in need.

"Wilson residence" came the voice on the line.

"Emily, it's Peter," he said. "I wonder if I could trouble you with a favor."

"Hello, Peter," she replied. "What sort of favor do you need?"

"A young widow has shown up on the parish door with her daughter, and it seems she's pretty hard up. Is your father's cottage still empty? Do you think you might feel like letting it temporarily for a very small price?"

"Well, this is unusual, I must say," she replied. "Is she from the area?"

"No, she's from Kent," he answered. "And if I may say it, she appears to be quite alone in the world, too."

"What brings her all the way to Cornwall?" she asked.

"I'm afraid I didn't get that far."

There was a pause on the end of the line.

"It's a very small house," she answered. "But I suppose if she wants to give it a try, they could be comfortable enough."

"How much would you charge?" he asked.

"Let's let her get her feet under her first. She can have the use of it for a couple of months. Is she looking for work as well?"

"I believe so, but she does have her little girl to look after."

"That's terrible, to be widowed with a young child," she answered. "Tell her not to worry about anything. The place is sitting there empty. I'll put the key under the flowerpot in front, and you can let her in yourself within the hour."

"That's very generous of you, Emily," he replied. "You've got a heart of gold."

"I had a clear out a few weeks ago," she said. "I brought all Father's things over here so I could have them near. The cottage really has only the basics one might need, but I hope this helps the young lady."

"Enormously," Peter said. "I can't thank you enough." He rung off and went back down to the sitting room.

"Ah," he said, walking in. "I see Mrs. Heaton has brought in tea and sandwiches."

The tray hadn't been touched, so he went over and handed a plate to Catherine, who took it shyly. "Here you are, Catherine." He avoided looking Mrs. Carré in the eye as he handed one to her as well. Then he poured tea for the two of them and smiled. "Do you take sugar?" he asked.

She shook her head. "No, thank you. This is fine."

He helped himself to a sandwich, and only then did his guests lift theirs and take a bite.

Looking up, he realized they were as shell-shocked as any people he had ever seen. Although he was eager to share the news about the Duncan house, he waited until they were finished eating.

"I may have a spot of good news for you," he said at last when they were sipping their tea.

"What is that?" the woman asked.

"It so happens that a friend of mine has a small cottage stand-ing empty, and she said that you'd be welcome to use it for a little while until you get on your feet."

She set down her cup. "I don't know what to say."

"We'll go over and look at it after lunch and see what you think. Mind you, it's quite small, but I believe the two of you could manage."

"I thought perhaps you'd know someone who could let us a room," she said, looking embarrassed. "I didn't mean for anyone to be put out."

"It truly was empty, Mrs. Carré. My friend said you are welcome to stay until you sort out what you plan to do."

"That's too kind of you."

It was clear she hadn't expected so much. He put his cup on the tray and collected hers as well. "I'll take these things back to the kitchen for Mrs. Heaton, then I'll drive you over to see it."

When he returned, he led them outside and opened the door of his battered Austin 7. Mrs. Carré climbed into the passenger seat, and he took the child's hand and helped her up on her mother's lap. He drove through Saint Austell, pointing out local sites, proud of his village, thinking how it must seem to someone who had never seen it before.

A few minutes later, he pulled up in front of the small house, and they all stepped out of the vehicle. Peter went to the door and lifted the flowerpot, revealing a key. He held it up and smiled.

"Here we are, ladies," he announced.

He slipped the key into the lock of the green front door and opened it, stepping back so the two of them could enter. The large window was covered in heavy drapes, and the first thing he did was to pull them open, allowing the light to flood in. Dust motes floated in the air.

"There, that's better," he said.

Peter watched the two of them explore the room. There were two chairs in front of the fireplace and a large dresser full of china.

In the kitchen was a table and chairs. They seemed to be entranced with the place or perhaps with its possibilities. After a moment, he gestured to the other door.

"The only bedroom is here," he said, leading them inside. "I'm afraid it only has one bed, but it should be big enough for two."

The young woman turned toward him, her face full of emotion. "This is so nice. I wasn't expecting so much. I can't thank you enough for helping us."

He cleared his throat, uncomfortable with too much praise. "There's a small garden off the kitchen where Catherine might like to play, too."

At the mention of her name, the child darted into the kitchen and opened the door. Peter and Mrs. Carré followed her out into the garden, where a fat tabby perched on the low stone wall.

"And who do you belong to?" Mrs. Carré murmured.

"I believe that's Mrs. Rawling's cat," Peter replied. "She lives next door. Since this house has been empty for a few months, she's pretty much had the run of the place."

She walked over and touched the basket chair that sat under the large plum tree. He followed and handed her the key.

"Where are your things?" he asked.

"At the hotel near the station," she replied. "I haven't checked in yet, but they agreed to hold them for me."

"Why don't we go get them and then stop at the grocer for a few things? The cupboards are empty, I'm afraid."

She blushed. "I can't let you do anything else for us, really. I've put you to so much trouble already."

He smiled. "Nonsense. I'm happy to help, and it's much easier to cart things around in an automobile. It won't take long."

Their errands were done too soon. Mrs. Carré found a basket on the bottom shelf of the dresser and used it to transport her groceries back to the house. He would have lingered if he'd been given the chance, but he realized he was the one imposing on her, not the other way around.

"Please call if you need anything," he told her when he left. "I'm always available if you want to speak to me."

She smiled and waved as he got into his car, Catherine waving as well. The child clutched a doll in her arms, and he felt a great weight off his shoulders that he had been able to help two such needy people. That was his job, after all, to do good in the community and spread the love of Christ. Ordinarily, however, he didn't enjoy it quite as much as he had today. It occurred to him that as the war went on, there would be more and more people appearing at his doorstep in need of help. Lily Carré was merely a harbinger of things to come.

On Sunday, he thought of her as he fastened his clerical collar and again when he walked to the church. He was trying to contrive a reason to go and see her and Catherine when he noticed that they had come into the chapel and taken seats near the back. He was ridiculously pleased to see them and relieved that his sermon was short and uncomplicated, so his mind could wander a little to his subject of choice.

Mrs. Carré wore a yellow, flowery frock and sat with her handbag settled on her lap. Catherine's pink dress was the prettiest in the room. The two of them would have caught his eye if he were among a thousand women. Her husband had been the luckiest man in the world. How dreadful it was to have lost him at such a tender time in their lives.

He turned his attention to the sermon, scanning the crowd to take his mind off the newcomers. Gavin and Susie sat in the second row. His friend stifled a yawn, as usual, but Susie gazed at him with her normal intensity. When he thought of the attributes of good fruit, they were the first people who came to mind. Solid, reliable, kind. Always ready to do for others. He was blessed in his choice of friends, wondering what it must be like to be young with no one to turn to and nowhere to go. The idea intrigued him, and he decided to write his next sermon on the subject.

After the service, he stood at the back door, greeting his parish-ioners as they filed out of the building, the church bells ringing twelve o'clock. He shook hands and made small talk until Lily Carré and her daughter stepped out the door. He smiled, reaching forward to take her hand.

"It's good to see you today," he remarked. "How are you getting on?"

"Very well, thank you," she replied. She bent down and looked at the little girl. "Say hello to the vicar, Catherine."

The child ducked behind her mother's skirt but then peered out at him again. Obviously, she remembered the pleasant interaction from a few days earlier. He certainly hadn't forgotten it.

"Perhaps I'll see you this week," he said.

Mrs. Carré nodded. "Perhaps."

She took Catherine's hand and smiled before they walked away. He wasn't aware that he was watching them until a very pregnant Susie took his arm, shaking him from his reverie.

"Well, never you mind me, Peter Ashby," Susie Brooks said, giving him an arch look.

He tried to assume an innocent expression. "Susie, don't you look wonderful today?"

"She's lovely," Susie said, cocking her head in the direction of the woman he'd been speaking to. "I never thought I'd see the day a woman caught your eye."

"She has done no such thing," he protested, but he could feel his ears start to burn, something that wasn't lost on Susie Brooks.

She smiled in delight. "I can't tell you how happy this makes me."

"I don't know what you're talking about," he protested. "I am equally pleased to see all my friends who come out on a Sunday morning."

Even as he said it, he knew it wasn't true. There was something about Lily Carré and her daughter that caused a shift in his thinking. He tried to go about his business as usual, but the week passed slowly. He had difficulty concentrating on his sermon, his rounds, or anything else. Finally, on Thursday morning, he donned his jacket and drove over to the Duncan cottage, knocking on the door. Mrs. Carré answered it, an apron tied about her waist. It was the only time in his life that he had found an apron so fetching.

"Hello, Vicar," she said, smiling.

"Call me Peter," he said. "I was wondering, what do you say about a drive to the beach this afternoon?"

She hesitated for a long moment. "Call me Lily. But I'm not sure a drive to the beach would be appropriate."

"It's not for us," he maintained. "I thought it might be a good distraction for Catherine."

"Well, she would love it," she admitted. "And it would be awfully nice to have a change of scenery for a while."

Peter nodded. "Then let's do it this afternoon. I'll call 'round in a couple of hours. How does that sound?"

"You're too kind to us."

"You're doing me the favor," he answered. "I've been meaning to get out there for a while but haven't had a good reason to do it."

Two hours later, they were sitting on the sand overlooking the sea. Peter had brought a blanket, along with a hamper containing a thermos of tea and a packet of biscuits. Catherine accepted a handful and strayed toward the water's edge.

"Come here, Catherine," Lily said. "Let's take off your shoes first so you can get your feet wet."

She knelt down and untied the laces. Removing the socks, she placed them inside the small shoes. The child ran to the water's edge and let out a cry of happiness when she felt a wave wash over her ankles.

Lily moved closer, and Peter walked with her, watching the girl. The beach was empty, and the sun was warm but not too hot. They couldn't have chosen a better afternoon to get some sun.

"It must be hard to raise a child alone," he remarked, unable to take his eyes off Catherine.

Lily shook her head. "She's a joy every minute. I'm so lucky. I don't know what I'd do without her."

Catherine began to pick up stones on the beach and came running back to them when she got her first handful. The hem of her skirt was wet from the splashing waves.

"Look!" she cried. "I got these for Henry!"

"Who's Henry?" asked Peter.

"Someone from home," Lily said quickly. She reached down and took them from Catherine's hand. "I'll put these on the blanket over here, and you can find a few more."

The child nodded and ran back to the water's edge.

"Well, she's having a grand time," he said. "Would you like some tea?"

Lily nodded. "I'd love some, please."

He poured the hot liquid into two mugs and handed one to her. They sat on the blanket, watching Catherine and her unreserved delight.

"I can't remember the last time I felt like that," Lily confided. "Look at her. She's so happy."

"A little sunshine is good for the soul."

She turned to Peter. "Thank you for bringing us here today."

"My pleasure."

It was, he thought, the first time he had seen her let down her guard. She was a good mother, he could see that. Tender with her daughter. Attentive to her needs. Being a widow probably made her even more protective of her child than she might have been.

"You don't like to talk about the past," he observed, tapping his mug.

"You can't go back and change anything," she answered. "It's much calmer right here in the present."

"I suppose that's true," he replied.

He was happy, happier than he had ever been, not that he would trade his experiences at university or in London for all the money in the world. The things that happened in life shaped one for good or ill. Sometimes he believed that the terrible parts had the greatest effect. He'd been lucky never to have entanglements he could regret or experiences that embittered him, as so many people had. Still, there were moments of sorrow that come to all, and Lily, it seemed, had suffered more than her fair share.

Catherine returned with another handful of stones, which he and Lily rubbed on the blanket to rid them of sand. They were perfectly formed and smooth to the touch, some gray, some white, but all the measure of a moment he would remember for the rest of his life.

# 7

---

*Ava*

I believe there is a theory that men and women emerge finer and stronger after suffering, and that to advance in this or any world we must endure ordeal by fire.

—DAPHNE DU MAURIER, *REBECCA*

From the beginning, Ava hated the occupation. She was alone more than she had ever been before, with the children gone and Joseph putting in long hours at the docks. Regular avenues for social interaction stopped altogether. There were no knitting groups, no theaters performing plays, no women's organization meetings to keep them both industrious and entertained. Church choirs disbanded, the library stopped hosting activities for the children and book events for adults, social clubs no longer conducted bake sales. None of the villages across the island bustled with activity as they had before. People stayed close to home and avoided potential confrontations with the Germans. Even friends and acquaintances kept to themselves. Ava was fond of their neighbors to the east, the Walkers, an older couple whose grown children were near her age, though she hadn't seen them for months. Her own life was all-consuming at times, especially after having the children. With Henry and Catherine gone, however, life lost its rhythm. Normally, she and Joseph sat down a few times a day for a cup of tea and talked about life between chores on the farm, but now, he left early in the morning and returned so late that he was almost too tired to eat his supper.

Ava began each morning by doing the wash, wringing out every item and carrying them in a basket out to the clothesline. One by one, she pinned shirts and blouses on the line, stepping back to watch them flap in the breeze. Ordinarily, the line was full of Catherine's smocks and Henry's trousers. Now only hers and Joseph's hung there. Everywhere, all around them, were reminders of what they'd lost. It was becoming difficult to do everyday tasks and to carry on as if nothing were wrong. Even now, standing completely alone on their own land, she felt as if she would burst. Women weren't meant to be separated from their children. It was unbearable. Leaving the basket where it lay in the grass, she turned away from the house, looking out at the sea.

Walking across the field, she wandered to the edge of the small cliff, staring out at the waves. Normandy was somewhere across the Channel, a grim reminder that she wasn't alone in her sorrow. Tens of thousands of French mothers were suffering as well, along with millions of others across Europe. She'd read about the concentration camps in Europe and the atrocities being conducted there, people arrested and imprisoned or killed because of their ethnicity or beliefs. Men, women and children separated, tortured, and herded like animals. Homes destroyed, personal possessions confiscated without warning, degradations suffered that no human being deserved. She had never imagined such a scourge sweeping through civilized nations and putting their safety and security at risk, and yet it threatened to consume them all. She was suddenly ashamed of her own naivety and self-involvement. Only weeks ago, the war was a troubling concern far from their shores, but now it had spread like a cancer, at risk of engulfing the entire world.

Ava sat down and pulled her skirt over her knees, hugging them to her chest. At least her children were alive and well. She resolved to be thankful for that. So many women had lost everything that mattered, with no hope of seeing their children or husbands again, and while she didn't know precisely where they were, at least hers had reached England and safety. Ava couldn't let herself believe anything different. She held on to a scrap of faith that she would see them soon and that everything would work out in the end.

Closing her eyes, she felt the cool breeze ripple her hair. Behind her, she could hear the flapping of the shirts on the line, ahead of her the beating of the waves against the rocks. She sat like that for some time, listening and thinking. At last, she stood and walked down the long, winding path through the marsh grasses and eventually onto the shore. Bending down, she took off her shoes and placed them on a large, flat rock, then made her way down to the water below, wading in up to her ankles. The water shocked her with its coldness.

Since the children had been born, she had rarely been there by herself. They had always walked down as a family. Catherine liked to dig in the sand, and Henry looked for crabs, which he always brought over to show them. He also loved picking up sea stones, particularly the smooth ones, and Ava knelt now in the cold water, running her hand along the sand and rocks, looking for one the right size for his collection.

"Fraulein!" a voice called out. "What are you doing?"

She looked up and saw a young German soldier coming toward her. Hastily, she stepped back from the water and walked over to the rock, tugging on her shoes. She stood as he approached.

He was tall and blond, with an angular face and penetrating blue eyes, a few years younger than herself. She had never been approached by anyone on their beach before, and it was unsettling to be confronted by a strange man, no matter how young he was.

"Good morning," she said, at a loss for words.

They had been told to be polite to the soldiers, but she had no idea how she would react when she actually met one of them.

"What is your name?" he asked, never taking his eyes from her.

She was aware of her windblown, disheveled appearance. "Ava Simon. I live up there."

He frowned. "What are you doing here?"

Ava had no idea what to say. She pointed to the path from where she had come. "I'm going back to the house now."

As she walked back to the path, she was aware of his presence behind her. It was uncomfortable being so near a soldier, a situation fraught with risk. Her muscles grew taut with every step. She could be raped or worse, depending on what sort of man he was. She wondered how far he had walked along the beach, not to mention why he had approached her. So far, none of the soldiers had come to the house. Her heart raced as she hiked through the marsh grasses up the steep incline until she made it to the garden. He came up beside her, hands clasped behind his back, and gave her a look of approval.

"Is this your house?" he asked. His English was very good, and she wondered where he had learned it.

"Yes," she replied in a curt tone of voice. "This is my house."

"Who lives here with you?"

She looked up at him for a moment and then looked away. "My husband, Joseph."

"And where is he now?"

Ava got a sick feeling in her stomach. "He's in the village, at the docks."

The soldier looked around. "Who is doing all the work around here, then, Frau Simon? I see you have a garden and animals."

"I am," she replied. Although she didn't intend to, her chin jutted out as if defying him to argue with her.

He looked at her in astonishment. "It's a lot of work for one little woman to do."

"I was raised on this farm," she said, shrugging. "It's nothing new to me."

"My name is Becker," he said. "I'm here to inspect the house for radios. Have you any to turn in?"

She shook her head and led him to the kitchen door. "There was a radio, but it's broken now."

"Let me see it."

Ava turned around and led him to the shed, where the broken radio lay in a box in pieces. She stood there, silent, as he knelt and rummaged through it. After a moment, he stood and regarded her evenly.

"This isn't merely a broken radio," he remarked. "This has been destroyed. Let me check the rest of the house."

She went back to the house and opened the kitchen door for him to enter.

"After you, Frau Simon."

In the kitchen, she walked over to the table to put some distance between them.

"There are no radios in the house," she replied. It was true. She didn't want to lie if she could help it.

"That will be for me to determine."

He watched her for a moment and then went into the parlor. She listened as he moved about the house, making his way from room to room. He took his time upstairs, lingering, it seemed, in Henry's. She didn't want to be alone with him in the house when he came back downstairs, so she went out to the garden and put on her gloves, pulling at the weeds with a ferociousness that shocked her. She couldn't wait until she could look around the house to make certain that nothing was disturbed. It was tainted with his presence as it was.

Becker eventually came out of the house and walked down to the garden where she was working.

"There are no radios, I am happy to see," he said.

Ava didn't answer, rubbing her arm across her forehead where a layer of sweat had formed from the exertion.

"Where are your children?"

"They left the island," she said, trying to not betray her emotions.

"Were you afraid, Frau Simon?" Becker asked with a curious look on his face. "Afraid someone might bother your children?"

She turned away and went back to her weeding, trying to ignore him.

He cleared his throat. "I'll check the barn while I'm here."

"Certainly," she replied.

She held her breath as he strode away. If he was as thorough with the barn as he had been the house, he might find her parents' radio. For the first time, she questioned the wisdom of Joseph's decision to hide it. Yes, they wanted to be able to listen to the news from across the Channel in an emergency, but there were stiff penalties for breaking the laws, perhaps far worse than they realized.

Standing, she threw her gloves on the ground and went inside the house, hurrying from room to room. A few things had been moved, and the closet doors stood open, but he hadn't ransacked the house as she had feared. With a final glance into Henry's and Catherine's rooms to make certain everything was still in its place, she went downstairs and back to the garden as he was coming out of the barn. Her heart thumped at the sight of him.

"Everything looks in order," he said as he approached.

She nodded, uncertain what to say.

He looked at her for a long moment. "I'll be back, Frau Simon. Perhaps we'll have another look at your beach."

"Good morning to you," she murmured, unsure what else to say.

Then she went back to her weeding, donning her gloves and gathering tufts of earth—her earth—in her hands, willing the German soldier away. After he had gone, she went into the barn and climbed up the ladder high enough to peer into the loft. Nothing appeared to be disturbed, but she would talk to Joseph anyway. She could have been in grave danger if it had been found. And the one thing she knew at this moment was that she had to survive this war and this occupation, for her children's sake if not her own. Surely her husband would understand that.

Joseph, however, didn't agree.

"Now that he's been through the house and the barn, I doubt he will go in there again," he reasoned that evening when she explained what had happened. "We don't know how long this will last, Ave. We have to be practical. Say we're stuck like this for years, we need to have a way to find out what's going on."

She shoved a spoon into the potatoes and set it in front of him. "What makes you so certain another soldier won't come out and look for himself? Anyone could find it at any time."

"I'm more concerned about him approaching you alone on an isolated beach," he retorted. "You put yourself in danger by venturing into a remote cove on your own."

"It's no more dangerous than the house," she answered. "It was a terrible feeling, having him walk through every room, touching everything. I went outside and worked in the garden until he left."

"I'm sorry," Joseph said, standing up and coming around behind her. He slipped his arms about her waist and touched his face to her hair.

She wasn't in the mood for affection, but she didn't push him away. They had problems to solve, and she was alone all day on an isolated farm, having to deal with Germans going through her house while he worked in town among other people.

"Why didn't we leave with the children?" she demanded. "Damn the cows and chickens and the farm. We should have gone with them when we had the chance."

He slipped his arms from her waist and went back to sit down. "We're doing everything we can. You know that. I'm making some money. That has to mean something."

"How much good is it if we can't use it to get to England?"

"You're upset," he said.

"With good reason."

"Yes, with good reason."

She stood up and walked to the window. "I want to speak to Helen Matthews again."

"Who's that?" he asked. "The teacher?"

"Yes," she replied. "The one who was supposed to take care of Henry and Catherine."

He raised a brow. "Do you think that's a wise idea? You blame her for what happened, you know."

"Maybe she can tell us something," she answered. "Anything at all."

Joseph didn't answer. He knew better than to argue with her. The next morning, she wheeled her bicycle out of the barn and rode down to the school. The headmaster was coming out of his office when she entered the building, and she hurried over to him.

"Mrs. Simon," he said, looking at her with surprise. "What can I do for you?"

"I'm here to speak to Helen Matthews," she answered.

He shook his head. "I'm afraid she's not here just now. She sprained an ankle on evacuation day and has been taking some time off."

"It's urgent that I speak with her, Mr. Mackey," Ava replied. "She was supposed to go to England with my children and didn't go at the last moment. I need to know what happened."

"It's against policy to share personal information," he began. Then he looked Ava in the eye. "However, I understand your position. I think in your case it wouldn't hurt to allow you to speak with her. If you'll wait a moment, I'll get her address."

He returned a couple of minutes later and handed her a slip of paper.

"Thank you, Headmaster," she said.

The Matthewses' farm was only a couple of miles from the school, and Ava knew the area well. She cycled north, taking in the countryside. It would have been a good day for exploring if life was back to normal. Of course, she didn't know when things would ever be normal again. Ava approached the house, a neat and tidy stone building, perching her bicycle against a tree. Helen's mother answered her knock.

"Yes?" the woman inquired, wiping her hands on a cloth. The woman looked at her suspiciously, but Ava knew anything out of the ordinary made one nervous at a time like this.

"I'm looking for Helen, please," she said. "My name is Ava Simon. My son was a student of hers at Saint Martins."

"Won't you come in?"

Ava was led into the sitting room and was offered a chair. Helen's father sat across from her, finishing a cup of tea, which he set on the table.

"This is Mrs. Simon," the woman told her husband. "Her son was at the school."

"Did your son go to England?" Mr. Matthews inquired, leaning forward, concern etched on his face.

"Yes," Ava said. "And my four-year-old daughter as well."

"I'm sorry to hear it," he said, reaching for a cane. "That won't be easy for you. My grown daughter left on the ferries, and we can't stop worrying about her, either."

"I'll get Helen," his wife said.

Mr. Matthews stood. "I'll let you have your chat, then."

Ava looked about the room. It was the home of a working-class family, the same as her own. Like many of the islanders, they lived on a budget, making and growing what they could, living simple but honest lives.

A few moments later, Helen came into the room. She tried to smile.

"Would you like some tea, Mrs. Simon?"

"No, thank you," Ava replied a trifle sharply. "I just wanted to ask you about what happened the day the children left."

Helen sat down next to her, nervously smoothing her skirt. She was a pretty young woman with delicate features, which wore a pinched expression now.

"I sprained my ankle," she said weakly. "My sister turned up at the school determined to go to England. It seemed the perfect solution since I couldn't go."

"How did you feel about going to England, Miss Matthews?"

"I was apprehensive, to be honest," she replied. "We had just a few hours' notice, and we had no idea where we were going or any idea of how long we would be gone."

Ava wondered if Helen had truly been hurt or if she had merely been afraid to go. However, that wasn't her greatest concern. The welfare of her children was the only thing she cared about.

"Your sister wasn't a teacher, then?" Ava asked.

"No."

"What is her name?" Ava continued. "Can you tell me something about her?"

"Her name is Lily Carré," Helen answered. She pointed to a photograph of a beautiful young couple that rested on the table between them. "She and her husband live in Saint Peter Port."

"She's married?" Ava said, shocked. "And she wanted to leave her home to go with a group of children she didn't even know?"

Helen sighed. "I was surprised myself. I knew she was unhappy, but I had no idea she would resort to such a thing."

"You're saying your sister left her husband and went to England on her own? Were they having marital problems?"

"That's really not for me to say. I shouldn't have been so forth-right. But the truth is, she wasn't happy and wanted to leave the island."

"Did she say what her plans were? Does she intend to stay with the children until we can come to get them?"

"We only spoke for a few minutes that morning," Helen admitted. "But Lily is a deeply caring person. She had both Henry and your daughter by the hand. I know she wouldn't allow anything bad to happen to them."

"But what of her husband?" Ava persisted. "And does she have children of her own? Did she leave them behind?"

"I haven't spoken to Ian, but I believe there may have been a falling-out." Helen clasped her hands on her lap. "And no, she didn't have children, although I know she wanted them desperately."

Ava stood. This was getting her nowhere. "I don't know if we'll get any word through the newspapers about our children, but if you by chance get a letter from your sister, could you please let me know?"

"Of course," Helen answered. "If I hear anything, I'll contact you at once."

There was nothing more to say. Ava went outside and got on her bike, feeling frustrated. There were no answers to be had, only more questions. Even Lily Carré's own sister didn't understand why she would have taken such an impulsive step.

She was stopped by a soldier on her way home, compounding

her misery. They seemed to be everywhere. In fact, most days, she found herself waiting for Becker or another soldier to arrive without notice. Every sound—the weather vane creaking, a gull landing on the roof, the sound of an automobile in the distance—made her nerves grow rigid. Joseph came home late each evening, eating a steady diet of potatoes without complaint, but it was clear they were growing more brittle by the minute. The uncertainty was getting to them, and there was no way to calm the waters of their souls.

She decided to go to the church one afternoon to speak to the vicar. As much as she loved their home by the sea, she loved the city as well: the tall houses lining the port; the narrow, winding roads where bunting was strung between buildings on special occasions; shops bedecked with flowers during more peaceful times; and markets full of every sort of bread and cheese and meats, a temptation no one could resist. Saint Peter Port was a beautiful, even joyous city, the crown jewel of the island. She quickened her pace as she bicycled along the empty roads. She was glad she had gotten out until she came to a roadblock with several soldiers standing in a line. It was jarring to see them in their green uniforms, guns held aloft.

"Name, please," one said, stepping forward.

"Ava Simon."

"What is your business in town?"

She felt a surge of annoyance at the question but kept it to herself. "I am going to the market and to church."

"Church?" another said, smirking. He turned to his comrades. "This one is going to church."

The men laughed and Ava stood there, wondering at his remark. Finally, the soldier turned back to her.

"Yes, by all means, Frau, go to church."

They stepped back and allowed her to cycle between them. Her cheeks burned, knowing they watched her as she rode away. She quickened her pace and hurried into town, slowing down only when she saw traffic coming in and out of the main roads.

Ava took a deep breath and resolved to continue her errands. She went to the boulangerie, where there at least nothing seemed to have changed. The comforting smell of bread met her at the door, and she went up to the counter.

"Two loaves, please," she said, opening her handbag to take out a coin.

"I'm sorry, ma'am," said the girl behind the counter. "But we are only allowed to sell one loaf per family now."

Ava nodded. "One loaf, then."

Ordinarily, they would eat most of a baguette and save the stale ends to feed the chickens, who went after them enthusiastically. But now she could see with rationing that there would be little to feed them, fewer scraps every day. She thought of Henry and Catherine and said a prayer that wherever they were, there was plenty of food and they wouldn't have to go hungry. It wasn't much, but it was all she could do for them now.

Leaving the shop, she headed toward the church. It was a familiar route. While Saint Peter Port was Guernsey's capital and its most important city, it was still a charming, small town. The harbor view of dozens of pale, whitewashed buildings with their pink roofs and the church steeples peering out from above gave her a lump in her throat each time she saw it. Through the years, she often stopped into the empty chapel during the week for a moment of peace. Like the high street, with its stately stone buildings and narrow lanes, it was as comforting to her as her mother's embrace. Things wouldn't always be like this, she reminded herself. Guernsey wouldn't suffer under an occupation forever. She parked her bicycle outside. Removing her scarf, she tucked it into her bag and pulled open the heavy wood doors.

She froze in the doorway, stunned by what she saw. Everything had been moved. Pews were pushed out of the way, chairs knocked over and kicked into corners. Signs were tacked up, although they were in German, which she couldn't read, apart from "Heil Hitler." Most alarmingly, the altar was draped in the Nazi flag. When she recovered herself, she searched the building for the vicar, but he was nowhere to be found.

Leaving the building, she retrieved her bicycle from where she had leaned it against the wall and walked it down the street. A woman near her own age was walking in her direction, and she stopped to speak to her.

"What happened at the church?" she asked.

The woman looked around to make certain no one was listening. "It's not just this one. It's happened all over the island. The clergy have been sent home, and the Germans have staked their claim."

"But what about services?" Ava pressed.

"There are no more services," the woman said, lowering her eyes. "Excuse me, I must get home."

Ava turned and watched her hurry away, then went farther into the town until she reached the square. The drone of planes overhead sounded closer every moment. She clapped her hands over her ears at the deafening roar. They flew far lower than usual, likely trying to intimidate the very people who were powerless to fight back. A minute later, the air was swirling with white sheets of paper like large flakes of snow, drifting to the ground below. She picked up one and studied the German words filling the page, although it didn't matter what it said. Crumpling it in her hand, she threw it back onto the ground. She would be damned if she would learn to speak German. This was the Bailiwick of Guernsey, not an outpost of Nazi Germany. They were a self-governing land and would be so one day again.

Two impulses rose inside her like bile. The first was that she had to fight the Nazis with every breath of her being, and the second, that she must buckle down and comply with the occupation if she wanted to be reunited with her children after the war. Turning toward home, she wondered which of the two demons on her shoulder would best the other. At this point, she didn't really know.

# 8

---

*Lily*

**Because I want to; because I must; because now and forever more this is where I belong to be.**

—DAPHNE DU MAURIER, *JAMAICA INN*

After the day at the beach, Lily decided to avoid Peter as much as she could. She wasn't looking for a man in her life, even one as charming as Peter Ashby. It was enough of a challenge learning how to bond with Catherine; she didn't need to complicate her life further. Fortunately, every day the two of them spent together felt more natural than the day before. Lily tried to convince herself she had done the right thing, saving the child from the devastating circumstances that would have awaited her in a place like Manchester. In her stronger moments, she believed it was the best decision for Henry, too, even if he didn't realize it yet. He was too young to care for a four-year-old on his own, and taking on such an enormous responsibility would have stretched him to his breaking point. Children weren't meant to be the provider and protector of others. They were meant to be cared for themselves. But the guilt was strong, at times overpowering. She would never forget their mother screaming for them as the bus pulled out of the schoolyard, and Henry had heard it, too. She lay awake many nights, wondering if he had nightmares about it. He was too young to be on his own, and if anything happened to him, it would be her fault. Lily prayed for him in those dark hours, that he would be able to cope with his newfound situation. She told herself she couldn't have taken both of them, even if she'd wanted to. There were many impediments to having two children: the expense of feeding them, the care and attention involved. Not to mention the house was barely big enough for her and Catherine, however much it was a godsend.

What she didn't admit to herself was that she wanted Catherine almost from the first moment she had seen her. Throughout her childless marriage, she had dreamed of having a daughter to spoil, to dress in pretty clothes, and to have as a friend and confidante when she herself was old. Every woman must feel the same, she was sure. She delighted in Catherine's elfin face and dazzling eyes, her hair as golden as the sun. Not every child was as perfect as she was in disposition, either. Lily comforted herself that the girl could have fallen into the wrong hands, being left to someone who wasn't kind and didn't treasure her and care for her as she would.

It was a miracle that they had found each other under such difficult circumstances. Nothing less than a miracle, indeed. Thousands upon thousands of Guernsey children had been scattered to the edges of the kingdom, and they had to find comfort and safety wherever they could.

To her relief, Catherine had begun to trust her and even become attached to her. Sometimes at night, the child folded herself into her arms to be held. Lily allowed the relationship to develop slowly. She felt if she provided a loving, safe environment for her, Catherine would adjust. Guilt gnawed at the back of Lily's mind because she had done something wrong. Many things, perhaps. But her motives were pure. She'd found a child who needed to be cared for in the midst of war, a child too young to travel unaccompanied by a parent. The war had made orphans of them all. Lily never spoke of Henry or Catherine's parents to her, but she did find a glass bottle and saved the stones the child had collected from the beach, a silent reminder of Catherine's other life. However, she didn't allow herself to think about what would happen in the future. It would have to take care of itself.

Peter, on the other hand, was a complication she could not afford, a danger to them in ways he would never understand. He was inquisitive about her past, and if he discovered what she was doing—that she had taken another woman's child—he could report her to the authorities. When she made the decision to seek help from the church, she'd expected to find an older, fatherly vicar to give her advice, not someone like Peter.

He was a compelling man, always smiling and so full of life. She knew from the first day that if she allowed herself, she could fall in love with him. It was obvious from even the smallest reaction she had to him. At the beach, they had brushed shoulders once or twice, and the touch had sent a tremor up her spine.

But she had lied to him about many things, and good relationships couldn't be based on lies. She wasn't a widow. She wasn't Catherine's mother, as he assumed. She wasn't a pauper, as she had led him to believe; she had a handbag full of pound notes, although she needed to make it last for as long as possible. But Lily couldn't talk to him about any of these things. He would never understand, not to mention it would hurt him to realize he had been deceived. He saw her as a decent and honorable woman, showing respect for her and her circumstances.

Together, she and Catherine were forging a good life. They fed Mrs. Rawlings's cat with a small dish of milk each morning. They took walks in the town and stared in shop windows, sometimes buying a ribbon for Catherine's hair. In the evenings, Lily took the girl on her lap and read her stories. On Sundays, they went to church. It was the life she had craved since childhood and of which she had been deprived, the life she would have had with Andrew if he hadn't been so tragically killed.

She regretted nothing about leaving Guernsey. She missed her parents and Helen, but she had to let them go. If she stayed, she would remain forever at the mercy of a cruel man. The future was what was important. The war threatened England, but she felt safe, hoping that perhaps in this remote village, they would remain untouched.

On Thursday, she got up and went into the kitchen to make tea. The previous week, she had perched three small pots of red geraniums on the windowsill to brighten the room. The sight of them now brought a smile to her lips. She watered them after putting on the kettle to boil. The cat caught her eye outside the window as it ran along the fence, master of all he surveyed. Lily sorted the tea, humming to herself. They had a good life here. How could she possibly have been happy in a huge, empty home with Ian when this was all she required?

Catherine slept in a little longer that morning and came padding into the kitchen a half hour later, her hair askew. Lily smoothed it down with her fingers.

"What would you like to do today?" she asked, setting a bowl of porridge in front of her. "Shall we take a walk?"

"Could we go to the beach with Peter again?" the child asked, dipping her spoon into her bowl.

"Well, he's very busy, you know," Lily replied. "He has the church to take care of and lots of people to look out for. We mustn't take up all his time."

"He'll say yes, Mama," she cajoled. "Please?"

Lily turned in surprise, catching her breath. It was the first time she'd ever been called Mama, and her heart brimmed with love for this beautiful child.

"Well, perhaps we can ask him what he's doing later," she conceded. It was hard to deny her anything.

However, the gray skies out the window quickly turned to rain. A trip to see Peter would have to wait. Lily realized she was as disappointed as Catherine.

"I bought you something," Lily told her. "I've been saving it for a rainy day."

Catherine jumped up to see what it was as Lily took down a parcel from the dresser and unwrapped it carefully. Inside there were sheets of crisp white paper and a bright tin of colored pencils. Catherine reached a tentative hand in and lifted one of them, touching the point with her finger.

"Do you like to draw?" Lily asked.

Catherine nodded.

"Have you ever tried it before?"

The child shook her head and Lily laughed.

"Then today, we will learn together, you and I," she said.

She cleared the table and set out two sheets of paper and placed the colored pencils in a glass between them. First, she would draw an object, and Catherine would try to imitate it, but soon the girl was making pictures on her own. They worked on drawings all afternoon.

They were the fortunate ones. Lily scoured the newspapers for information whenever she could, aware that everyone she'd left behind was now suffering under German occupation. If Catherine's mother had kept her there on the island, she would have been in danger, too. But fortunately, she'd had the courage to send her child to a safer land, and for that, Lily would always be grateful.

The next morning, there was a knock at the door. Lily hesitated before she answered it. Unbidden knocks could mean that someone had uncovered what she had done. While she believed she had rescued Catherine, others might question the lawfulness of her decision. In her darker moments, she wondered if Catherine could be torn from her arms and relegated to an orphanage while she was consigned to sit for years in a cold, hard cell for taking a child that wasn't her own. Yet there was no one she could ask and no way to find the answer. Reluctantly, she opened the door. It was Susie Brooks, to whom she had been introduced at Holy Trinity a few weeks earlier. Lily opened the door and led her inside.

"Good morning," she said, curious at the sudden appearance of Peter's friend. "Please come in."

Susie was at least eight months pregnant, and she entered the house, settling herself into one of the chairs at Lily's invitation, holding her swelling belly.

"May I get you something?" Lily asked. "Perhaps some tea?"

Susie shook her head. "I'm fine, thank you, Mrs. Carré. I came to offer you a proposition, if you're interested."

"Please, call me Lily."

"And I'm Susie," she replied. "I'm in need of some help before my baby arrives and for a while after. I was thinking three or four hours a day, for a few weeks. I wondered if you might be interested. I'm afraid we wouldn't be able to pay you much, but meals would be included."

"That's very kind of you," Lily answered, relieved. "I would be happy to help you. Of course, I have Catherine…"

Susie smiled. "Bring her with you. She'll be good company for my daughter. They're only about a year apart, aren't they? I thought you could do the cooking and cleaning and keep an eye on Alice. We could pay you a little something each week until I get back on my feet. Perhaps by then, something better will come along for you."

Lily nodded. "I'd love to. Thank you so much. You've all been so welcoming to the two of us."

"Wonderful," Susie said. "That's settled. When would you like to start? To be honest, I'm ready to get off my feet any time."

"What about this afternoon?" Lily asked. "I'll make dinner."

"You're a godsend." Susie reached into her handbag and took out a list and a packet of money. "This is what we'll need from the market, if you don't mind."

"I'm actually glad for something to do," Lily said. She meant it. It would likely be good for Catherine, too.

"Well then, I'd better go. My neighbor is watching Alice for me, and I promised I wouldn't be long." She took Lily's hand. "I'm so glad you're here. This means a lot to me. I'm sure we'll be great friends."

After she'd gone, Lily turned to Catherine. "We're going to have some fun today. First, we'll go to the market and then to a friend's house. Won't that be nice?"

Catherine nodded, although she wasn't paying attention. She'd lost interest in her drawing and had decided to find the cat.

The Brookses' house was typical of the area: a stone cottage with wisteria climbing around the eaves and a white wooden gate out front. Lily shifted the basket of vegetables and sausages on her arm and lifted the latch, walking with Catherine to the front door. She knocked and stepped back, waiting.

"There you are!" Susie said when she opened the door. "Come in, won't you?"

A ginger-headed girl a little younger than Catherine appeared behind her mother and gave them a shy smile.

"This is Alice," Susie said. "Alice, this is Catherine and her mother, Lily."

The girls began to talk almost at once, and Susie showed Lily to the kitchen. After a few days, she realized that coming to the cottage was the best part of their day. The children got along well, and cooking and cleaning for the Brookses assuaged some of the guilt she felt at the way she'd attained her current happiness.

Over the next few weeks, Lily began to relax, convincing herself that everything was all right.

In some ways, she had saved Catherine, who might have been overlooked or even abused in the crowded, meager conditions the evacuees were forced to endure. The child could have been lost or even injured in the chaotic circumstances to which they were subjected. By taking her, Lily had rescued her from a desperate situation and was giving the child a solid, happy life. They had a comforting routine. Her relationship with Susie was friendly, and though she kept Peter at arm's length, Lily enjoyed going to Holy Trinity: the walk to the church with Catherine in their Sunday best, slowly becoming part of their community, and the sunny sermons Peter gave, reassuring his flock during the strained days of war.

Susie's labor began a couple of weeks later, and Lily was in the house when the contractions started. They were slow and steady at first, though she rang for the midwife anyway. Having never gone through it herself, she was nervous for Susie. So much, she believed, could go wrong.

She had never been present at a birth and had never expected to be. She found it nothing like she had imagined. Although she was relegated to fetching towels and hot water, she lingered at the edge of the room, watching the writhing and moaning of her friend. It was a long and difficult process. Occasionally, Susie's screams pierced the air, though Lily could hardly comfort the children due to her own fear. She fed them and sent them downstairs to play while she went back to the birthing room, mesmerized by the horror of such pain and suffering.

"Push," the midwife ordered.

Lily moved closer for a better look. A round, bloody ring encircled the baby's head, which had begun to crown. The midwife held out her hands, waiting for the child to be born. It slid out on the third push, facedown, arms slack at its sides, limbs limp from trauma. The midwife cleaned out the infant's mouth and nose and then wrapped it in a towel. There was so much blood—on the baby, on the sheets, streaking down Susie's limbs. It was horrifying. Yet the infant began to mewl, and the mother and midwife smiled, letting Lily know the birth had been a success.

It was a healthy baby girl. Lily left them to sort out the next steps and returned only to put fresh linens on the bed an hour later.

"What do you think?" Susie asked when she returned, clearly proud of her newest child.

"She's beautiful," Lily answered.

The baby was so small and fragile, she was afraid to come near. Tiny feet kicked in the air, and she reached down and touched one, reveling in her feather-soft skin, by far the softest thing Lily had ever touched. The baby's ribs were visible, and her hands reached out, tiny fingers opening and closing in the air. Lily was fascinated, staring at the child in wonder.

"It takes you back, doesn't it?" Susie murmured, pulling her dressing gown around her. "Was Catherine as little as this?"

"Yes," Lily answered, wishing she knew the answer. But of course, she must have been. She was still so small now.

She watched Susie swaddle the baby in a blanket with deft hands, as confident in what she was doing as Lily could imagine.

"She's even smaller than Alice was," Susie remarked. "It's hard to believe time has flown by so quickly. You should have seen me then. I was so happy to have a baby, I could hardly put her down. I suppose all mothers feel the same."

She leaned back on the bed and lay the baby against her chest. The infant stopped mewling and began to relax as Susie rubbed her gently on the back.

Lily was still reeling from the experience. She couldn't help but wonder if it had been as difficult for Catherine's mother to be delivered of her children. No wonder the woman had screamed at the bus, frustrated that she hadn't even been able to tell them goodbye.

"Is there anything better?" Lily murmured, trying to keep her murky thoughts at bay.

"Nothing in the world," Susie answered.

Lily left the room and found Catherine and Alice. She sat with them for a while and then, giving Catherine a pat on the head, went into the kitchen to make a pot of soup. After half an hour, she went in to check on Susie, who had put the baby into the cradle next to the bed and fallen asleep herself. She drew the blanket over her friend's shoulder and, glancing at the baby to make certain she was all right, turned and closed the door behind her.

Later, Lily heard the sound of the baby waken and begin to cry. She went back to the room and smiled at Susie, lifting the squalling red-faced infant from the cradle and placing her in her mother's arms. Susie opened her gown and lifted the baby to her breast, where she settled down and latched onto the nipple. In the past, Lily would have felt devastated at the unfairness of living a life with no children. Plenty of women had children who didn't treat them well and certainly didn't deserve them. Not Susie, of course, but many others she had observed through the years. Until that moment, Lily hadn't realized how deep her envy was of other women, having this experience and knowing the joy of having a child of their own. But for the first time, she wasn't envious at all. She stepped into the doorway and watched Catherine playing with Alice. She finally had a child in her life, and it didn't matter to her in the least if she had birthed her or not. She, like millions of women all over the world, was finally experiencing the joy of motherhood, and she wouldn't trade it for anything in the world.

She turned back to Susie and smiled.

"Can I bring you some tea?" she asked.

But Susie was so engrossed with her baby, she didn't hear a thing.

Gavin soon arrived home to see his wife. As Lily prepared the evening meal, there was a knock at the door. She left the kitchen to open it, and when she did, Peter was standing on the step. He smiled when he saw her.

"Come in," she said as he stepped through the door.

Catherine looked up from where she was sitting on the floor and jumped to her feet.

"Peter!" she cried.

She ran to him as if he were her favorite person in the world. He laughed and lifted her into his arms. Gavin looked at Lily and raised a brow, making her blush. It was obvious to them all that there was an attachment forming among the three of them. Peter gave the child a squeeze and set her down next to Alice.

"And what have we here, ladies?" he asked, kneeling next to them.

"We're giving our babies some tea," Alice said matter-of-factly.

"Oh, I see," Peter replied, a serious look on his face. "And what do they like for tea?"

"The same things we do, silly!" Catherine answered.

Lily couldn't help being touched. Not all men were good with children, but Peter treated them as if they were the same as anyone else, talking to them with unmistakable warmth. She watched as he went over to sit next to Gavin.

"Congratulations are in order, my friend," he said.

"Thank you," Gavin replied. "She's another darling, just like her sister. Isn't that right, Alice?"

"How's Susie?" Peter asked.

Lily didn't stay to listen to their conversation. She went back into the kitchen and set the table for Gavin and Alice and laid a tray for Susie, which he could take to her whenever she wanted it. Removing her apron, she hung it on the hook and straightened her dress before walking back into the front room.

"Come on, Catherine," she said. "It's time to go."

"Thanks for your help today," Gavin said, standing. "We appreciate it."

"You're welcome," Lily answered. "Everything is ready in the kitchen for you, and I set a tray for Susie for later. We'll see you tomorrow."

"I wasn't planning to stay," Peter said, standing. "Why don't I drive you home?"

She looked down, afraid her cheeks were growing pink. "We can manage, thank you."

"Nonsense," he said. "I'm going that way anyway."

They said their goodbyes and, taking Catherine's hands, left together.

"I was hoping I'd see you," he murmured after they had left the house and were seated in his car.

"Can we go to the beach again?" Catherine asked.

"Hush now," Lily said. "It's not polite to ask for things."

He looked at the two of them and raised a shoulder. "I'll talk to your mother about it. How's that?"

Lily couldn't look at her, afraid she would give her secret away. But instead, Catherine settled down in the seat between them and leaned against Lily as they rode in silence back to the small stone house. It was if they had done it a thousand times before.

# 9

---

*Henry*

It started on a rainy Monday. The wind had been blowing for hours, and rain beat against the windows of the dormitory with a viciousness Henry had rarely seen. Though it was only early afternoon, the temperature had dropped, and he put on his sweater to get warm. Crawling into his bunk, he rolled over onto his side and stared at the wall. He'd been there long enough that he knew every crack and crevice. He'd come to think of the tiny lines as a sort of map, as if he could figure out how to get from Manchester—or wherever they were now—back home. It was quiet in the room, no sound apart from the storm raging outside. Several other boys were asleep. Afternoon exercises had been canceled for the day, and there was little else to do.

Henry remembered rainy days at home. Mum would make treats for them, and sometimes she would sit with him and Catherine to work on a jigsaw or read a book. She was pretty, his mum, with blond hair and large blue eyes. She was small but strong, and he had never seen her shirk any job for any reason. She was a hard worker and could be serious at times, but she had a good sense of humor, too. What he really loved about her, though, was that she was a good person, like his father. They were always doing things for others and setting an example for their children. Many times, he had gone with her when she had volunteered at the church or taken food to someone who was sick. He was proud of her, so proud that he could burst. And his father was special, too. He was gentle and good, unlike some of the other fathers Henry had seen. A few of his friends had hot-tempered, cantankerous dads that made Henry glad for the upbringing he'd had. Even at nine years old, soon to be ten, he knew the difference between good and evil when he saw it.

However, he also wondered if having parents like that made him softer than he should have been, for there was little kindness among the ranks of the boys sequestered in the dormitory. He'd noted the lack of good humor among them, but a few were downright mean. On the day of the heavy rain, as he lay with his face to the wall, drowsy and nearly asleep, he felt a strange tickling sensation in his ear. He jumped up and shook his head, only to see a beetle fall from his ear and crawl under the bed.

Four boys stood a few feet away, convulsing in laughter. The oldest was named Richard, and even though he hadn't had a problem with him yet, Henry had kept his distance. He could see what sort of person he was, the type who always convinced others to get into trouble.

"Stop!" he cried.

Richard stopped laughing and took a step closer. "Oh, he wants us to stop, does he, boys? Do you think we should?"

"You don't put beetles in people's ears," Henry said. He could still feel a twitching feeling, and he knew that every time he lay down, he'd be afraid they'd do it again.

"Well, I do," the boy said.

Richard was at least three years older than he was and much taller as well. He stepped forward and gave Henry a shove. Henry looked about, but no adults were around, and all the other boys sat up silently, paying attention.

"Please don't," Henry said, trying to be calm.

"'Please don't'!" one of the other boys said, mimicking him. Richard and his friends all began to laugh.

Henry tried to walk around them to go outside, even in the pouring rain, when another of the boys—Timothy, he thought—grabbed him by the collar.

"Where are you going?" he asked, keeping hold of Henry, who tried to squirm away. "We're talking to you."

"What do you want?" Henry asked.

It was a serious question. He understood that the boys might be bored and looking for a bit of fun, but perhaps if they thought about it, they would realize it wasn't a nice thing to do, picking on smaller children for amusement.

The older boy considered the question for a moment. "What do we want? Hey, boys, what do we want?"

They came up with some vulgar and offensive ideas, as Henry stood there perplexed. He'd rarely been in a situation where there weren't adults around, and he wasn't used to handling problems like this. He took a step back, watching them.

"I think this one needs a knock on his noggin," one of the others said.

Before he knew it, fists pounded at him from every direction. Someone grabbed a handful of his hair. He swung his arms out but didn't connect with anything. After a couple of minutes of grappling, one of them, he wasn't certain who, punched him in the stomach. Henry collapsed onto the floor, moaning and holding his stomach as the boys laughed and walked away. After a few moments, Henry pulled himself up, the eyes of all the younger boys on him. He crawled back into his bed, turning his back to all of them.

Nothing else happened for the rest of the evening. In fact, things were calm for a couple of days, and Henry started to believe the worst was behind him. He thought a lot about Catherine these days, and not knowing what had happened to her was taking a toll on him. Was she in a dormitory somewhere for girls? Was she the smallest? Did older children put insects in her ear or hit her, too? Surely not, since she was so young. He hoped the lady was taking good care of her. He wished he could remember the woman's name, but he had heard it once, perhaps twice, and he hadn't paid attention. He didn't know he would need to remember it. Miss Matthews was her sister, though, which was a comfort, because as soon as he saw his parents, he would tell them she had taken Catherine somewhere, and they could sort it out. However, it was hard to imagine her being in a good place. All the people he had seen so far were fairly desperate. In his darker moments, he wondered if he should stop thinking about Catherine entirely since there was nothing he could do about finding her. Yet he knew the answer was no. His parents wouldn't stop worrying about her, and he was the only one who knew who she was with. He couldn't allow himself to think that the two of them had been separated as well. She had been kind, Miss Matthews's sister. She had held Catherine's hand and talked to them both very nicely. He had to hope for the best.

A few days after the incident, he was eating in the cafeteria when someone walking by pushed his face into his plate. He hastily wiped stewed cabbage from his chin and looked around, but he couldn't identify who had done it. A day or two later, he was tripped in the corridor on the way to class.

His stomach was in knots. He began to have trouble eating. His desire to go home was so strong, he didn't know if he could make it through another day. Still, he didn't tell the adults. Aside from Miss Fairley, there was Mr. Humphreys, the teacher, Mr. Davies, who coached the cricket team, and a handful of other grown-ups who appeared to have some authority or supervisory role at the school, though he didn't know quite what their jobs were. Miss Fairley was the only one he usually spoke to, and even then, she was in charge of a large number of children and only had so much time for them all. Not to mention that she looked almost as lost as they did.

He wondered what her life was like before the evacuation. She was a teacher, but she didn't wear a ring, so she probably didn't have a husband. She was pretty, and all the men teachers noticed her—he'd seen them looking at her when she wasn't paying attention—but she didn't seem to have any interest in them herself. He credited her with good sense, since they didn't appear to be terribly nice. Mr. Humphreys had long teeth and hair that always needed to be cut, and Mr. Davies was too gruff and abrasive for a person like Miss Fairley. If it were up to Henry, she wouldn't settle for less than she was worth. He was careful not to talk to her too much, though, for it would be another reason for the boys to tease him. They'd pestered poor Wilf Dobbins about missing his mummy until the boy cried whenever they came near.

One Saturday morning after breakfast, Richard and his friends approached Henry in the dormitory when most of the others were outside. Henry had hoped for some time to think about his favorite books and his special spot at home where he could find the best frogs when they interrupted his thoughts and came up to him.

"Wotcher up to, Simon?" he asked, crossing his arms.

"Nothing," Henry replied.

"He's up to nothing," Richard told his friends.

"You mean he's good for nothing," one of them answered.

They all laughed and bumped elbows over the enormity of his

wit. Henry waited patiently. It was going to get worse, he knew. Much worse.

Richard reached over and tweaked his nose and then kicked him in the shin. Other feet, clad in dirty shoes, kicked out at him as well. Then one of the others punched Henry in the eye, knocking him off balance until he fell back against the wall. Anger rose in Henry's chest, and he started breathing harder. He tried batting away the feet and then swung an arm, connecting with the side of someone's head. When the boy went down, he fell on top of him and got him in a choke hold. Everyone in the room started shouting as Henry pulled the boy this way and that. He was in control of the situation until a pair of arms went around his waist and someone tried to pull him off. Henry let go of the boy but squirmed out of the arms that grabbed him and reached out and punched the boy straight in the nose.

"Henry Simon!" Mr. Davies cried, once again taking hold of him. "We won't have violence in our camp."

Breathing heavily, he stepped back, realizing Mr. Davies was the one who had tried to pull him out of the fight. The other boy lay on the ground, pretending to be more hurt more than he really was. He'd given the boy a drubbing, but no worse than Henry himself had gotten.

Mr. Davies pointed to the door. "March yourself to the office at once."

"But, sir—"

"To the office."

Never in his life had Henry been in trouble, and never had he been in a fight. As he straightened himself and walked down the hall, he wondered what his father would say. Surely he wouldn't want Henry to be beaten up day after day. He would want the boy to defend himself.

Mr. Davies followed him down the corridor and into the office, where he directed Henry to sit in a chair in front of all the teachers and administrators. Mr. Davies explained the situation to them, and the headmaster stood, a stern look on his face.

"I'm afraid we can't tolerate this behavior at our camp," he said firmly. "You know, we were trying to make a decision today, and I think you've made it for us. We've been told that a few of you will be moved into homes in the countryside. You'll be the first one to go, Henry."

He looked from one adult to the other around the room. Everyone looked down except for Miss Fairley, who stood in the corner, watching him carefully.

"Henry's not a bad boy," she said, interjecting herself into the conversation. "I'm sure he was simply defending himself against the others."

"We can't condone this sort of behavior," Mr. Humphreys said. "If it happened once, it can happen again."

It was decided. After supper, Henry's things were packed, and he stood with Miss Fairley in the dormitory, trying to deal with the rush of emotions inside him.

"Perhaps you'll get to go to a place that has more room to play," Miss Fairley said. "It could be for the best."

"I don't want to leave," Henry argued, feeling miserable.

The truth was more complicated. He didn't care about the camp; he just didn't want to leave Miss Fairley. It wasn't the same as being with his mother, but he didn't want to keep losing people and having to start all over with new ones. Miss Fairley was kind, and he couldn't be certain at all that anyone else he met would have the good nature of this gentle teacher. She reminded him of home and of his school and better times.

"I'm afraid we don't have a choice," she said.

He appreciated how she included herself in his misfortune. Her eyes were so kind, Henry wanted to hold on to her and never leave. But he didn't. Men, even young ones, couldn't allow themselves such weakness. He tried to swallow the lump coming up in his throat, and she didn't make things any better when she brushed his hair back from his face to get a better look at his black eye.

"You need a compress on that," she said, standing. She came back a few minutes later with a cold, wet cloth and held it out to him. "Hold it over your eye, just there."

Henry obeyed. After a few minutes, the throbbing lessened, and he stood. Miss Fairley moved over to a desk in the corner, and he was grateful it was only the two of them in the room. He thought for a moment and then removed his shoe, fishing the ten-pound note from the toe. Then he walked over to Miss Fairley and held it out to her.

"What's this?" she asked, shocked to see such a large sum held out in front of her.

"I had it in my bag since we left Guernsey, Miss," he said.

"Then it's your money, Henry," she said, looking him in the eye. "You shouldn't wave it about. Someone might take it from you."

It made him feel better that she recognized there was something of a criminal element in the boys' dormitory.

"I want you to have it," he insisted.

"But why?" she asked, looking confused. "You may need it for the trip ahead."

"They'll take care of me because I'm young," he reasoned. "But you have no one here to take care of you."

She got the same look on her face that his mother did whenever he had been especially good. Reaching out, she took him by the shoulders and drew him close.

"I'll pray for you, Henry Simon," she whispered.

They heard the crowds coming and pulled apart. Miss Fairley gave him a long look and then, slipping the money down the front of her blouse, she sat down at the desk once more and went back to work on what she was doing. None of the other boys noticed anything when they burst through the door, laughing and talking. Henry went back to his bunk and sat there, staring at his wall.

Within an hour, he was packed up and shipped away on another train, trundling off deep into the night.

# PART THREE

# 10

OCTOBER 1940

*Lily*

> I wanted to go on sitting there, not talking, not listening to the others, keeping the moment precious for all time, because we were peaceful all of us, we were content and drowsy even as the bee who droned above our heads.
>
> —DAPHNE DU MAURIER, *REBECCA*

Gradually, Lily and Peter became a couple in the eyes of the village without even realizing it. Parishioners began to notice when he shook her hand and held it a moment longer than anyone else's after the Sunday morning sermon. He sat next to her whenever they were invited for dinner at the Brookses' or when they attended an outdoor music concert. When Holy Trinity asked for volunteers to feed the poor one Saturday a month, Lily offered her services, and Peter tied on an apron as well and positioned himself next to her. It was inevitable that at some point people should begin to think of them together. Mothers stopped pushing their daughters toward the eligible vicar, for it seemed he wouldn't be eligible for long.

Although she tried to keep up her guard, Lily loved being near him. Goodwill generated from him in a way she had never seen in anyone before. It was particularly noticeable in the compassion with which he served those in need. He knew everyone who came in and treated them with dignity in the midst of their troubles.

"Have you seen the papers?" he asked one Saturday morning when they were washing down tables after ladling food.

"Not today," she replied, looking up. "Why? Has something happened?"

She was always interested in hearing what was happening in terms of war efforts, having a keen interest in Guernsey's situation in particular. From what she had read so far, the occupation was troubling in many respects. Bus service had been stopped, automobiles confiscated or allowed for official German business only. It was a hardship for the elderly. Younger citizens could bicycle about, but people like her parents weren't healthy enough to cycle for miles to get a loaf of bread. She felt a twinge of guilt as she realized that she and Ian would have taken in her parents and allowed them to live in comfort and security if she had stayed behind, but it was too late to think about all that now.

Bombs had destroyed several buildings on the island as well as homes. Food was becoming scarce, another problem for those who didn't have money. Citizens were intimidated and bullied, in some cases imprisoned.

"Since London and Kent were bombed last week, the government has become concerned about the southern and eastern coasts," Peter continued, unaware of her troubled thoughts. "We're the most vulnerable to an invasion. They're talking about their options to defend us, should the need arise."

"How exactly could they do that?" Lily asked. She had hoped Cornwall was far enough from the front lines that the threat would be substantially less.

They sat down to talk in the empty church hall. Peter had sent everyone else home.

"They're going to close the beaches," he said, sighing. "They plan to block them off with barbed wire and land mines to try to stop the Germans from having a place to land. I've even heard they're going to destroy piers and docks so there will be no way to get up on our shores from a submarine or boat."

She put down her cloth and smoothed her skirt. "I thought we were safe here."

Peter nodded grimly. "As a matter of fact, I did, too. But we will get through this, I promise." He reached out and touched her hand. "You're not alone, Lily. You and Catherine, I mean. I'm here for you. I won't let anything happen to you."

"You're a good vicar."

"That's not what I mean, and I think you know it."

She did, though it was a comfort to hear him say the words. He didn't rush things, however, treating her with respect at all times, but the few weeks she had known him felt like a lifetime.

"Well, I'd better get Catherine," she said, standing. "We need to get a few things at the market before we go home."

"Shall I drive you?" he asked.

"I need the exercise," she answered, smiling.

Peter stood. "Can I come by tomorrow evening for a while?"

Lily hesitated and then nodded. "How about eight o'clock?"

"Perfect," he said.

She went to collect her things and to pick up Catherine. It was early afternoon, and the two of them walked to the market. She wished sometimes she had a garden of her own, but there wasn't space in her temporary quarters to plant anything. She was careful buying fruits and vegetables, making them last. Catherine was sometimes fussy about the lack of variety in their meals, but it was wartime, and they had no choice. They filled a basket and paid for their purchases before walking home.

Lily couldn't help thinking about what Peter had said. As much as she hated to admit it, a woman and child alone were more vulnerable at a time like this. It was one of the reasons she took Catherine to church, to build a sense of community. She had hoped they would be far enough away from London and the threat of imminent attack, but it was clear they weren't. There was nowhere to go now that would be safe. If necessary, they could seek shelter with any number of people they'd come to know in the past few weeks, especially the Brookses, but it occurred to Lily that Peter was alone, too. Alone, and just as in need of comfort as she was.

The following evening, he knocked at her door. When she opened it, he smiled.

"Is Catherine asleep?" he asked.

"As a matter of fact, she is."

"Come out and talk to me for a few minutes, then."

They left the door open and wandered a few feet from the house until they were standing under an old oak tree. Peter took her hand and brought it to his lips. She pulled back at the unexpectedness of the gesture.

"Why don't we get married?" he said suddenly. "I want to have you and Catherine with me to protect you. I don't like the two of you being on your own."

"You can't marry me simply because I'm a widow, Peter," she replied, trying to keep her tone light. "I have no desire to be a burden to you or anyone."

"That's not what I mean," he said, shaking his head. "I'm in love with you, Lily. And unless I'm entirely mistaken, you feel the same way."

She wanted to tell him how she felt, but nothing could erase what she'd done. And while she could live with it herself, she didn't want to force a lie onto him as well.

"Marry me."

"It hasn't been a year, you know," she protested. "What would people say?"

"We're in the midst of a war," he said. "No one is thinking about anything but trying to survive at a time like this. It's easier to do it together. And you don't have only yourself to think about, you have Catherine. She'll be so much better off if we're both caring for her and making certain she's all right."

"You have so many people to be responsible for already," she countered. "You're the caretaker of an entire community."

"There's strength in numbers," Peter replied. "And even a vicar needs love and assurance at the end of the day."

She turned away and leaned against the tree, thinking. "When you marry someone, you take them on, even with all their problems. And I'm afraid I come with more than my fair share."

"It wasn't your fault, if that's what you're thinking," Peter replied. "I know only too well how often a widow blames herself when her husband dies, as if she were responsible. That couldn't be further from the truth."

"I do feel guilty," she confessed. "And perhaps one reason it has been difficult to talk about it is because my marriage wasn't perfect."

This was the closest she had ever come to telling the truth. She turned and studied him, trying to imagine what he would say if she told him what had really happened.

He stood back and shoved his hands into his pockets. "Lily, I may be a vicar, but I'm really just a human being with faults and foibles of my own. In my official capacity, I've borne witness to the fact that marriage is, frankly, difficult at times for nearly everyone. To make a good marriage, one has to apply a great deal of thought and often forgiveness on a routine basis. There are no husbands or wives anywhere in Cornwall, or even in the world, that haven't had their share of troubles. Everyone says or does things they shouldn't. It's how we deal with it that matters."

When she didn't answer, he stepped closer. "I see that you're fighting a war with your past and feel you're losing. You're not forgiving yourself for something you've done, perhaps. But I can promise you that just as Christ forgives his children, we are to accept that forgiveness and in turn forgive ourselves."

"You make it sound so easy," she said.

"I see what a good person you are," he said. "And I'm asking that lovely, dear person to say yes to my proposal of marriage and become my wife."

She allowed him to pull her closer, and their lips met. For a few moments, everything else in the world was forgotten. If God truly forgave her, she no longer had to worry about leaving Ian, or abandoning Henry at the train station, or her guilt about her plans to keep Catherine for the rest of her life. If sins were forgiven, she could be whole again and start anew. And Lily desperately wanted to start anew. When Peter pulled back from their embrace, she looked up into his eyes.

"There's nothing in the whole world I want more than to marry you," she murmured, touching his arm.

He laughed and pulled her closer. "Now that's the answer I was hoping for."

They kissed again and then he let her go, reaching for her hand. Once again, she looked down, watching as their fingers intertwined. They fit, as though they were created to go together. A thought came unbidden to her: she didn't remember Ian ever taking her hand. It was such a simple gesture, one that meant true love and devotion, and she had never felt it from the one man to whom she had pledged her troth. Through the years, she'd wondered how many women married only to find life wasn't anything like what they had been promised. But Peter Ashby was different. Anyone who married him would know deep and abiding love and a friendship that would bind them together until the end of time.

Later that night, she sat in bed, holding Ian's ring up to the light. It was time to sell it. She couldn't ask Peter's opinion, because he would take a sentimental view, saying she should keep it for the fond memories or to pass on to Catherine one day. It was a beautiful ring, but it was also a symbol of the worst time of her life. She had to think of the here and now.

The following day, she left Catherine with Susie and walked across the village to a jeweler's, clutching her handbag to her chest nervously. If Peter ever asked about the ring, she could say it had gone missing or that she had sold it to buy food.

"How may I help you?" asked the middle-aged man who sat behind the counter.

"I have a ring I want to sell," she replied.

When she pulled it from her bag, his eyes visibly widened. It was clear diamonds weren't commonly traded in the current climate, particularly not one the size of hers. Lily held it out for his inspection.

"What can you give me for it?" she asked.

He cleared his throat. "Well, I'm afraid I certainly can't give you what it's worth."

Lily was torn. In the end, she decided that a lesser amount would be easier to explain if and when she needed to. They settled on a price, and she pocketed the pound notes without a second thought. It was the right thing to do.

Now that it was agreed they would marry, Peter was full of plans and ideas, and Lily allowed him to have his way. This was his first and only marriage. It had to be perfect.

"I have a friend in a nearby village who could perform the ceremony," he said one morning after the Sunday service. Lily had lingered in the chapel until everyone else had gone, and he came inside and lifted Catherine onto his lap. "We could drive up there in a couple of weeks and come back the next day."

"Will we bring Catherine with us?" she asked.

"Just this once, I think it should be the two of us," he replied, trying to gauge her reaction. "What do you say?"

"All right, but who will watch her?"

"We could ask Gavin and Susie," he said.

"I don't mind leaving her there for a short time, but Susie shouldn't have to worry about her for an entire day. She has the baby to think about."

"Then I'm certain Mrs. Heaton would do it."

Lily had been to the vicarage on a few occasions, most recently to announce their engagement to a small group of friends. Mrs. Heaton had been pleased for the two of them and had welcomed Lily into the fold.

She nodded. "I think that may be best."

"So let's plan on two weeks from yesterday," he said. "And it's time to think about moving into the vicarage."

She would be sorry to leave the small house. It was her first home with her child, the first place she had ever lived where she got to make all the decisions. But she was eager to start the next part of her life. Catherine had her clothing and a few toys, and she had a smattering of art supplies and a handful of books she had collected over the past few weeks, but they didn't have much else. Everything would fit into the Austin in a single trip.

"I have another question for you," Peter said, smiling. "What do you think about another child?"

"Another child!" Lily repeated. "But we have Catherine."

"I love her like she's my own," he answered. "I utterly adore her. But she might like to have a little brother or sister, like Alice."

Lily couldn't bring herself to reply. Of course she wanted a child with Peter. He was the man she loved. But she was afraid to get pregnant, having never been pregnant before. It was simply another way for her past to interfere with her present. Peter would no doubt ask her constantly for comparisons between the pregnancies, and it would be a difficult subject for the entire nine months.

Another problem occurred to her. She had never handled a newborn before. She might be a perfectly terrible mother, uncertain what to do and how to react. With a five-year-old child, she would be expected to be an expert on the subject rather than the unexperienced person she actually was.

However, at other moments, she imagined carrying Peter's child and raising him or her together. Catherine would soon be going to school, and she would have long days on her hands once again, just as she had gotten used to filling her days caring for a child. It was something she would have to ponder.

The day of the wedding arrived before Lily was ready. Peter brought them to the vicarage to drop off their things and to let Catherine settle in before they left. He took them upstairs to one of the bedrooms and opened the door.

"Look, Catherine," he said. "Come see what I have for you."

It was a small room, but there was a bed draped in a white quilt with a cardboard box sitting in the middle. She went over and peered inside, squealing when she saw its contents.

"It's a kitten," he said. "And this is your new bed, in your new room."

Catherine looked up at Lily, who nodded. "That's right, darling. We're moving into Peter's house. We're going to be a family."

"Will you sleep here with me?" she asked, scooping the tiny creature into her arms.

Peter laughed. "No, but she'll be next door with me. Let me show you."

He ended up giving her a tour of the entire house, ending in the kitchen, where Mrs. Heaton gave her an apple.

"And now," he said. "Your mama and I are going to take a short trip, but we will be back tomorrow."

"That's right," Lily cut in. "Mrs. Heaton will look after you. You'll sleep in your new bed and look after your kitten until we get back."

"What are you going to name your new friend?" Peter asked, stroking the kitten's head.

"Rosie."

He smiled. "A good name, indeed."

"Don't you worry, Mrs. Carré," Mrs. Heaton said. "We'll be fine. There will be lots of things to do."

"Thank you," Lily replied.

"I'll have to get used to calling you Mrs. Ashby," she said, dusting flour off her hands. "Congratulations to you both!"

"We won't be far away, Mrs. Heaton," Peter replied. "We're going to the church in Polperro. A friend is the vicar there, and he is going to marry us in the church, nice and proper."

"Oh, but I wish we could all see you wed," she protested. "If it wasn't for this awful war, ruining people's lives."

"With rations and shortages, it doesn't feel like the right time for a large celebration," he said, smiling. "This is the right way for a wartime wedding. Think of the story it will make for our children and grandchildren."

Lily knelt and took Catherine into her arms. "You be a good girl for Mrs. Heaton, won't you, darling? Peter and I are getting married, and when we come back tomorrow, he will be your new papa. You'll like that, won't you?"

"Can I call you Papa?" she asked, looking up at him.

He bent and kissed her on the top of the head. "It would be my greatest pleasure."

Lily released Catherine and stood. They were going to be a family, the three of them. It was the most wonderful thing she could imagine. When she looked up, Mrs. Heaton was smiling.

"Good luck, you two," she said.

"We'll see you tomorrow," Lily replied.

"Come on, darling," Peter said. "Mustn't keep them waiting."

Lily stood, reaching out one last time to touch Catherine's face. They hadn't been separated since the day they met. Months had passed since then, although it was still a short time to affect such a change in the child's life. She rarely spoke of her family, and Lily did everything she could to keep the girl focused on the present and the life they made together. They slept in the same bed; they were side by side every single day. Was it enough to keep Catherine from thinking about her past and revealing it to Mrs. Heaton in a moment of reflection?

Yet she couldn't keep Peter waiting. She would have to make up a story if Catherine said anything unusual and hope that she could smooth it over. She was going to be married to a man she loved and was starting a new life. It was important to consider what she was about to gain rather than what she might lose.

Peter took their cases to the car, and she lingered in the doorway before reaching for an umbrella in the stand. A light rain was falling, and she hurried to join him as he opened the door for her, smiling as she stepped inside. She had to remember this was a happy day, the happiest day of her life.

Within minutes, they were on the way to Polperro. The beauty of Cornwall still astonished her, and she was grateful once again that she had not gotten on a train headed to Manchester all those months ago.

"You're going to love this place," Peter said. "When the war is over, I'll bring you and Catherine back for a proper holiday. It's wonderful in the summer."

"She'll love it," Lily replied. "You know how much she loves the beach."

"It's one of the reasons I came back myself," he answered. "London is full of fun, interesting places, and I'd love to show you Oxford, too, one day. But this is home."

"It's my home, too, now," she said, smiling.

"I can't tell you how happy that makes me." He glanced up from the road. "You know, I still can't believe how you simply walked into my life one day when I least expected it. And with the loveliest child I've ever seen. I want you to know I'll be a good father to her. I'll be the very best I can be."

"I know you will," she said. "And she already loves you. This proves my theory that everything happens for a reason."

He tapped his thumbs against the steering wheel and started humming a tune. Lily leaned back against the seat and relaxed. It was going to be all right. Peter loved her as much as she loved him. They were meant to be together. Difficult things happened to everyone, and the right thing to do was to move forward and make the best of the here and now. She exhaled as if she'd been holding her breath forever. She was safe here with Peter. Nothing could happen to her now.

The rain grew steadily harder. A couple of hours later, they reached their destination. Peter drove them through the village and to the port before taking her to the church.

"Look," he said, pointing at the boats bobbing in the harbor. Even in the rain, it was beautiful.

"It's lovely," she remarked. "We have to come back someday."

"It's a promise."

They drove up to the old church and parked outside. He came around to the passenger door, opening it as he held out an umbrella.

"Is it bad luck to be married on a rainy day?" she asked.

"There's no such thing as bad luck."

He put his arm around her and led her across the gravel walkway. Halfway to the church door, Lily stopped, turning to face him. The rain pelted on her shoes, and she was getting a chill, but she suddenly began to panic. This marriage was a mistake, and she couldn't do it to him. Not after how wonderful he had been to her and Catherine. The umbrella did little to keep them from getting soaked, and rain spilled from their shoulders.

"Come on," he urged. "We'll be as wet as otters if we don't get inside."

"Wait," she said, putting her hand on his chest. "This is an important decision. Getting married is for the rest of your life."

He laughed. "You almost sound like you're trying to talk me out of it."

"Perhaps I am," Lily said, brushing her hair away from her face. "I am not a perfect woman. I have more flaws than you know."

Peter looked at her for a moment. "And I want to spend the rest of our lives getting to know every single one."

"I mean it, Peter. I'm not good enough for you."

"Don't say that," he replied. "You're the only woman in the entire world who is good enough for me. You're the only woman I could ever love."

"I don't deserve you," she whispered.

"Whatever you've done that makes you think you're not worthy isn't the main part of your character," he answered. "I see the real you. The good person, the loving mother, the heart that does for others without complaining. You're not only going to be the best wife I could possibly have, but you'll make an excellent vicar's wife as well."

"Do you believe that?" she asked. She wanted to believe it. With all her heart, she hoped it was true.

"I do," Peter replied. "Now, let's go inside out of this rain and get married."

Lily allowed him to lead her into the church. It was a handsome old stone building, and there was a comforting sense when one stepped inside and stood on the flagstone floors. The ceiling was high and the acoustics powerful. Even the sound of a dropped piece of paper echoed against the stone walls. The pews were at least two hundred years old, and she walked over to one, rubbing the weathered wood. Looking up, she saw a small vase of flowers near the altar. She realized then that she had no flowers to hold in her hands. Perhaps it was a sign.

They took off their sodden slickers and propped the umbrella against the wall in the back of the church. Peter straightened his jacket and tie while Lily took out a mirror and repaired her hair. For a moment, she gazed at her reflection, thinking of the first time she had come to a church and gotten married.

Ian had been a handsome bridegroom, and even though she hadn't been in love with him, on that day, she felt that she might be able to love him in time. It seemed half the island had come to the wedding of the prominent young barrister and his lovely bride. She remembered the service; it hadn't been emotional for her, though her mother and sister had cried. To her, it had been a call to arms to get on with her life and stop thinking about the past. It was a chance to live in a grand house and bear children, giving her a purpose, raising the next generation of young Channel Island citizens who would be beautiful like their parents and go on one day to have productive careers and homes of their own. She would spend twenty or twenty-five years raising them and then sit back and enjoy the grandchildren that would inevitably come.

That had been the plan. Instead, the large home had been empty and silent with only the two of them in it. She used to wander from room to room, ordering new wallpaper for the sitting room or paint for the hall. She'd been consumed with projects that grew meaningless over time. Her life had been given to a house that wasn't her own, and she had little to show for her years of effort. She'd never had anyone of her own to love until Catherine had come into her life, and she knew exactly what she had been missing.

And now, Peter stood before her, believing that she was good enough to be his wife, a tidal wave she couldn't resist. How drastically life had changed in only a few months. She stared into his eyes, thinking him the best person she had ever known, wishing only that he had come into her life so much earlier, before she had ruined herself with lies.

"Marry me, Lily Carré," he murmured, bending near.

"Always," she replied.

He kissed her there, under the solid wooden beams where angels perched on Sunday mornings, lifting the spirits of all who entered. Everyone, perhaps, but married women who were committing bigamy in the middle of a dreadful war.

"So here's the happy couple," a voice called out.

"Jack!" Peter replied. He loosened his hold on Lily and walked over to shake his friend's hand. "So good of you to do this. It means so much to us. Excuse me. Jack, this is Lily, my fiancée. Lily, this is Jack Carlisle, a great friend from Oxford who's ended up in this part of the country, to our good fortune."

"Very pleased to meet you," Lily replied, holding out her hand.

"I see why you're so keen to wed this one," Jack said to Peter while shaking her hand. "You look like a pair of bookends, if I may say so myself."

"So what about the formalities?" Peter asked.

"We'll go into my office to take care of the paperwork first, and then we'll come back and get started," Jack replied.

Lily could feel her heart begin to pound. She knew she didn't have the required papers for a marriage to occur. Perhaps fate would intervene and prevent the marriage from happening after all. She followed Jack down the hall to his office with Peter at her side.

"Birth certificates, please," Jack said.

Peter took his out of the breast pocket of his coat and handed it to Jack. Lily removed hers from her handbag and gave it to him as well. He looked it over for a minute and then glanced up.

· "So you've been married before," he stated.

"She's a widow," Peter said.

"Have you got the marriage license with you?"

Lily shook her head. "I'm afraid not."

He cleared his throat. "What about the death certificate? I'm sorry, I have to ask."

"My daughter and I had to leave in a hurry," she said. "I was unable to bring everything with me when we had to move."

"Can't those things be sent for?" Peter asked. "Copies can come from a government office in London or wherever later."

"It's standard procedure," Jack replied.

Peter smiled. "I can vouch for her, Jack. And we'll get you whatever you need as soon as we can."

After a moment, Jack nodded. "Of course, of course. Anything for you, Peter."

He handed them the marriage license, and Peter signed it, then Lily. Afterward, Jack added his own signature as officiant.

"To the chapel, friends!" he said, smiling.

They walked back and continued toward the altar, each with their own prayers. Lily knew the substance of Peter's: that the war would spare them and this country, that their marriage would be blessed and happy, that children would follow, and that they would live a long and joyful life. Lily's were somewhat different. She prayed she wouldn't be punished for her sins, that Peter would never know the hurt and pain she was causing him even then, standing at the altar by his side, and that Catherine would be theirs forever, joining them in the beginning of a new life full of hope.

Peter took her hands in his as they listened to Jack perform the service. Near the end, she looked down at her hand, which until recently had borne Ian's ring. Instead of a sparkling diamond, Peter slid a plain gold band onto her finger. It was perfect. She stared at it, thinking of the promise she was making to him. She lifted her eyes and looked at him as she clasped his hands tightly.

Afterward, they shook hands with Jack, Peter most effusively, and they gathered their things and went back to the car, darting between raindrops along the way. He drove them to a small inn where they were to spend the night. He brought the cases up to the room and then, leaving her to unpack their things, went downstairs to order supper for two. While he was gone, Lily stood at the window, looking out at the sea.

How momentous this day was. How terrifying and wonderful, all in the same breath. She wanted to be a good wife to him. He deserved the best woman in the world to live at his side, but he would never forgive her if he found out the truth. She wondered if it was possible to close her eyes and begin again, as if she were a bride about to embark on her life for the first time, without the memory of ill treatment at the hands of a cruel man. Hadn't she deserved more than a man who hurt her? Didn't she deserve the chance to love and be loved freely, without fear?

"A penny for your thoughts," he said, suddenly appearing beside her.

She started and then shrugged.

"You're nervous, aren't you?" Peter asked.

Lily nodded. "It's silly, I know."

"It's not silly at all," he replied. "This is a huge step for you. I can't even imagine how you're feeling. Listen, the rain has stopped. What do you say to taking a walk along the shops for a while? How does that sound?"

"Perfect," she replied.

They bundled into their coats and went down the stairs and out into the road. He reached for her hand. They wandered for a long time together, in no rush at all, and talked about many things.

"I didn't think how hard this might be for you," he said. "And Catherine, too. She must miss her father terribly."

Lily didn't answer. She didn't even want to contemplate the thought. He kissed her slowly, and they turned to walk back to the hotel, hands still intertwined as if they'd been joined forever.

"I've got a rough interview today," he said the first day he was back on the job. "A woman in the parish is seeking help because her husband has been abusive. I'm trying to counsel them both, although I wonder if it wouldn't be better for her to leave him than for me to send her back into the fray. Surely God doesn't want people to suffer."

Lily looked up, remembering mornings where Ian was standing

as close to her as Peter was now. How he smiled sometimes with his teeth clenched together, as if anything could set him off into a wretched mood. She was often that very thing.

Unaware of her turbulent thoughts, Peter straightened his cuffs, watching as she hung her dressing gown next to his.

"I can't tell you how happy this makes me," he said, smiling. "Us, together. Perfectly happy."

She smiled, thinking how handsome he was, particularly first thing in the morning. Kindness and good looks in the same man seemed an unbearably good fortune. He lifted her case from the floor, reaching in a hand to prevent something from falling out. Her smile slipped when she realized what was inside.

"What are these?" he asked, lifting the letters tied in a ribbon.

Her heart skipped a beat. "Letters from my mother."

Another lie. Somehow, Lily knew, this had to stop.

"Ah," he said, handing them to her. "You won't want to part with those."

However, she realized, that was precisely what she must do. After breakfast, when he kissed her goodbye and left the vicarage to go to the church, Lily took the letters and went downstairs, building a fire in the hearth. When it was burning sufficiently, she pulled each one from its envelope, reading them all for a final time before consigning them to ashes. Andrew had loved her, and she him, but now she enjoyed a mature, proper love with a man who adored her, one who must never be hurt.

When she was finished, she sat still on the floor, the blue ribbon still in her hands. Catherine came downstairs and sat next to her.

"What's that?" she asked.

Lily smiled. "It's a ribbon for your hair."

Catherine allowed her to pull back some locks and tie it around them, securing it with a bow.

"That's my beautiful girl," she said.

She watched the child run off into the kitchen to wheedle a treat from Mrs. Heaton. Then, in spite of herself, she lowered her head and began to cry.

# 11

---

*Ava*

**We can never go back again, that much is certain.**

—DAPHNE DU MAURIER, *REBECCA*

Over the next several months, some of the German soldiers rotated off the island, harsher ones taking their places each time. There were fewer smiles from the officers than there had been in the early days of the occupation, fewer compliments to the pretty, young island girls, and more arrests taking place each week. Becker remained in Guernsey and still came to the farm every week or two, without purpose, it often seemed, and as friendly as he tried to be, Ava remained cold when faced with his attempts at conversation. He had a shrewd eye, however, and she never wanted to goad him into being the crueler version of himself, the one that would tear apart the house and barn and discover the contraband radio in the hayloft.

She never forgot it was there. It was burned into her consciousness as if with a branding iron. Some days, she thought of throwing
it into the sea and watching as it washed out from the channel
toward the ocean. She was still angry with Joseph, although she no
longer mentioned it. Sometimes it seemed as if the two of them
were prisoners of an altogether different sort: two people forced
to share the same house without any ability to communicate with
one another. He was irritable and silent, while her anger was on a
slow burn. She went through the motions, cleaning and cooking
and milking and harvesting vegetables, but her heart was set on one
thing only: the return of her children.

She did have her own little rebellion, one she told to no one.
Residents of the island had been forbidden from going to the
beaches. The Simons had their own isolated stretch of sand, and
when she walked down where Becker had found her once before,
she could sit inside a hidden cove in the salty sea air and listen to
the waves beat the rocks, a reminder that there was another world
outside the limits of their farm, where people, somewhere, were
free. It was better than thinking of the shortage of food on the
island, the hoarding and the reduced rations, the tractors sitting
idle in the fields while they did the backbreaking work by the sweat
of their own brows. Here, in this inlet, she could watch and think
and transport herself to another place and time while she waited for
America to make up its mind about the war.

If she wasn't careful, she could spend the whole day there. But there were chores to be done, shopping to be accomplished with what money they could rub together, and a household to run. One day, she noticed that Joseph had closed the door to the children's rooms so he wouldn't be constantly reminded of their absence. The action hurt her further. She wanted to talk about them and think about them, insert them into every conversation. Perhaps men were weaker than women, she thought, who had the propensity to torture themselves on any subject on which they become obsessed. Women were the analytical ones, thinking everything through, trying to reason what should be done and why, when men often wanted to let things be.

One morning, Ava went to the barn after Joseph was gone and retrieved a fishing rod, walking down the path to the beach. It wasn't easy to catch fish there, but Joseph had done it on several occasions through the years, and if he could do it, she could as well. She was sick of their steady diet of potatoes and carrots, and they hadn't seen meat for weeks. The thought of a sea trout or salmon sounded appealing and achievable. Tucking the rod under her arm, she climbed down the rocky bank and onto the beach. The clouds were dark, threatening rain, but she had worn her stoutest rubber boots and her mackintosh just in case. After a few minutes, she realized it wasn't as easy as it looked. It was challenging to position oneself on the rocks and get comfortable enough to stand with a pole for an indeterminate length of time. The wind had picked up somewhat, adding to the difficulty. Still, she persevered. A quarter hour passed, and nothing tugged on the line. She tried to concentrate not on the weight of the rod, which grew heavier with each passing minute, but on the things she would do with Catherine and Henry when they came home. She imagined Henry getting lost in stacks of books at the library and Catherine tugging at her skirt as they passed the candy shop, begging for sweets. Her mood lifted as she meditated on the thought of them all together again, living their ordinary life, putting the occupation and the separation behind them. There was peace in that moment. The inlet was quiet, with no boats to be seen, even out on the horizon. She stood, tossing the line out every now and again. She could be as stubborn as any old fish.

Ava suddenly heard the sound of boots crunching on the gravel nearby, and she froze, afraid to turn around to see who was approaching.

"Frau Simon!" Becker called.

She turned and looked at him, almost relieved. "Becker."

He shook his finger at her. "How did I know I would find you down here?"

"I'm hungry," she said, deciding to tell him the truth. She was too tired to invent an excuse anyway. "I'm tired of potatoes. And there are all these fish in the sea, just waiting to be caught."

He made his way down the path to stand near her. "You know you're not allowed to come down on the beach."

"I'm not escaping," she retorted. She gestured to her rain gear. "How far do you think I could get, anyway, in these boots and this coat?"

"Have you caught anything yet?" he asked, looking about.

She had forgotten to bring a pail and any other equipment were she lucky enough to catch something.

"No," she admitted. "But I haven't been here long."

They were silent for a few minutes. She threw the line back into the water and waited, both for a nibble on the line and a decision from Becker. Clearly, he was trying to make up his mind what to do about her.

"You're making things difficult for me," he said at last.

She glanced at him under her lashes. "What do you mean?"

"I can't be seen to show favoritism to any of the locals, you know," he said. "It undermines the respect you should have for authority."

"I do have respect for authority," she said quietly. "I am also starving."

He glanced at her, and she knew that in spite of her coat, he could see she was too thin. It wasn't only a lack of food that was a problem; it was a lack of desire to eat when she didn't know where her children were. What if Henry and Catherine were not being fed properly? What if they went to bed at night with empty stomachs, crying themselves to sleep?

She shook herself. She had to stop. It was always easier to assume the worst, that they were starving somewhere without her and had forgotten their parents and their home. But that wasn't likely, no matter how much she might torment herself.

Before either of them could speak, there was suddenly a tug on the line, and the pole was nearly jerked out of her hand. She gasped, straightening the rod. Gripping it tightly, she pulled back against the weight of the fish, anchoring herself with a foot on a large rock. Neither of them spoke, although she was aware of Becker watching her with interest. Who would win, woman or fish? She fought as hard as she could to hold on to it, reeling in the line as fast as she could. Just as the rod was about to slip away, Becker reached around her with both arms and gave the rod the final pull to bring the fish to shore. They fell back together, landing on the sand, and Ava scrambled to her feet to make certain the fish was on dry land.

"It's a codfish," he said, an admiring tone in his voice. "I was beginning to think you were reeling in a shark or something."

"Are you a fisherman?" she asked.

"I used to fish sometimes when we visited my grandparents in Densborn," he replied, coming over to inspect her catch. "That's a good-sized one you have there."

The fish was about eighteen inches long, and they studied it as it flopped about on the sand. She took off her boot and gave it a swift blow to the head, watching as it went still. When she looked up, Becker was giving her a lopsided smile.

"I never thought I'd see something like this today," he said, scratching his head.

She bent and took the hook from the cod's mouth and then lifted it in her arms.

"Now what?" he asked.

"Now I cook it, if I have your permission."

He squinted at her, thinking. "Don't come down here again, Frau Simon. You don't know who might find you here."

She nodded and began walking back to the house. She might not do it again for a few days or even weeks, but she would be back.

"Frau Simon," he said to her retreating back. "Ava."

She stopped and turned to look at him.

"Don't flirt with danger," he said, following her to the rocky path. "If you do, you'll be the one who gets hurt."

She nodded and turned away, not ready to consider the meaning of his words and, even less, the implication of him telling her.

That afternoon, she made a fish pie. She chopped the fish, along with strong, fragrant leeks, a smattering of flour with milk and parsley, and then spread mashed potatoes on top, using a fork to make swirls in the potato as her mother used to do. The smell filled the house, a smell she quite enjoyed.

Joseph arrived home earlier than usual that evening, still preoccupied and weary. He grunted a greeting to her and then sat down at the table and ate her fish pie without even noticing what he put into his mouth.

The following day, Ava knew she had to get out and see a fellow human being or she would go mad. She decided to visit the Walkers, whom she hadn't seen in months. A wave of shame crept over her as she realized she should have checked on them sooner. Hoping to avoid roadblocks, she decided to check on the couple and see how they were faring under the current conditions. Securing a box of vegetables in the basket of her bicycle, Ava donned a straw hat and began to pedal down the road. It was a cool day, though the sun was shining, and she was glad for her cardigan.

She wondered what life was like for Joseph on the docks, if he was able to shut it all off and concentrate on lifting box after box, doing hard physical labor without comment. He had retreated somewhere deep inside himself, and she was forced to cope without him.

Marriage could be a challenge during difficult times, she knew. She'd seen her parents go through similar things when her father was ill in his last months. Her mother, always patient, had become less so at the time when it was most necessary. It was wearing, caring for someone for months on end, putting oneself at the last of the list, and soldiering through. It was hard to forgive yourself when patience wore thin and energy flagged. It was difficult to remember they were only human, and humans had a very definite breaking point. She'd never thought she could be angry with her husband over his own grief and despair, although perhaps it was because there was no one to shelter her from her own.

Ava had hoped their relationship would be as solid as the Walkers' had always been. They were elderly, with grown children.

They didn't attend the same church as the Simons, so Ava didn't see them often. In fact, they hadn't had a long visit since their barn burned down in 1939 and Joseph and Ava had seen the blaze in the night sky and come rushing to their aid.

They kept to themselves like the Simons and most of the farm families on the island, and privacy was respected for those who wished it. People had lives to lead after all.

Ahead, she spied their house and increased her pace to reach it quickly. Everything appeared still and quiet. The sun bore down on the hawthorn trees that grew in the front of the property, shading the front door. She cycled up to the front of the house and then leaned her bicycle on the railing.

Ava inspected herself before she knocked. She hadn't thought much about her appearance in the last few months, and it was obvious now. Her shoes were scuffed, one of her wool stockings had fallen down, and her hair was flat and lifeless when she removed her hat. She pulled up the stocking, though it didn't really matter in the broader picture. She was alive, which was all she could think about.

She knocked once and then twice. After a moment, she heard a sound inside and stepped back as the door was opened.

"Yes?" Mrs. Walker inquired, peering at Ava as if she couldn't remember if she recognized her or not.

"Mrs. Walker, I'm Ava Simon, from the farm down the road. I thought I might come over and check on you."

For a moment, the woman didn't move, then she stepped back to allow Ava to come inside. The room was dark, and it took a few seconds for her eyes to adjust. A musty smell she didn't recognize assailed her, and her first thought was that the curtains needed to be taken down and washed. As she looked around, she realized the entire place could use a good scrubbing.

Ava handed Mrs. Walker the box. "I brought you a few things from my garden."

"That's very nice of you, I'm sure," the woman murmured.

When she didn't move, Ava touched her arm.

"Is everything all right?" she asked. "Would you like to sit down?"

The woman nodded, and Ava walked her into the kitchen and helped her sit in a chair. She placed the box of vegetables on the table.

"I'm sorry to burst in without calling first," Ava said.

"We haven't been quite up to company," Mrs. Walker replied.

"Is your husband working outside?"

The older woman shook her head. "Oh, no. George has been ill as a matter of fact. I'm afraid I'm barely managing."

"Who is bringing you food and supplies?" she asked.

"The Partridges have a boy who runs errands for us," she answered. "Our son was killed at Dunkirk. He never married, and our daughter went to the States last year with her husband. We haven't been able to get much help at all."

"What can I do for you?"

The answer was forestalled as Mr. Walker called out. Instinctively, they both stood, and Ava followed Mrs. Walker into the darkened bedroom. Thick curtains blocked out the light, and she hovered in the doorway, not wishing to intrude.

The man was in pain; that much was clear. Ava watched Mrs. Walker wet a cloth and hold it to his forehead, though limbs thrashed about in the bed. He coughed violently, his eyes clenched shut.

"Is he running a fever?" Ava asked.

He was in so much discomfort he hadn't even noticed someone else was in the room.

"He hasn't had his insulin," the woman muttered.

Ava felt a surge of alarm. "Do you have any?"

"I don't think there's any on the island."

"Who's your doctor?"

"Dr. Evans. He came by last week and said things don't look good."

"Where's your telephone?" Ava asked. "I will ring him."

"It hasn't worked for months," the woman replied.

"Well, I'm going to get him," Ava said. "Mr. Walker needs to be in the hospital."

"I don't think he can be bothered, Mrs. Simon," Mrs. Walker said, turning to look at her. "They don't have the medicine he needs, either."

"Well, we'll make certain that if it's here, he gets it," Ava answered.

She went outside, taking her bicycle from where it had been perched against the house. Then she began to cycle as quickly as she could toward Saint Peter Port.

She was stopped at the roadblock.

"What is your destination?" one of the soldiers asked, taking a look at her identification.

"I need to see a doctor. One of my neighbors is unwell."

He handed back her papers. "What business is it of yours?"

"A sick neighbor is always one's business," she replied. "Unless you're a heartless human being."

"Suit yourself," he finally answered.

The four men moved aside so she could pass, and as she did, she turned back to look at them. "Why do you always stop me when I'm going into town?" she asked, pushing her hair out of her eyes. "Surely a woman on a bicycle is no threat to any of you."

"We follow orders," one of the others said, rifle held aloft. "We can't get lax and let you islanders run all over the place unsupervised."

"We've done it for hundreds of years, and nothing has happened yet," she retorted.

The first soldier stepped toward her, frowning. "Don't be disrespectful, Mrs. Simon. Otherwise, we might have to take you into custody."

She looked at him for a moment and nodded, walking her bicycle until she was out of view before she got back on and cycled down toward the village. Her anger was getting the best of her, she knew. She didn't want to be taken to jail, but neither would she be able to keep silent forever.

It was suddenly clear to her the reason behind Joseph's lack of communication, his gruffness every evening when he came home. He was as angry about their lot as she was, stifling his complaints in order to prevent her own from becoming unbearable. Yet how long could they go on like this? she wondered. How much could people stand to bear?

In the village, the isolation of the countryside was replaced with a bustle of activity. Seeing automobiles on the street jarred her, though she knew the soldiers had appropriated them for their own use. A few Guernsey men ran errands for the Germans as well. She made her way to Victoria Road and cycled until she found Dr. Evans's office. He wasn't their doctor; they went to Dr. Bellamy in Port Road, but she was acquainted with Dr. Evans and had no inhibition about walking into his office.

She went up the steps of his building, opening the door. No one sat at the reception desk, and there were no patients waiting to see the doctor, so she walked through and tapped on his office door.

"Yes?" a voice called out.

"Dr. Evans?" she said as she opened the door.

"Mrs. Simon," he said in surprise. "What may I do for you?"

She came in and closed the door behind her. "Where is everyone?"

"My secretary quit because she lives too far away to come in every day," he replied. "And my nurse was taken on at the hospital after the bombing."

"You're here alone," she remarked. "Do you still see patients?"

"When I can," he answered. "It's not as easy for everyone to get around as it was before."

Ava sighed. "I've come from the Walkers, Dr. Evans. Mr. Walker, he's doing quite poorly. His wife said he doesn't have his insulin. I thought I could get some for him and take it to them now. Or perhaps he should be admitted to the hospital."

"There's no insulin on the entire island," he replied. He looked weary, as if he never slept. His white coat was rumpled. He didn't look at all like the professional she had known him to be. "The occupation hasn't been going on long, and yet look at us. They've broken us in a matter of months."

"But what will happen to him?" she persisted.

"His body will start to fail," he answered. He sat on the edge of the desk and sighed. "I'm going to be honest with you. Without the insulin he needs, he won't make it. And in his rather weakened state, I don't expect it to take long."

"Our medical supplies come from England, then?" she asked.

"That's right," he answered. "And with all communications cut off from Britain, we have no way of getting things like insulin that we desperately need."

"Have you talked to someone?"

He nodded. "I've spoken to everyone I can think of. The

bailiff, a few of the senators, and every other doctor on the island. It's a damnable situation, but for the life of us, there's nothing we can do."

"Should he be in the hospital, then?" she asked. "I mean, if there's no other option. He's dying right there at home."

"I offered to bring him to the hospital myself, but he refused. Some people prefer to spend their last days at home."

"But it's not fair," she protested. "He wouldn't be dying if it weren't for the Germans being here."

"What about you?" he asked. "How is your family?"

Ava sighed. "My children went to England with the evacuation. We have no idea where they are. My husband took work at the docks trying to get us enough money to get out of here, should there be another chance."

He shook his head. "There won't be another chance, Mrs. Simon. You know that. We're trapped. All of us. Trapped like the sitting ducks we always were."

"Where's your wife?" she asked.

She had seen the woman on a number of occasions and knew her to be an attractive person in her forties, rather elegant, she had often thought.

"Trying to keep our home together, I suppose," he replied. "I'm not much company these days, but I don't know who is. We're all suffering in some way or another."

"What about your children?"

"My daughters are married and live nearby. My son joined up to help with the fighting."

"I'll keep him in my prayers," she answered. "God bless him, trying to save us."

Dr. Evans stood, putting his hands in his pockets. "I have to apologize, Mrs. Simon. I shouldn't have spoken so frankly. Sometimes I think I'm losing my mind."

"We all are, I'm afraid." She crossed her arms, thinking. "Is there anything I can do for the Walkers? Any way to ease their suffering?"

"Without his medication, I can't think of anything," he replied. "He's dying a slow and painful death, like several of my other patients. We have to pray for them. That's all we can do right now, unfortunately."

"Thank you for your time," she said.

He nodded, watching as she left the office. Closing the front door behind her, she got on her bicycle and girded herself for the long ride back to the Walkers'.

The weather had grown cooler, and she rode out of the village under an overcast sky. Once, she stopped to button her cardigan and tie her scarf over her head. She was troubled, seeing a competent doctor reduced to helplessness due to factors outside his control. Somewhere on the island, some must be thriving, but it was hard to know who it could be at such a time.

Perhaps those who collaborated, she thought. Do favors for the Germans and have better food or a vehicle to drive or entertainment at one of the clubs that catered to those willing to mingle with the enemy. But the rest of them were coping with broken families and dying loved ones and hardship unlike any they had ever known.

When she reached the roadblock, she handed the familiar soldiers her identification and kept her mouth shut, vowing not to anger them further. She didn't like it, but she had to stop attracting negative attention. She thought of Joseph and how he must feel the same way. He had to deal with more soldiers than she did.

Her legs ached as she rode the final mile, and she parked her bicycle in front of the Walkers' door, tapping on it as she entered. When there was no response, she pushed open the door.

"Mrs. Walker?" she called.

Again, there was no answer. She went into the kitchen and found it empty, glancing out the window into the garden. After a moment, she walked down the silent hall and to the bedroom door, opening it slightly. Mrs. Walker lay on the bed next to her husband, neither of them moving. A few seconds passed before she realized they both were dead. She looked down and saw a bottle of poison lying on the floor, seeping the last of its contents onto the woolen rug.

Ava turned and vomited in the corner of the room before dragging herself out of the house and throwing herself onto the ground outside. She wept until she could not shed another tear, then stood, covered in dust and dirt from head to toe, and walked her bicycle the rest of the way home, where she would notify the authorities and then crawl into her bed, not to come out for the rest of the day, if ever.

# 12

---

*Henry*

Henry was driven to the train station by Mr. Davies, a disappointing development, indeed. The man hadn't spoken a word, as if Henry were the most objectionable boy in the world. Staring out the window, oblivious to his surroundings, Henry tried to tell himself it didn't matter where he lived as long as he could go home to his parents one day. He was feeling a surge of emotions all at once. Fear of the unknown by being sent off, this time alone, to a place he had never seen and people he did not know. Shame, for he had acted impulsively and would perhaps disappoint his parents. Hunger, because he had missed his evening meal in the rush to get him on the evening train in time. And not least, guilt, for he was leaving Miss Fairley on her own with the meanest boys from Guernsey as well as the dimmest teachers, men who didn't even know how to sort out who was at fault in a simple case of bullying. Not to mention another move, which took him even farther from Catherine and their parents.

He was also tired. He'd grown accustomed to his schedule at the dormitory. One needed to know when things were going to happen in order to cope with new situations. He tried to imagine what it would be like in Yorkshire, where they were sending him, but the only piece of information he had been able to discover was that there was a request for a boy to stay in a town called Middleham, and the administration in Manchester had left the selection to the headmaster.

It didn't help that others might also be sent away from the dormitory sooner or later. It was terrifying to be the first. To comfort himself, he thought of his parents and what they would be doing right now. His mother would be setting the table for the evening meal, probably her specialty, a thick chicken stew. His father would finish the last of the day's chores. If Henry were home, he would be writing an assignment to turn in to Miss Matthews the following day; otherwise, he would be reading a book. On colder nights, he liked to lie on his stomach in front of the hearth and read by the flickering firelight. He had started *The Wind in the Willows* two days before the evacuation and had to leave off without knowing what would become of Rat and Toad. Suddenly, he realized the copy sitting on the table by his bed belonged to the library. He worried that he would be gone so long that the fines would add up to more money than he or his parents could ever repay.

The combination of the swaying train, the endless, aching worry, and his empty stomach all exhausted him. Henry lay down on the seat, the jerking motion of the train eventually lulling him to sleep. He had no idea how long he had slept when he was nudged by the train guard and awoken. Rubbing his eyes, he sat up and looked about. The train had stopped and the carriage was empty. He hopped to his feet and ran to the door, jumping down the steps. Looking about, he tried to figure out where he was supposed to go when a hand took hold of his shoulder. He flinched, turning around to see who it was.

"Just a minute there, lad," the guard said. His face softened when he saw he had startled Henry. "I'm sorry. I didn't mean to frighten you. I'm supposed to take you to the waiting room until someone comes for you."

Henry nodded, his stomach grumbling. He followed the guard into the building and was directed to take a seat, watching the activity buzzing around him as people gathered their luggage and headed for their various destinations.

"Now, don't you go moving from this spot, you hear?" the guard said. He was around forty, a tall and lanky man. He lifted his cap and scratched his head, studying Henry. "Your teacher said you're being picked up here at this station. If you'll wait here, I'll find out who is coming for you."

Henry leaned back on the wooden bench and brought his rucksack up to his chest in a defensive position, not that it contained anything valuable now that he'd given his money to Miss Fairley. He was proud of his impulse to give it to her. No one else seemed to care about her from what he could see. He only wished there was something to eat in the bag, but unfortunately, there wasn't. If he'd known he was going to be shipped off, he could have snuck some bread into his pockets.

Twenty minutes later, the guard returned with an old man. The elderly gentleman pushed up his cap with a finger and inspected Henry, not finding anything particularly interesting about him.

"Is that all you have?" he asked, pointing to the sack.

Henry nodded. "Yes, sir." It didn't seem like much to him, either.

"Well, let's get on, then."

Henry didn't move for a moment, afraid to leave this well-lit room and go out into the darkness with another stranger. However, the guard tilted his head and nodded.

"Go on w'ye," he said. "Don't keep the man waiting, son."

"Yes, sir," Henry answered.

They walked to a car that was one of the oldest Henry had ever seen, a jalopy that looked like it had seen better days long before Henry was born. The engine sputtered and then started, and Henry felt it jerk as it lunged forward onto the road. The sky was growing dark, and as they drove through the center of Middleham, he sat up in his seat to inspect the village at dusk. It was a nice town, if small. It bore no resemblance to Guernsey, but it had a pleasant look. They didn't stay in the village, however. The old man took a road that led out into the hilly countryside, rocks crunching under the wheels of the old car.

Soon it was too dark to see much but the road, which was ill lit by the sputtering headlamps on the vehicle. The fear, the exhaustion, the hunger—everything conspired to make him tired, and he struggled to stay awake. He bit his tongue to try but eventually succumbed to the rocking motion of the jalopy and the stress of the day. When he woke, they were parked in front of a gray stone house, and he was being nudged once again.

Grabbing his pack, he slung it over his shoulder, hopping out of the car. Then he followed the man to the front door. In spite of himself, he began to shake. The suspense, however, did not last for long. The door opened, and an elderly woman waved them inside.

"Come in, come in," she said.

Henry obeyed, waiting patiently for her to say something. She was short, not much taller than he was, with paper-thin skin and ruddy, pink cheeks. When she leaned in closer, he noticed she smelled of lavender.

"And who might you be?" she asked, looking at him up and down.

"Henry Simon, ma'am," he replied. "From Guernsey."

She looked up at the old gentleman. "You have good manners for a boy," she remarked, nodding her head.

"Aye," the man replied. "Is that all you'll be needing?"

"Yes, thank you, Mr. Timmons."

As she walked him to the door, Henry took a step closer to a small room where a single plate sat on a large wooden table. He looked at it longingly and then realized the woman was standing beside him.

"I imagine you're a hungry lad, aren't you?" she asked.

Her voice was curious but kind, and he nodded.

"Well, put your sack here, and you can sit at the table."

He did as he was told as she went into the kitchen, propping his elbows on the table and resting his chin in his hands. He jerked them down again when she returned.

"Some beef soup for you," she said. "And a glass of milk."

Hungrily, he guzzled the soup and then downed the milk in gulps. He suddenly realized his mother would scold him for such behavior at home. But the woman simply watched him with interest.

"Didn't they feed you there where you were?" she asked.

"Not since breakfast," he said.

"I'll get you some more milk and some bread to go with it."

After he had finished his meal, he thanked her again, and she led him up a creaky staircase, opening the door at the top of the stairs. It was a real bedroom with a bed and dresser like his room at home, not a lumpy old cot in a makeshift dormitory. It was also a room with a door. He liked it, but still, he was nervous to be alone in a house with a stranger.

"Do you need anything else?" she asked.

"No, thank you," Henry replied. "Is this where I will sleep tonight?"

"This is your room now, Henry." She pointed to a door down

the hall. "My room is just there, and my sister's is next to mine. Wake me if you need anything."

He nodded and then went into his room and shut the door. Opening his pack, he took out his pajamas and changed. There was a basin and pitcher on the dresser, and he washed his face and hands. He would try to remember everything his mother had taught him so she would be proud of him when he finally got home. Then he crawled into the bed and, laying his head on the pillow, fell instantly to sleep.

The next morning, the door was cracked open, and Henry sat up, realizing he wasn't alone. He started when he saw a dog lying on the end of the bed, stretched out near his feet. The creature fluttered an eye and looked at him, waiting to see if Henry was friend or foe. He'd never had a dog before, but he understood the gesture. Reaching out a hand, he patted him.

"What's your name?" he asked.

In answer, the dog gave a wag of his tail. Henry patted his head and then swung his feet over the edge of the bed and began to get dressed. He had few choices in the way of clothing, but he wore his least wrinkled shirt and trousers. When he stepped onto the landing, the dog jumped off the bed and joined him. They followed the smell of bacon down the stairs and into a large kitchen.

Two ladies were cooking at the stove, and he hesitated in the doorway, waiting to be noticed. They were chatting quietly, one holding a spoon and the other with a cookbook in her hand.

"What do you think of a cottage pie for tonight?" the tall one asked, her back to Henry.

"Ah, there he is!" the other exclaimed when she caught sight of him. It was the same lady he had seen the night before. "Come in and sit down. Let us have a look at you."

Although he had no wish to be inspected by anyone, he hadn't the means to resist, studying them carefully himself. The two women were clearly sisters. The one he'd met the evening before was the shorter and stouter of the two, with graying hair pulled into a knot. The other was taller, but he was unable to tell if she were older or younger.

"I'm Maisie Nicolls," the taller one said, nodding. "I understand you've already met my sister, Millie."

Henry cleared his throat.

"Who is this?" he asked, pointing to the dog.

"Why, that's Toby," Millie Nicolls said. "He's a border collie we got from the Simpsons three or four years ago. We've raised him from a pup. I had to open your door last night because he was scratching to get in and see who was in there."

"He woke us both, but bless you, he didn't waken you," Maisie added.

"What do you like for your breakfast?" Millie asked. "I made everything just in case."

Henry smiled for the first time since he'd left home. "Some bacon, please. And egg. And is that toast?"

Maisie nodded. "Now we know what he likes, Mill."

"I usually have porridge at home," he confessed, afraid that now he had done so, bacon would no longer be forthcoming on future breakfast menus. On Guernsey, he wasn't accustomed to eating a large meal in the morning. It had been unusual for his mother to make so much food on the day he and Catherine left, but he knew she was trying to find a way of telling him how much she would miss him.

"Well, you'll have bacon and eggs here," Millie replied. "All this fresh air makes one a bit peckish."

"Here, boy," he said to Toby.

The dog lifted himself from his spot on the floor where the sun streamed through the window and went over to Henry. He let Henry reach out a hand and stroke his head, basking in the attention. Then he reached out a paw to tap Henry on the leg when he stopped petting him.

"Look, he likes it!" he said.

"Of course he likes it," Maisie said, raising a brow. "He's a dog. Dogs always like to be petted."

After he ate and they talked him into giving them his other clothes to wash, Henry took Toby outside to explore. The house was situated on the top of a slope that led down into a verdant, lush valley. Beyond it were hills for as far as he could see and a stream that bisected the back of the property between the house and the valley below.

He wandered down to the stream and knelt by the water. Bits of algae floated on top, and beneath, a shoal consisting of hundreds of tiny minnows darted this way and that at his approach. He'd read somewhere that they lived on a diet of microplankton and larvae, and he determined to inspect it further over time to be certain.

He spent most of the day outdoors, and that became his habit: breakfast and talking with Millie and Maisie, wandering the hills and streams, returning in the late afternoon. It was a beautiful place, the hills dotted with heather. He had never known such freedom. If only his parents and Catherine were here, everything would be perfect.

"Will I go to school?" he asked his caretakers one evening.

"Of course," Millie replied. She was the softer of the two, although they were both sympathetic to a boy alone in a foreign country looking for some stability. "You'll go when it starts in September."

"A bus will pick you up in the mornings and bring you back in the afternoons," Maisie said. She had a sharp eye and seemed to know what was bothering Henry before he did.

There were still several days to go before he had to worry about it. He ate his meals listening to the Nicolls sisters talk about the goings-on in their area. It was pleasant enough, but having Toby changed everything. His parents had never allowed him to have a dog at home, no matter how much he had begged for one, because of the chickens and the livestock. Here, however, Toby became his constant companion. They inspected the hills and dales and brooks, venturing farther each day. He discovered that there was a library in Middleham, and on Saturdays, when they were driven into town by Mr. Timmons to go to the market, they stopped into the library at Henry's request. There, he checked out *The Wind in the Willows*, a book on English pond life, and another on the Yorkshire Dales. He wanted to know everything about the place so he could describe it to his parents when he saw them.

Maisie and Millie Nicolls had their quirks. But he was happy to be there nonetheless. On Sundays, the three of them dressed in their best clothes and went to church, where Henry prayed for Catherine. They asked him a couple of times about his family, and he was able to talk about his parents, but when he tried to talk about his sister, tears stung his eyes. For now, they thought it best not to press him further.

"May I have a piece of paper?" he asked Millie one evening.

She glanced up from her knitting. "Of course," she answered. "It's in the drawer of the desk there. Take as much as you want."

"I want to write a letter to my parents," he ventured, glancing up to see if the idea was acceptable.

"We can't mail letters during a war," Maisie said, looking up from her needlepoint for a moment and then back down again. "Not to an island that is occupied."

"What does that mean?" he asked.

There was a long hesitation before she replied. "No boats can carry mail there while the war is going on."

"Oh," he answered.

He wouldn't argue further, but the war couldn't last forever, and he wanted to get word to his parents that he was all right. He decided then and there to start writing letters to them and hope one day they could be mailed and set his parents' hearts to rest.

Taking a few sheets of paper and a pencil, he slipped from the room and went upstairs, shutting the door behind him. He put the paper on the desk and sat down, staring at it, thinking. It was difficult to know how to begin, but he wanted them to know everything. Taking the pencil in hand, he began to write.

*August 30, 1940*

*Dear Mum and Dad,*

*This will be a long letter to catch you up on what has happened to your son, Henry. First, Catherine and I went to England with Miss Matthews's sister. Miss Matthews did not come with us on the boat. I think she must still be there on the island. That same night, after we arrived in Weymouth, we were given train tickets to a town called Manchester. Only, there was a big problem. When I got on the train and went to find a seat, I found out that Miss Matthews's sister and Catherine hadn't gotten on behind me. I don't know what happened. One minute they were there and the next they were gone. Can you please ask Miss Matthews if she has had a letter from them, so you can know where they are?*

*That night I was taken to an abandoned old school with a lot of other boys and a few teachers. Miss Fairley, from my school at home, was very nice to me and made us all feel safe. There was one big room for eating, one for a classroom, and another for sleeping and that's it. We weren't allowed to go in any of the other rooms. Whenever it rained, we couldn't go outside and there were no books and nothing at all to do. The food was not as good as yours, either, Mum. There were a lot of beans and porridge and not much else.*

*Things I liked: the classes, even though the teacher was boring; the exercise in the afternoon (cricket, Dad, I was learning to play); the woods behind the old school where I could walk around and be by myself a lot. Things I didn't like: the food; the hard, lumpy old cot; sleeping in a room full of strange boys who make lots of noise at night (and especially I didn't like being away from Catherine since I am supposed to take care of her.) Also, the boys from my old school were mean to me and they picked on me and it wasn't my fault but when I tried to stop them, I am the one who got into trouble. So I was sent away.*

*Now I am near a town called Middleham with two old ladies who are quite nice. Though not as nice as you, so don't worry about that. There are hills as far as you can see, and the earth smells very good. Until I see you again, I plan to take a lot of hikes to explore every stream and wood.*

*I forgot to tell you the best part. They have a dog. His name is Toby and he's a border collie.*

*He's a good old thing. He follows me everywhere. I think he's my best friend for now.*

*I miss you and I will never forget you. I hope you will not forget me, either. I also hope you will forgive me for losing Catherine. I promise it didn't happen on purpose.*

*I am, ever,*

*Your loving son,*
*Henry*

*P.S. Please take The Wind in the Willows back to the library so we don't get into trouble.*

He took to writing a letter every Sunday, and by 1943, there was a large box full of them, none of which were ever mailed.

# PART FOUR

# 13

---

*Lily*

> Every moment was a precious thing, having in it the
> essence of finality.
>
> —DAPHNE DU MAURIER, *REBECCA*

The war had been going on for years; sometimes it felt like forever. In 1942, the Cornish town of Bodmin suffered a blitz of its own a mere twenty minutes from Saint Austell when two German airplanes dropped a succession of bombs on the unsuspecting village. The gasworks company was hit, causing an explosion the likes of which the town had never seen. Homes and businesses were destroyed. Hospitals were full. Air raids kept everyone ill at ease, waiting for the next attack. Lily was frightened that the devastation of war had come so close. Throughout that year and into the next, the English coped the best they could with what they had at hand: building victory gardens to supply herbs and vegetables, rationing food, men volunteering to join the forces, women going work to support the war efforts. Churches, like Holy Trinity in Saint Austell, took in the poor and displaced, helping them relocate after losing their homes and livelihoods. Everyone did their part, even children. Catherine helped her parents serve food on Saturdays, carrying bowls of soup and plates of food to those in need. No job was too small or unimportant at a time when the fate of the nation hung in the balance. Winston Churchill set out a plan for postwar reconstruction in 1943, leading Britain to hope that the war would soon be over.

"It is our duty to peer through the mists of the future to the end of the war," the prime minister stated, "and to try our utmost to be prepared by ceaseless effort and forethought for the kind of situations which are likely to occur. Speaking under every reserve and not attempting to prophesy, I can imagine that sometime next year—but it might be the year after—we might beat Hitler, by which I mean beat him and his powers of evil into death, dust, and ashes."

The newspapers had printed the speech, and Lily and Peter read it several times, willing it to be true. They felt fortunate to be together and in a position to do for others as well, but they looked forward to a time of peace.

"I can't believe we've been married three years already," he said one evening, looking up from his newspaper as she came to join him in the sitting room.

"I know," she answered.

She set down a tray on a low table and poured them each a cup. It seemed impossible that three years had gone by. She loved being a vicar's wife, although her role was tailored more to wartime needs rather than the ecclesiastical. She didn't give teas at the vicarage or spend her days organizing church bazaars. Her role, first and foremost, was to support her husband, whose responsibilities became heavier with each passing month. They were fortunate to have grown into their roles together.

There were changes in their family as well. Catherine had started school the previous fall. On the first day, they walked her to the building and introduced her to her teacher, Miss Penny. Lily and Peter were given the chance to look at the classroom, a small but cheerful room where a cluster of nervous six-year-olds were gathered, awaiting the start of their educational careers. Peter was proud, bragging how easily Catherine took to it, but Lily was silent all the way home.

She was consumed with guilt after the experience, although she couldn't explain it to her husband. It wasn't her place to be there when Catherine reached this milestone. The child's real mother deserved that honor. Lily didn't even know the woman's first name, but she thought of her frequently. Did she think about Catherine on a daily basis? She knew that if for some reason she was parted from Catherine, she wouldn't stop thinking about her for the rest of her life.

All around them, people's lives had changed. Gavin had been conscripted in 1941 and was now a lieutenant commander with the army. Susie had gone to work at a military installation as a typist, leaving Alice and the baby with her mother. Peter hadn't signed on due to his role as a clergyman, but he had discussed the possibility. Lily held her tongue, knowing she didn't have the right to influence him, but she didn't know what she would do without him.

They tried to settle into a routine, though it was marred by the occasional air raid. Between their duties and responsibilities, they made time whenever possible for leisurely Sunday lunches. Saturday afternoons were spent with Susie and the children, either taking them on picnics or playing croquet in the garden. On the rare occasion, they had cider in the pub with friends. Lily sometimes wished she had met Peter when she was young, though she didn't allow herself to dwell on those thoughts for long. They had each other now, and that was what mattered.

The velvet bag full of pound notes remained undisturbed in a dresser drawer. Lily never told Peter about the money, and there was still a good deal of it left. Occasionally, she took a few pounds and bought a new dress for Catherine or a tie for Peter. The few times he inquired about the new items, she told him they were gently used hand-me-downs from a parishioner. He never questioned her about it. She could easily have purchased all the clothes she pleased. However, she never bought anything for herself. Everything she had was for her daughter and husband.

As harried as they were, all business of the day was curtailed at dusk. Lily and Mrs. Heaton made blackout curtains for every window at the vicarage and strictly followed the rules. Their counterparts in London observed blackouts in order to avoid attack by enemy bombers, but in the seaside towns of Devon and Cornwall and Sussex, they were primarily observed to prevent enemy ships and submarines from making landfall on their shores. They never used electricity or lit the stove after dark, learning to manage by candlelight like their parents before them. In the evenings after Peter walked Mrs. Heaton home, he and Lily and Catherine sat in the parlor, taking turns reading aloud. Sometimes they simply watched Catherine play or draw, content to be together. So many others didn't have that privilege, Lily knew, and they didn't take it for granted.

After Catherine started school, Lily volunteered at a local hospital several days a week. She and Peter had discussed the possibility of her joining the Women's Land Army, which assigned women to jobs in dairy, agriculture, or local factories, but in the end, she offered her services to the nearest hospital. Peter had decided that since he could walk to the vicarage, she should take the car when she went to work. He drove her into the countryside to let her practice on empty roads. On her first day to drive herself to work, she was nervous. She had never driven on her own before. The Austin was several years old, but she still didn't want to nick the paint or put a dent in the fender.

"You can do it," he said, leaning against the car. "Just remember what we talked about when we practiced."

She took a deep breath and started the car, then took her foot off the brake.

"I can do this," she murmured to herself.

"See? It's easy," he said.

Peter stood back and waved as she pulled away. It was frightening at first, having the power of a vehicle in her hands, but as she became accustomed to it, she loved the freedom of driving. She had never expected to operate a vehicle, always having been driven in the past. Ian certainly wouldn't have allowed it.

During the week, she went to the hospital most days. There, she changed into her uniform and assisted in all variety of tasks, taking medication to patients, rolling bandages, getting water for those who couldn't lift a glass, swabbing floors, and folding sheets and towels after they had been laundered. No job was insignificant when lives were at stake.

"Mrs. Ashby," one of the head nurses said one morning. "Would you take Mr. Potter a fresh pillow, please?"

"Yes, ma'am," she answered.

She put down the broom where she had been sweeping the corridor and went to the supply closet to find what she needed. Extracting a pillow from a shelf, she took a fresh pillowcase from another and put it on neatly.

Mr. Potter was an acquaintance, having attended Holy Trinity until a year or so earlier, when his lumbago began to trouble him. She had once taken a meal to his home when his wife had passed away. He was nearly eighty years old, with snow-white hair and long, arthritic fingers. She had heard once that he had been a pianist, but after retiring, he and his wife lived quietly in Saint Austell, setting up easels and painting side by side, sometimes on the beach and occasionally in the village square. She had seen a photograph of him and his wife from the early days of their marriage. Betsy Potter had been his second wife, his first having died in childbirth. He didn't remarry until his fifties, and Betsy had been a woman of his own age. They had been friends for several years before deciding to marry. Lily knew nothing of what happened to his child, but she did know that losing his second wife had been as painful as losing his first.

"Mr. Potter," she murmured as she pulled back the curtain.

"Hello, young lady," he replied.

She smiled. He always called her "young lady," despite the fact that she was nearly thirty now.

"Hello yourself," she said, smiling. "How are you this morning?"

"Quite well," he said, sitting up. He tried to straighten his pillow, and she walked over with the new one.

"Here you are," she said. "I brought you a fresh one. Lift up and I'll get this settled for you."

She replaced the pillow and removed the first, which bore spatters of blood. He'd had stitches in his forehead from a recent fall, and the wound wasn't healing quickly. Placing the pillow out of sight, she returned to his bedside and smiled.

"What else may I get for you?" she asked, smoothing his blanket and sheet.

"A pint would do."

"I'd bring you one if I could," Lily answered, leaning in conspiratorially. "But I think it might get me sacked."

Mr. Potter laughed. "There's a good girl."

"I can bring you a cup of tea if you like."

He patted her hand. "That should do quite nicely."

She removed the old pillow and took it to the laundry and then went to pour him a cup in the kitchen. Moments like these were atonements, she often thought. She was a good person, capable of doing good deeds, just as she was meant to. Sometimes she thought of her life in Guernsey, which had revolved entirely around Ian. He wasn't one for philanthropy or do-gooding, as he called it. He was a successful barrister, but Lily had long suspected that the person he most intended to benefit from his work was himself, in order to propel his career. She was a rich man's wife; she was meant to make him look good in the eyes of the community. The difference between Ian and Peter was that Peter was beloved, just for being a kind and caring person. How lucky she was that she had been brave enough in 1940 to walk away from a life of misery. From Ian's perspective, he would mock her for living in a drafty old vicarage, the hours she spent sweeping hospital floors, even the simple tasks of learning how to bake bread. He would never understand a life without servants, in particular the idea that one could be a servant to others.

When the tea was ready, she took it to Mr. Potter and chatted with him while he drank it. He reminisced about Betsy and long afternoons trying to capture the precise color of the wind and the sea. After he was finished, she took the cup and drew the curtain so he could rest. She would describe those moments to Peter that evening. He would understand, which was why she had married him.

On her breaks, she sat in the hospital lounge with the newspaper, scanning it for signs of Guernsey. It wasn't likely that she would hear news of her family, but she kept abreast of the general climate of the occupation. The food shortage was still troubling, but she had read accounts of islanders growing and harvesting their own vegetables. Many she knew were already well experienced in the art of growing produce. She wondered about her sister often. Had Helen fallen in love and gotten married? Was she taking good care of their parents? Did she think of Lily from time to time? Mainly, however, she wondered if Helen regretted not getting on a boat to go to England when she had the chance, because war or no, in spite of rationing and blackouts and bombings, England was far better off than the Channel Islands, which were trapped in Hitler's grasp.

Sighing, Lily put the papers aside and went back to work. That evening, she had hardly been home for a few minutes when there was a knock at the door.

"I'll get it, Mrs. Heaton," she called out.

When she opened it, Susie stood there, out of breath.

"I've had a telegram," she said. "Gavin's been injured."

Lily led her into the parlor. "Come and sit. Tell me everything."

"I don't know anything yet," Susie replied, her hands shaking. "The telegram says that he was injured in the line of duty and is having surgery. How badly do you suppose he's hurt? And what would we do without him?"

"Don't jump to conclusions," Lily urged. "We won't lose him."

Gavin had come to mean as much to her as he did to Peter. They were family, as far as they both were concerned. Peter arrived home shortly after and knew immediately that something was wrong.

"What is it?" he asked.

He didn't say Gavin's name, but Lily knew he was thinking the worst.

"Susie got a telegram," Lily explained. "Gavin was injured and has been taken to surgery."

Peter sat next to Susie and took her hand. "We are going to pray for him, the three of us. He will be all right. His days on this earth are going to be long and joyful. He'll come back to you, Susie. I know it."

She fell into his arms and wept. Lily put a hand on her shoulder for a moment and then slipped out to make a pot of tea. When she returned, Susie was recovered.

Lily handed her a cup and nodded. "'Keep calm and carry on,' they say. Well, that's just what we'll do. That's what Gavin would want until he gets home to assure you he's all right."

Susie took the cup, nodding. "I just want him to come home. Everything else can be sorted out."

"You're a brave woman," Peter said. "The war has made all of us stoics. We have to keep going for the children and make certain this sodding war is ended. We have no choice."

Three days later, there was a second telegram, which stated simply LT CMDR GAVIN BROOKS RETURNING HOME FROM THE WAR STOP SHOULD ARRIVE SOON END.

Susie called to tell them the news.

"So you still don't know what happened?" Lily asked.

"I'll have to ask him myself," Susie replied. "But at least he's coming home."


The following Wednesday, Gavin indeed arrived in Saint Austell. Susie had stayed home from work, and Peter and Lily were there to see their friend with their own eyes. Lily brought a meal for them and even let Catherine stay home from school to help occupy Alice and her sister as they waited. It was nearly three o'clock in the afternoon before he walked in the door. It was clear from the look on his face he hadn't expected a welcoming committee.

Susie threw her arms about her husband before he'd even set

down his case. He held her close for several minutes and then turned and embraced his daughters. Then he shook Peter's hand and squeezed Lily's arm before Susie led him to a chair.

"Tell us everything," she said.

"I'm one of the fortunate ones," he replied.

He had been on a mission with four of his men, scouting enemy troops, when they'd been discovered by a lone soldier who lobbed a grenade in their direction. Gavin had been blown off his feet and knocked unconscious. Two of his men, both boys under twenty, were killed. The other two escaped with flesh wounds. They dragged their commander to safety and tried to stanch his bleeding. When they got him back to camp, the surgeon found he had chest wounds. The surgery to save his life was successful, but not all the shrapnel was able to be recovered. One piece was lodged danger-ously close to his heart, but they had to leave it or risk having him bleed to death.

He was being sent home, having done his duty to serve His Majesty and to defend the Commonwealth, although he would have gone back if they would let him.

"Well, I for one am delighted in the judgment of the doctors," Susie said. "I wouldn't send you back for all the money in the world."

Peter stood. "We won't tire you any further, Gav. Let me know when you're up to a pint."

Lily went to get Catherine, and they all went out to the Austin and climbed in.

"He looks better than I thought he would," Lily said in a low voice.

"I have to agree with you," he answered. He looked down at Catherine, who was listening. "And what is Mrs. Heaton making for supper today, I wonder?"

Lily smiled at the change of subject, always noting when he was considerate of Catherine. He was such a good father. They went back to the vicarage, drinking coffee and talking through the afternoon. It was a rare day off for both of them, and Gavin's safe return was a reason to celebrate. Mrs. Heaton had roasted a chicken stuffed with herbs, and the ubiquitous potatoes and cabbage were on the table as well.

During supper, Lily looked up and saw that Catherine was picking at her food.

"What's the matter, darling?" she asked. "Aren't you feeling well?"

Catherine put down her fork. "May I please be excused?"

"Would you rather some broth or something?" Lily asked. She felt a twinge of nerves. Her daughter didn't look like herself.

"No, thank you," Catherine replied. "I just want to go to bed."

"I'll be up in a few minutes," Lily said.

By nightfall, Catherine had a raging fever, and Lily felt more panicked than she had ever been.

"It's only a fever," Peter said. "Surely she's had fevers before."

Lily looked up into his searching gaze. She was tempted to tell him the truth. Instead, she took a deep breath.

"Yes, when she was small," she answered. She tried to recall what she had read about them. Hadn't she seen somewhere that infants ran fevers when they were teething? However, she didn't know anything about fevers in children of Catherine's age. "It's been a very long time."

"We can manage," he said. He smiled, trying to lighten her mood. "I don't recall you being this upset when I had a temperature with the flu last year."

"That's not true," she replied, trying not to let him see how upset she was. "And I spoiled you, if I remember correctly."

"Yes, you did," he admitted. "I seem to remember sweets being involved."

He went over to the bed and brushed Catherine's hair back from her face. "Let me get you a cold cloth, Princess."

Catherine murmured something unintelligible, and Lily sat next to her on the bed, taking her hand. She didn't know what she'd do if something happened to her. Fortunately, she was better the next day, and Lily breathed a sigh of relief.

The following Monday, there was a commotion at the hospital, and Lily ran to see what was happening.

"A bomb went off near the military installation ten miles up the road," the head nurse shouted. "All hands on deck! We'll need everyone's help to deal with this tragedy."

Within minutes, injured men began to arrive in various states, some mildly injured and others who were taken as quickly as possible into surgery. The ward, which had been calm until minutes earlier, was suddenly awash in the odor of unwashed bodies and smoke. Lily waded through the sea of men sitting on the floor in the corridors waiting for treatment.

"Look for people who need bandages, not stitches or surgery," a doctor told her as she approached. "Stitches are required if the cut is more than half an inch long or deep and won't stop bleeding. Get compresses for those."

She set to work, making compresses and giving them to the ones with the worst-looking injuries, then she and several others began bandaging some of the others.

"I'm out of gauze," she said to one of the nurses, a girl she recognized but had never spoken to.

"In that closet across the hall," the girl answered. "Bring as much as you can."

Lily turned, bumping into a gurney that had been abandoned in the middle of the corridor.

She gasped, wobbling for a second. The gurney was empty apart from a man's leg from the knee down, which had been ripped from a body in the blast. The head nurse put her hand on Lily's back.

"Are you all right?"

Lily tried to breathe. She nodded, tearing her eyes away from the severed limb.

"Wheel this to the room on the left, then, and get it out of the way."

Unclenching her hands, she took hold of the side of the gurney and rolled it into the room, taking care not to look at it again. Then she hurried to the closet and filled her arms with rolls of gauze.

It was real, this war. Until this moment, she hadn't seen the worst of it, the dying, the dead, severed limbs on a gurney in the middle of a ward, which would now be seared into her consciousness forever. She threw herself into her work for the next few hours, until her back ached and her heart was broken. Eleven men died that evening, sons and husbands and fathers whose families would have to be notified.

That evening, Mrs. Heaton set dinner on the table and Peter and Catherine carried on a conversation, oblivious to her silence. Later, Lily tucked her daughter into bed, thankful they were safe for the time being. But she became more watchful, ever cognizant of her responsibility to keep this child from harm, now and forevermore.

# 14

---

> If only there could be an invention...that bottled up
> a memory, like scent. And it never faded, and it
> never got stale. And then, when one wanted it, the
> bottle could be uncorked, and it would be like living
> the moment all over again.
>
> —DAPHNE DU MAURIER, *REBECCA*

Every summer, Guernsey was alive with wildflowers. Before the war, it had been a mecca for European artists who came to paint the island in its glory. The Simons' property was no exception, with bright, colorful blooms bursting through the ground in spring and dotting the horizon for the duration of summer. This year, when Ava noted the first Saint Peter Port daisy making its way through the earth after the rough winter months, she kicked at it, loosening it from its roots, and then reached down, ripping it from the ground. She put it down to a black mood, but a few days later, when she saw a patch of white blossoms taking root near the vegetable garden where she was turning the soil for the new crop, she attacked it with a hoe and beat at it until she nearly lost control.

Life was infuriating. She missed the children with a consuming passion. Although the Red Cross stated their intention to account for every child and get word at least once to their parents during the occupation that they were safe, she and Joseph had waited nearly three years in vain for news.

"How much longer?" she asked him at supper one evening. "Why haven't we heard something yet?"

"There are thousands upon thousands of displaced women and children," he said flatly. "It takes a long while to get word to everyone."

He'd stopped telling her that they would hear soon. She knew it was because he could no longer in good conscience promise her something that was already proven untrue.

"None of their clothes will fit when they get home," Ava continued. "I could make a few new things, but what if they are too small by the time we finally see them?"

"Ave," he replied.

"And Catherine's bed!" she argued, brushing off his attempt to stop her complaining. "She won't be able to fit in it if she gets much bigger."

"I promised I'll make a new one, and I will," he replied.

He never got around to it. He was one of the lucky ones who still had a job, though he was now paid in Deutsche marks instead of pounds, which was all that was accepted in the shops now. Not only had the Germans forced them to alter their monetary system, but they had the audacity to change their time zone to reflect the time in Berlin rather than London. The old ways were being stripped away one by one.

"I'm tired of not knowing what's going on," he said one evening when he was particularly agitated. "Every day I have to resist the impulse to steal a boat and make my way to England myself."

Ava looked up, shocked. She was mending a tear in one of his shirts, biting the thread between her teeth after tying the knot.

"At least you see people in town," she said, bristling. "I can't leave the house without an inquisition."

"No one knows anything," he told her. "Even Mosier, the foreman, only does what they tell him. We have no idea what's in the shipments the Germans get from Le Havre. Maybe it's munitions, for all we know. Guns to kill us with."

Ava dropped the shirt into her lap. "You can't mean that, Joseph. They wouldn't do that, would they?"

"Aren't people dying already?" he argued. "What about the Walkers? People are being driven to kill themselves when they can't eat or get medicine."

She set the sewing aside. It was her turn to try to stem the tide of his depression. "But we have our health. We have hope. We're going to see Henry and Catherine again."

Joseph stood and headed for the door.

"Where are you going?" she asked. "It's already dark."

"Where do you think I'm going?" he answered. "To get the radio."

"You can't," she argued, jumping from her seat. "We need to get rid of it before we are caught. They could kill us just for having it, Joseph."

"Did you know that they're teaching the children to speak German in the schools?" he asked, pausing with his hand on the doorknob. "Thank God ours are in England."

Ava was shocked. The majority of children had been evacuated three years earlier, but more than two thousand who hadn't still went to schools on the island. However, she hadn't known they were being taught the language of their captors. It seemed particularly cruel.

"It's been three years," he said, staring at her. "Three long, miserable years. We've been prisoners for every minute of that time, Ave. I want to know what's happening in the world. I can't wait a minute longer."

He threw open the door and went out into the night. Ava followed him to the door. The wind blew in from the south, a warm breeze that lulled them into a false sense that spring was coming. Grabbing a stole from the arm of a chair, she threw it around her shoulders and followed him toward the barn.

The world was still and silent, as if war had never come to the island. She was as frustrated as Joseph at the lack of information and help, but she was afraid to do something so dangerous after all this time.

The barn doors creaked as they opened, setting Ava's teeth on edge. Joseph took a lantern from a hook on the wall and lit it with a match. Holding it in his left hand, he made his way up the ladder to the loft. Ava stood in the doorway, afraid to speak. Any noise could attract the soldiers who patrolled up and down the lanes at all hours of the night, looking for resistance fighters and collaborators. Several English soldiers had made it across the channel over the last few months and had been arrested and shot for espionage. The residents who harbored them were arrested as well. The islanders were sick of the censorship, the curfews, the interrogations conducted on a whim, the perpetual state of anxiety and fear. The Germans had built observation towers to make certain English soldiers could no longer invade and get a foothold on the island.

It was no surprise that Joseph's resolve had been crushed. Ava felt as though hers had been gone for a long while already. She barely went through the motions to get through each day. In fact, she was surprised she hadn't been the one to cave in first. But the cost was too great. She hadn't waited all this time to lose her children forever.

Overhead, she could hear the scuff of his boots on the boards, the lantern barely lighting the barn enough for her to see anything.

He dug through the hay, then she heard him pull the radio from where it had been hidden. With some difficulty, he made his way down the ladder with it, handing it to her before going up to retrieve the lantern.

Ava held it out, arms extended, as though a dead child had been thrust into her hands. She drew in her breath and went to stand near the door, listening for unwanted noises outside. After he climbed down again, he put out the lantern and hung it once again on the hook and then closed the barn door behind them.

Silently, she handed the radio to him. For one thing, it was heavy, and for another, she had no desire to touch it any longer than necessary. She followed him back to the house and then closed and locked the door behind them.

"Where are you taking it?" she asked.

"To our room," he answered.

She followed him, aware of the creaking of the stair as they went up. They went into their bedroom and shut the door behind them. Even in their own home, she didn't feel safe. It was cold outside, and the window hadn't been opened, but Ava went over to make certain it was shut fast while Joseph plugged in the radio, turned down the volume, and began to work the dial.

All they heard for a few minutes was static. Once, a German voice came through, but he turned it quickly to search for another channel. Finally, he finessed it just enough to hear a scratchy, hard-to-hear voice.

"It's English!" he said.

Ava held her breath as he moved the radio in different positions until he finally got a better signal. They sat down on the bed and listened to the news being read by a presenter whose voice they didn't know. Before the war, they often listened to the BBC news programs, but it seemed strange to hear one again for the first time in so long.

"December was a difficult month for the troops," the presenter said. "On 7 December, a raid was conducted in the Bordeaux harbor. Twelve men were involved in the dangerous mission, with only two survivors. No further details are known at this time. On Sunday, the thirteenth, Jews in Britain observed a day in mourning for victims of the Nazi genocide. Jews from all over the country marked this grim occasion. Churchill continued to try to console the nation, after forty thousand English have already been killed in air raids over the last two years…"

Ava stood and went into the corridor, closing the door behind her. The world had fallen apart before their very eyes and they were powerless to do anything about it. It didn't strengthen her resolve to hear about death and suffering. In fact, it threatened what little sanity she had left. She didn't even want to be in the same house with it. In spite of what they had suffered, they had to keep hope alive.

Leaving the house as soundlessly as possible, she made her way toward the beach. Moonlight lit her way down the familiar path as she slowly and carefully stepped through the marsh grasses and rocks to the beach below. She pulled her wrap around her, perching on her favorite rock. Drawing her knees under her skirt, she listened to the comforting sound of the waves lapping on the shore. They would all stand here again one day, she knew it. Joseph and Henry would fish together or set out in the boat, and she and Catherine would make castles in the sand. She had to believe it. Otherwise, life wasn't worth living.

Forty thousand English dead from the air raids alone. She could hardly conceive of the number. It meant the Germans had reached English shores and bombed their cities. Ava had strongly believed the English wouldn't give up, and they had not. They were still trying to infiltrate France and get information to stop the Nazis as recently as two weeks earlier. That was all she needed to know. The islands might be suffering through an occupation now, but England hadn't surrendered. Their children, she prayed, were in the countryside somewhere, far from straying bombs. She had to believe that. They'd all seen the Luftwaffe flying over the island toward England. They'd heard planes shot down in the distance. She had known a battle was raging over their heads, but until she heard that number, it hadn't felt real, and it deepened her feelings of sorrow. So many people lost in this war, so many lives ruined with no end in sight.

She finally stood, realizing she had to go inside sooner or later. If she were lucky, Joseph would destroy the radio and they could get on with their lives. Nothing about Catherine or Henry would be broadcast over the airwaves. There was nothing more they could know. The war still raged around them. Their children were still gone. Three years had passed, and she couldn't help but wonder: How much longer would the suffering go on?

A sudden banging noise came from the direction of the house. Ava tried to make her way back up the path, but going up was more difficult in the dark than going down. She heard shouting, and her heart caught in her throat. She fell to her knees to avoid being seen and inched her way up the gravel path.

When she neared the top of the crest, she squinted, trying to see what was happening. A scuffle had broken out. She could just make out Joseph's voice as he argued with a handful of soldiers. She heard the sound of an automobile engine being started, and she stood, running through the grass, trying to get to her husband. As she ran, a hand came out of nowhere and grabbed her arm. She was swung back toward the soldier, and they were so close, she could feel his breath on her face.

"Another suspect, I see," he said. His fingers bit into the flesh of her upper arm.

She tried to jerk away, but his hold was too strong. "Let me go," she said.

Ahead, she heard the sound of the car as it sped off toward the town, and she tried to pull away to follow it.

"My husband!" Ava cried.

"Let's go into the house," the soldier ordered.

As they approached, two others met them at the door.

"I found this one hiding near the beach," he told the others.

"State your name," said a familiar voice.

Ava looked up at Becker. An odd feeling of relief flowed through her. "Ava Simon. I think my husband has been taken."

Becker led them into the house and back into the kitchen. "Have a seat," he said. Then he turned and conferred with the others in German.

She knew better than to speak, waiting until the three of them were finished and turned to look at her.

"We have some questions for you," the first soldier said. "Captain Jager is coming to talk to you."

Ava sat rigidly in the chair. "Where was my husband taken?"

The soldier pointed a finger at her. "You don't get to ask questions. You get to answer them, do you understand?"

She nodded, looking up at Becker and the third soldier, who had turned to leave. Becker gave her a nearly imperceptible nod.

"We'll be back in a few minutes," he said.

That was almost certainly for the soldier's benefit, not hers. She felt the color drain from her face and resisted the urge to pull the wrap more closely around her shoulders. She didn't want to make a single movement that would attract his attention. The behavior of the Germans toward the islanders who had committed offenses was inconsistent at best. Some were released with a warning, others shot, the rest taken to prison camps. It was terrifying. Ava berated herself for leaving the house when her husband needed her most. However, a person can only stand so much. Listening to the voice traveling the airwaves across the channel was frustrating in more ways than one. The English were free, if under siege, and able to talk openly about the war and its effect on the residents of their hemisphere. The islanders were not. They cowered in their homes in fear, unable to get outside information or to resist their captors in any way without the pain of death being forced on them.

A long half hour later, the soldiers returned, this time with their captain, who came through to the kitchen, where she and the soldier still sat waiting.

"Mrs. Simon," the officer said. "I need a word with you."

The soldier stood at attention and then moved to the back of the room.

"Out, all of you," the captain stated, waving his arms.

She was exhausted from sitting so still, but she tried not to move lest he get angry. It was past midnight, and she was tired and cold and numb. She simply wanted the inquisition to be over.

"Who was your husband collaborating with?" Captain Jager demanded when they were alone.

He stood over her, arms behind his back, pacing. It made her even more frightened. She started to get up from her chair, and he put his hand on her shoulder and pushed her back into it.

"He wasn't a collaborator," she replied.

"Who did he plan to give his information to?"

"No one," Ava said. "He wasn't working with anyone at all."

"Oh, come now," the captain answered. "He comes into contact with a great number of people at the docks. Are you expecting me to believe that he was collecting information that he was not intending to share with the resistance?"

"We only want to know where our children are," she said miserably, bowing her head. "We haven't had any word of them since 1940."

"Excuse me," he replied. "Did you really think you would hear your children's names on British radio? Because a few little orphans from Guernsey won't be of much interest to the general public as it might be to you."

"They're not orphans," she retorted. "They're children who want to come home to be with their parents."

"That is not my concern," he said. He stopped pacing and went over to the stove. "Why don't I put on some tea, Frau Simon? I think we are going to be here for a while."

Ava bit her tongue to stop herself from telling him to keep his hands off her things. Instead, she waited as he filled the kettle with water and lit the fire on the stove. Then he came and sat down across from her.

"Where are they taking him?" she asked.

"Your husband, the traitor?" he answered, turning to look at her. "Probably they will shoot him."

She rose from her chair angrily. "He is no traitor. You know the government and the people of this island have been cooperating with you to the best of our ability. He wanted to know if England was safe, if our children were in peril or not. You can't let them shoot him. You can't!"

"I don't think it is in your best interest to tell me what to do," he said, raising a brow. "And I believe I told you to sit down."

She sank into her chair, gripping the edge of the table in her hands. "They won't hurt him, will they?"

He walked over and took down two cups and then turned to her. "It's very important that you tell me the truth, Frau Simon. Is your husband a member of the resistance or not?"

"No," she replied. "He most certainly is not."

The kettle shrieked, and he stopped and poured them each a cup of tea, setting one in front of her. He stood to drink his, leaning against the sink. "You know the penalty for lying to a German officer?"

"I wouldn't lie," she answered.

"Why did he keep a radio?" he continued.

"We were desperate. We turned in one, but he wanted to keep the other in case there was anything we needed to know."

He slapped his hand on the table. "We shall tell you everything that you need to know."

"Do you have a family, Captain?" she ventured. "A wife and children back home?"

He frowned. "My family is none of your affair."

"Surely you want them to be safe," she persisted. "To know where you are."

"You couldn't possibly care about such a thing."

She folded her hands in her lap. "I'm merely saying that all families in both our countries are suffering at a time like this. My family has suffered, too. We're frightened for our children and for our freedom."

"Aren't you going to drink your tea?" he inquired. "Or don't you touch tea that was made with German hands?"

"I'm worried about my husband," she answered. "I can't think of anything but knowing he is safe."

He finished his cup and set it on the sink. Then he turned and took his hat and placed it on his head. "He won't be shot for a first offense, but he will be sent to a prison camp. It was a crime to keep a radio after they were strictly banned."

He walked toward the door, and she followed him.

"Thank you for telling me," she said.

"Stay out of trouble, Frau Simon," he replied. "Consider yourself duly warned."

The following morning, she got onto her bicycle and rode toward the town, unable to stay cooped up any longer. She felt like a caged animal. Her identification was requested at the checkpoint, and she gave it with no comment. When she got closer to Saint Peter Port, there were other people bicycling on the same road. She stayed carefully behind them. The islanders had been warned not to ride in groups or even side by side. They were to travel in single file and not get too close to one another.

She went about her business, buying bread, getting a packet of bandages for the knee she had scraped on the rocks the night before, stopping at the docks to watch the men working there, although her true purpose was to look for Becker. She lingered as long as she could and then gave up. It was as she was about to get on her bicycle and begin the trek home that she saw him standing across the street from where she was. She walked her bicycle in his general direction, careful not to approach him directly.

"Frau Simon," he murmured when she came near.

Ava looked up at Becker. His eyes, as blue as the sea, stared back at her. It was ridiculous, she thought, that the only person who seemed to care about her in the middle of the war was a German soldier.

"How are you?" he asked in a low voice.

"I want to know where my husband was taken."

"I'll see what I can find out," he murmured. He glanced around. "You need to be careful. You were nearly arrested with your husband last night."

Then he turned and walked away. She took a deep breath and walked her bicycle toward the church. She didn't go inside but instead sat in the shade of the ancient oak tree under which she had played when she was small and talked with friends as a young wife and mother. It was a comfort at a time when there was little to be had.

Did God still answer prayers? she wondered. She wasn't certain. Instead of being reunited with her children, she had lost her husband, too. Things were getting worse, not better. Eventually, she forced herself to get up and start back toward home. She wondered if it was safe to stay there any longer by herself or if she should try to find someone to live with until her family came home.

The next day, Becker showed up at the door. She let him in, looking up at him, hoping for answers.

"Did you find out anything?" she asked.

"He's been sent to Alderney," Becker said. "To the prison camp there."

Alderney was one of the smaller of the Channel Islands. Ava had been to Jersey and Sark but never to the small, northernmost island off the coast of Brittany, which was only three miles long. However, she felt some comfort in knowing he hadn't been sent to France. Or worse, Germany or Poland.

"What do you know about it?" she asked, desperate for information.

He shrugged. "Not much. Just that some of the nonviolent offenders have been sent there. I haven't seen it for myself."

"Why did this happen?" she asked. "Were they watching us? Hoping to catch him in the act of resistance and take him prisoner?"

"What good does it do to ask why things happen?" he answered, shrugging. "Bad things happen because we live in an imperfect world. It's as simple as that."

"What am I going to do?" Ava asked.

The only answer was the ticking of the clock. Becker stood there, waiting for her to speak. But she couldn't. She had lost everything. She didn't know if she could even go on living. Before she could react, he reached out and then, without a word, pulled her into his arms.

# 15

---

*Henry*

There were days when Henry felt guilty because he loved Yorkshire so much. It had taken time to adjust to living with Miss Maisie and Miss Millie, who were eccentric and sometimes difficult, but his life with the Nicollses was a great improvement over what it had been in Manchester. Millie was forgetful and vague. She would send him for a newspaper, and when he returned, she would ask him to buy some butter, not realizing she had already sent him into town. Maisie was gruff, but Henry came to see it was her tough northern exterior, developed over many years of looking after Millie and herself. She growled at him impatiently at times, which taught him the rules in a hurry.

However, they had their good qualities as well. Maisie had a sharp sense of humor, making wry cracks and giving him sideways glances that always made him laugh. Millie fussed over him and made his favorite things to eat. Neither of them had ever been around children before, and each in her own way had a strong desire to spoil him. Shortly after his arrival, he was given a bicycle. The women had contrived with the postman to ask on his rounds if he could find one that could be loaned to them for the indefinite future. One was promptly found and donated to the boy. It was scuffed and dirty when they got it, but even though he didn't mind, Maisie set about cleaning it and applying a fresh coat of blue paint. When she finished, Henry couldn't imagine anything better. He found a discarded bell in the shed and attached it to the handlebar so that when he came near the house, he could ring it to let them know he was home.

He also had unexpected freedom. In Guernsey, his roaming was frequently curtailed by boundaries set by his mother, but here, Maisie and Millie had no idea what to do with a young boy and treated him as though he were a young adult. He didn't take advantage of the privilege, being conscientious, but he liked being able to traverse the village on a regular basis, making friends with many of the people who worked there. Occasionally, he earned a shilling taking messages or delivering packages from the butcher, where he sometimes stopped in to get a scrap for Toby along with the evening meal. Maisie gave him a jar, and he saved his meager shillings for the day he would go home.

"Your birthday is coming up, young man," Maisie said one day. "You're twelve this year."

Henry looked up, surprised she remembered. But, of course, it was his third birthday with them.

Millie looked at the calendar, a frown creasing her face. "It's only a week away," she said. "And we haven't much sugar."

"Sugar?" he asked.

"For a cake," Maisie explained. She turned to her sister. "Don't worry. We can borrow some if we can't buy it. What sort of cake do you plan to make?"

"A spice cake," Millie answered.

"That's a very good cake indeed," her sister said, nodding.

On the day, they woke him with a birthday song. They brought him breakfast in bed and didn't mind when he fed part of it to Toby. That evening, Millie produced the promised cake, and there was a small gift wrapped in brown paper and tied with string sitting beside his plate.

"What is it?" he asked.

"You have to open it to see," Maisie said, raising a brow. "Surely you're old enough to figure that out."

Millie clapped her hands together. "Go on, then. Let's see it!"

Henry lifted the package, surprised at its heft. He took his time untying the string, lifting it off with a flourish that delighted Millie. The paper crinkled as he unwrapped it, and when he saw what it was, he gasped in excitement.

"It's a magnifying glass!" he exclaimed.

"Perfect for an explorer like you, I should think," Maisie replied. "It belonged to our father. He would be pleased to know you have it."

"Happy birthday, dear Henry," Millie added.

"Yes, Henry," Maisie said. "A very happy birthday to you. And now, let's have some of Millie's cake."

The cake was good, and the attention was nice, but Henry would have given anything to be back at home. He smiled, grateful for what he was given, but wondered when, if ever, he would see his family again. What were they doing right at this moment? Sometimes he liked to picture them going about their daily business. In his mind, he always imagined he was with them.

School was another pleasure for Henry. At first, he had difficulty with his teacher's thick Yorkshire accent, but Mr. Hall never seemed to mind if he was asked to repeat himself. For some reason, he thought it a sign of Henry's ability to pay attention, a quality several of the other boys lacked. Henry especially liked it when he read to them, long, interesting chapters of various books about pirates and knights and adventure. No teacher had ever read aloud so much in Henry's experience. He sometimes remembered his school in Guernsey where, four years ago, Miss Rayburn had rapped his knuckles anytime he couldn't say his times tables fast enough. Miss Matthews had been an improvement because she was kind and ran a pleasant, quiet classroom, but she was no longer his favorite since she had set Catherine and himself adrift, causing them to be separated. Henry wasn't one to hold a grudge, but if someone had to be blamed for their predicament, it was her. If she had stayed with him and held on to their hands, he never would have lost his sister.

The camaraderie among the boys was strong, but Henry particularly liked a boy named Percy Wilkins. Percy was Henry's age, although shorter and noticeably thinner. His glasses perpetually slipped down his nose when he buried himself in a book. He was always reading, every time Henry saw him. Even Henry didn't like to read as much as Percy. One day, he decided to do something about his friend's lack of ambition. It was a Friday afternoon, with the weekend stretching out before them to do as they pleased.

"Let's walk down and look at the dales in the morning," he said, gathering his books and shoving them into his bag. He and Percy left the classroom and went out to find their bicycles.

"I don't walk down there," Percy answered after a moment. "It's too far."

"No, it's not," Henry argued. "Not if you bring something to eat for later."

Henry had a habit of stuffing food in a satchel and slinging it over his shoulder, ready with fortification should he need it. He suddenly couldn't think of anything better than Percy joining him. The boy wasn't shunned by the others, but he was often left behind, obviously due to his reticence about physical activity.

"Come on," Henry implored. "I'll bring the food. All you have to do is come with me."

Percy reluctantly agreed, probably to get Henry to stop asking him. "I'll bring something to eat, too," he said.

The next morning, he met Henry at the house, a knapsack of

his own slung around his chest, which slapped against his side with every step. Henry petted Toby, who scratched on the door to be let out. Maisie opened it and handed Henry a packet of food.

"What's this?" he asked.

"A sandwich and some tea," she said. "Don't be late." It was as much as directive as she ever gave.

Henry nodded and waved. "We won't!"

The boys set off along a path that was Henry's favorite. He was proud to introduce it to his friend. The air was cool, almost cold, but they wore stout coats and boots and hats on their heads. Above them, the sky was dotted with clouds, and occasionally they could see a sandpiper or linnet flap their wings and glide from tree to tree, promising spring in the not-too-distant future. Henry and Percy walked until they came to a bridge that led across a wooded area, where the only sound was the chatter of woodcocks nesting in the undergrowth. At the end of the path, they walked a few yards and then went through a small wooded area. Sometimes Henry stopped there and sat in the shade or to stop the wind that tore through his coat on blustery days. This day, however, the wind was still, and he led Percy through to the other side, which opened to a path along the ridge of a hill that had been well trodden.

"How much farther?" Percy asked.

Henry stopped. He could walk all day if he wanted, but he realized Percy wasn't able to go as far on his first attempt. Shrugging, Henry pointed ahead. "There's a good spot up there."

Percy nodded and fell in step with him again. The hills and dales stretched as far as they could see. A few dozen sheep dotted the landscape to the left, and to the right was a swell. Henry led him to the crest, then dropped his bag onto the ground at his feet.

"Isn't this grand?" he asked.

"Grand, yeah," Percy answered. He placed his bag on the ground as well and then sat down beside it. "What did you bring to eat?"

Even Henry knew that the food was the most important part, and they tore open their packs to see what was in store. Henry had a hard-boiled egg, a Marmite sandwich, an apple, and a flask of tea. Percy's mother had packed ham and crusty bread with cheese, two pickles, and a carrot, which he snapped in two, handing half to Henry.

"Let's share everything," Henry said. He wouldn't mind having some of that ham.

Percy got into the spirit, and they spread everything out and divided it in halves.

"I've never done anything like this before," Percy said in wonder. "I've only ever eaten at the table."

"At home in Guernsey, my mother always let me explore," Henry told him. "But this is far better for having a good look 'round."

"Where is Guernsey?" Percy asked.

"It's an island between England and France," Henry replied. "It's very nice there. My mum and dad are there, but my sister and

I were sent to England until they can come and get us or until the war is over, whichever comes first."

Henry hadn't been told he was there for the duration of the war, but he inferred it from everything he had seen and heard since this whole thing had begun. He had already been making plans to get home as soon as the Germans were out of Guernsey. He scoured the papers as vigorously as Maisie. Millie didn't like to be bothered with news. Her world changed little one way or the other. Henry's plan, as he saw it, was as follows: first, he would wait until the war was over, hopefully quite soon; then, he would take the shillings he was earning running errands for the butcher and buy a train ticket to Weymouth. He knew he had docked in Weymouth when he had first arrived in England and that they offered ferry service to the island. He would get aboard one of the boats, then he would be taken back home. He could imagine the look on his parents' faces when he suddenly walked up the hill from Saint Peter Port and came up to the door. If he was lucky, Catherine would already be there, and he finally could stop worrying about her.

"Can we do this again sometime?" Percy asked, drawing Henry's attention back to the present.

"Of course we can," Henry replied. "Whenever you want."

Percy nodded. "Next Saturday, then. My mum was awfully pleased for me to have a special thing to do."

They packed up the food that they hadn't finished to save for later, if they got hungry again.

"Are we going home now?" Percy asked.

"No," Henry said. "Not yet. There's lots more to see. You're not tired, are you?"

Percy shook his head. "Not since we rested for a while."

"Well, we'll go a little farther, up along that ridge there," Henry told him. "And we'll be sure to stop and rest on the way back."

"All right," his friend answered.

They walked for several minutes until they came to the high part of one of the hills. It had a ridge that was steeper than Henry expected, having not ventured quite so far on his own before.

"How much farther?" Percy asked.

"Just a little way," Henry told him.

Henry's boot slipped on a slick stone and he nearly fell, righting himself quickly. He found a stick and used it to point the way. Then he stopped and surveyed the area below.

"Look at this!" he cried.

They paused, both breathing heavily at the exertion, looking down on the valley. The nearer hills were green and mossy looking; the farther ones appeared a deep, midnight blue. Marsh grass swayed in the breeze, and the herblike scent of heather rose up from below. Henry pulled off his cap and tucked it into his bag and then unbuttoned his coat.

Percy pulled off his cap as well, his mouse-colored hair flattened down on the top of his head. He had an enormous grin on his face that revealed his two crooked front teeth, the first time Henry had ever seen them. He smiled at his friend as well, and then Percy punched him on the arm.

Henry reached out and punched him back to return the compliment. Then a loud droning noise came from overhead, and they looked up, shading their eyes against the sun.

"It's a German plane!" Henry shouted, trying to make himself heard over the roar of the aircraft.

They stood rooted to the spot. The plane flew lower than they expected, and suddenly, gunfire rained down upon them.

"Get down!" Henry yelled.

He dropped down and flattened himself on the ground. Percy jumped down as well but lost his balance and began to tumble over the side of the ridge. His boots scraped on the gravel as he tried to right himself, but he didn't have the strength. Henry jumped up and ran after him, shouting his name, the sound echoing through the valley. Percy fully lost control, heading for a rock that protruded from the ground, and even with Henry's cries, he could do nothing to stop his own fall. He hit the rock at great speed and then lay still upon the ground.

Henry skidded on the rocks in his urgency to get to his friend, righting himself and carefully making his way down to the place where Percy lay.

"Percy!" he shouted.

When he reached his friend, he dropped to his knees and touched him on the arm. Percy lay on his side, a thin line of blood dripping from his scalp.

"Percy!" he said again, shaking his shoulder. "Can you hear me?"

The boy didn't move. Quickly, Henry tried to assess the situation. The blood on his scalp was minimal, coming from a small cut over his left temple. Henry put his ear near Percy's mouth and listened to him breathing. Then he stepped back and looked over the rest of his friend's body. One limb was bent at an odd angle, though he didn't appear to have been hit by the gunfire. Henry shook him by the shoulder, and after a moment, Percy's eyes fluttered open.

"Are you all right?" Henry asked.

Percy moaned in pain.

Henry leaned forward. "What is it? What hurts?"

"Everything," Percy replied.

"Can you sit up?"

"My ankle," his friend answered. "I've hurt my ankle."

Henry made a mental calculation. It was too far to go for help, and if he did, he risked the possibility of Percy falling even farther down the ridge.

"Try to sit up if you can," Henry said.

It was a difficult prospect. Percy groaned in pain as he tried to sit up.

Henry looked at him seriously. "Can you use your arm?"

"I think so."

"We have to get back up to the top of the ridge," he stated. "Can you stand?"

In truth, Henry was terrified. If they tried walking back up the ridge, Percy could lose his balance again and this time fall even farther. He might even drag Henry down with him.

"I can't."

Henry looked at the leg in question, lifting the trouser leg and inspecting the bruise that was already forming around his knee.

"I'll have to drag you up," he stated.

He took off his coat and knelt.

"What are you doing?" Percy asked.

"You'll have to hold on to the end of the coat as hard as you can while I pull you up. Just don't take hold of the sleeves."

"Why not?"

"Because they'll rip clean off," Henry reasoned.

Percy held on to the end of the coat, and Henry pulled him a few feet at a time. After a minute, Percy realized he could use his good leg to get some traction and to help lift his weight. While Percy was the smaller of the two, it was still a great weight for another boy to pull up the side of a steep hill.

"That's it," Henry said as they made progress.

First ten feet, then fifteen. Henry promised himself not to look up, because it would be easy to get discouraged. He concentrated on pulling Percy a couple of feet at a time.

After the first several minutes, they stopped to rest, and then Henry nodded.

"Okay, let's try again."

The slippery, gravelly slope a test of their will, it was twenty minutes before they were back on the top of the ridge. Henry dropped the coat and put his arms around his friend, pulling him the last few feet onto level ground. They dragged themselves away from the edge and collapsed.

"How are you doing?" Henry asked, nearly out of breath.

"I think it's broken," Percy said, stifling tears. "I can't move it at all."

Even though they were now on the top of the ridge, it was still too far to go for help and to leave someone alone in such pain. Henry stood, thinking. He found their discarded bags and slung them over his shoulder, then faced his friend.

"If we can get you to your feet, you can hold on to me, and we can get back to where people can help us. You take the stick."

Percy nodded, grimacing. "I'll try."

It was difficult. Henry's back already ached from the task of dragging Percy up the ridge. It took everything he had to get Percy on his feet. At last, his friend was standing on one leg, his arms around Henry's waist with Henry supporting him. Percy kept the bad leg lifted, and they tried to take a step forward. It nearly brought them both to the ground.

"We have to do it together," Henry said. "Try to watch what I'm doing."

They took a tentative step forward and then another. Henry considered the path they had taken to get there. They'd gone over a bridge, through a wooded area, and then walked at least ten minutes past the spot where they had eaten their lunch. He couldn't possibly get his friend through the woods on his own. His hope was to get him back to the place where they had eaten lunch and then go for help from there.

The ten minutes it had taken for them to walk from the woods to the ridge was three times that on the way back. They stopped many times to allow them both to rest and once for Henry to roll up the leg of the trouser of the injured limb and have another look. It was swelled and bruising. Quickly, he rolled the trouser down again, and they found their way back to the place they had stopped before. Henry helped Percy sit down on the ground and then turned to face him.

"I have to go for help," he said.

"No!" Percy cried. "Don't leave me."

"I can't get you through the woods by myself," Henry said.

It was true. Even if they could have navigated the uneven ground, the rocks and sticks and fallen trees with three working limbs between them, Henry's back was aching, and he couldn't carry him another step.

"Here," he said. He took off the bags and set them on the ground, opening one of the flasks. "Have a drink of this."

Percy obeyed. Henry took out the sandwiches and lay them by his friend.

"You can eat something if you want," he said. "I'll run through there, and when I find someone, I'll bring them back to help us."

Percy looked terrified. "What if you don't find someone?"

"I will," Henry assured him, even though he worried about the same thing himself. "And I'll be back as soon as I can."

Percy nodded, accepting the inevitable. He couldn't have gone any farther anyway.

Henry turned and ran back in the direction from which they had come. He loped through the woods, swatting at tree limbs, and tried to ignore his own feelings of trepidation. What had he been thinking? he wondered. Why had he allowed them to get so far away from the main road? He had endangered both of their lives. It didn't bear thinking if he couldn't find anyone to help them. He ran until he was out of breath and just then came to a clearing.

Ahead, he saw the bridge and ran toward it, panting. Stopping to lean against the rail, he looked about. There was no one in sight. Earlier, he thought he had seen people there, but he couldn't be certain.

"Help!" he cried, hoping someone would hear him.

When no one answered, he crossed the bridge, telling himself to keep going. He finally spotted a couple of hikers a few years older than he was and shouted in their direction.

"Help!" he called to the two of them. "My friend is hurt."

The two young men approached, and Henry got a good look at them. One was tall and thin with unruly blond hair, and the other was a foot shorter. His dark hair fell over his brow.

"What happened?" the taller boy asked.

"The Germans shot at us!" Henry replied.

The second frowned. "I thought I heard gunfire. Were either of you hit?"

Henry shook his head, out of breath.

"Where's your friend?" he asked.

"Through the woods, on the other side. He fell down the side of a hill, and his ankle might be broken."

The second youth stared at him for a moment. "The two of you were up there alone?"

"Yes," Henry admitted, hanging his head.

"That's a long walk for the two of you."

He gave Henry a suspicious look, as if the two of them had been up to no good, instead of recognizing that they were explorers, just as he was. Older teens were like that, Henry thought, always distrustful of the motives of children, even when they were the same as their own.

"I know it was a long walk," Henry said, shaking his head miserably. "We thought we were fine."

"Come on," the first boy said. "We'd better get him out of there."

Henry nodded and trotted on ahead, leading them back through the woods and eventually into the clearing where Percy lay waiting.

The dark-haired boy knelt and looked at Percy. "Which leg is it that's hurt?"

Percy pointed to the offending limb, wincing when the young man pulled up his trouser leg. He nodded for his friend to have a look as well.

"We'd better get you out of here," the first said.

Between the two of them, they lifted Percy, who put his arms around their necks as they hefted him up the best they could. Henry gathered their things and led the long procession back to where they had started their journey.

"We don't have a car," the first one said when they came to the road. "We rode our bicycles. We'll have to hope someone stops for us."

A few minutes later, a tan Standard Eight model stopped next to them, and the driver, an older man, got out. One of the young men explained the situation.

"We'll get you home, son," the man said to Percy. He opened the back door, allowing the boys to deposit him on the back seat.

Henry went over to the boys and held out his hand. "Thank you."

They nodded solemnly and shook his hand, and then Henry went around to get in the passenger side. He couldn't squeeze in the back with Percy stretched out across the seat.

"I think he should go to the hospital," the man said.

"Please, take me home," Percy begged. "It's not far."

Henry gave him directions, pointing down the road. "It's down there about a mile or so."

"All right," the man said, finally agreeing. "Let's get you home."

In a few minutes, they arrived at Percy's house, and Henry ran ahead to get his friend's mother. He explained what happened, knowing he would have to retell the entire thing to Maisie and Millie when he returned.

Later, the sisters were sympathetic, but Millie scolded him about going so far alone. He accepted the tongue-lashing without a word and, when he was released, collapsed into bed without supper. After the incident, he no longer ventured so far from home.

# PART FIVE

# 16

---

*Lily*

> The past is still too close to us. The things we have
> tried to forget and put behind us would stir again.
>
> —DAPHNE DU MAURIER, *REBECCA*

By 1945, Lily and Peter, along with many of their countrymen, began to believe the war was almost over. Surely it couldn't go on much longer. Cornwall had suffered several bombings, but their own community had escaped unscathed. They had gotten used to wearing their gas masks at regular intervals with equanimity, trying to be prepared rather than caught off guard. They learned to live with rationing. It was challenging to feed a family with so little eggs, milk, sugar, and other basic necessities, but how could one complain about a shortage of milk when their family, unlike so many others, was able to stay together? They learned to stretch the little meat they had in dishes like toad in the hole, using their one egg per week to make the batter. They plucked apples from orchard trees to make a crumble, which took less pastry than pie, and every meal was heavy on vegetables, which they grew in their own small garden. Lily felt sometimes that she served squash constantly, but Peter never complained. If pressed, he said it was easier to get through difficult times together with someone one loved, and they were lucky to have the food they had.

Their parishioners had more serious concerns, the death toll from the war growing each day. As the vicar's wife, Lily sat through innumerable funerals and squeezed a hundred hands, and with each one, she knew she was one of the lucky ones. Catherine was nearly nine now, smart and beautiful and everything she had imagined her daughter could be. She had bloomed under their care, and she loved Lily, but she was especially fond of Peter. Lily wasn't jealous; she adored Peter herself. She often wondered what life would have been like without him. It certainly wouldn't have been the perfect existence they had created together. Even Mrs. Heaton was part of the family. She had become something of a surrogate mother to all of them, a shoulder to lean on whenever things were difficult. In turn, Lily was able to give to the broader community in her role as vicar's wife. She often felt as if she were born for the role.

She kept a small stack of newspapers articles about Guernsey hidden behind the front cover of one of the books in Peter's library on a shelf he rarely used. She hadn't been able to learn anything about her family or Ian, but she had a tenuous grasp of the enormity of what it meant to live in occupied territory. The reports, often gleaned whenever there was a rare escape from the island, gave her a view of the suffering her fellow countrymen were going through. From time to time, she would read and reread them, then shut them away again. There was nothing she could do for any of them but pray for the war to end soon. She kept busy with her own family to care for.

Lily had never gotten pregnant, the only chink in the armor of their happiness, but infertility didn't get in the way of their good life. She was already a mother and Peter a father, for he couldn't love any child more than he loved Catherine. Now and then, she thought about her daughter's family in Guernsey. The war appeared to be drawing to a close, but there was nothing she could do about it now. The decision that had been made in a moment would last forever. Over the years, she realized she could never tell anyone what had happened when she left Guernsey. It was a secret she would take to her grave.

And then one day, she felt it: tenderness in her breast. Alone in the kitchen, she lifted her hand to touch it, smiling. They'd done it. They'd gotten pregnant after all. Catherine was at school and Peter was at the church. Even Mrs. Heaton was out doing the shopping. Lily went upstairs and took off her blouse, looking for any sign of fuller breasts. Of course, it was early. She couldn't expect all the changes to happen at once. And perhaps she wasn't pregnant. She had thought she was a year earlier and was nothing short of devastated when her time of the month came right on schedule.

Checking the calendar, she realized she was three days late. Still, it was too soon to get excited. She'd been busy and forgetful about her meals, and even then, she wasn't eating a great deal. But she resolved that if she hadn't started in a week, she would go to the doctor.

It was a long seven days, but at the end of them, she was convinced she was pregnant. After taking Catherine to school, she walked to the doctor's office. She had only seen him a few times, mostly to look after Catherine on the rare occasions she had been ill. He wasn't much older than Peter, a tall, dark-haired man who was quite likeable. She went to the office and was shown in by the receptionist after a few moments.

"What brings you in today, Mrs. Ashby?" he asked, coming around his desk to shake her hand. "Is Catherine well?"

Dr. Winbourne and his wife went to Holy Trinity and were very fond of Peter, and Catherine and herself by extension.

"I think I might be pregnant," she said, trying to control her feelings.

"What are your symptoms?" he asked, taking off his glasses.

"I'm ten days late, and I have some breast pain."

"Tender, swollen breasts are generally a good sign if one is hopeful of getting pregnant," he said, nodding.

She exhaled, relieved. "I'd love to have another child."

"Catherine would like a brother or sister, I'm sure," he said, smiling. "We'll do a quick blood test to find out."

"When will you know?" she asked, hoping it wouldn't take long to get the results.

"In the next day or so," he replied. "I'll call you at the vicarage when I have the results."

"Thank you," she answered. After the test, she gathered her things and made her way to the door.

Lily had no idea how she was going to wait even a day to hear the answer. Their lives would be forever changed if it were true. Peter would be ecstatic, but Catherine had been an only child for all the life she could remember. Then she reminded herself: this was how all parents felt when they were expecting a second child. It was natural that Catherine might be anxious, but it meant Lily and Peter would shower her with even more love and attention than ever. That evening, she took a bath in the warmest water she could get, having boiled three kettles in the kitchen.

"Are you feeling all right?" Peter asked, coming in to hang up his tie and unbutton his collar.

Her heart swelled just looking at him.

"I'm fine," she said, smiling. "A bit tired, so I thought I'd have a good, hot bath."

As she lay back in the tub, she listened to the sounds on the other side of the door. Peter was reading a story to Catherine, and another after she begged for a second. Then he told her to get

252 · JULIA BRYAN THOMAS

changed for bed and she could come down to the kitchen to join him for a glass of milk.

Lily smiled. Even if the pregnancy test was negative, she had so much to be thankful for. Not least never having to see Ian Carré again. She missed her parents and her sister, but not as much as she might have thought. She was completely immersed in her new life, as if she had been reborn, and she had never felt the sense of belonging that she had now. With or without another child, they were a complete family. She didn't want to lose sight of that. Smiling to herself, she got out of the bath and donned a dressing gown, thinking of the happiness they shared.

She didn't have to wait long for the news. Dr. Winbourne called at ten o'clock the following morning.

"Congratulations, Mrs. Ashby!" he said. "You're pregnant!"

Lily felt a lump come into her throat. "Really?"

"Absolutely," he answered. "No doubt whatsoever. Call the office next week to set up a physical examination."

"I will," she said. "Thank you."

She hung up the phone in a daze, smiling to herself.

Mrs. Heaton came in, drying her hands on a towel. "I heard the telephone," she said, "but I had my hands in soapy water."

"That's all right," Lily replied. "It was for me."

She wanted to confide in the older woman, but it was only right to tell Peter first. Lily kept to herself for the rest of the day, even allowing Mrs. Heaton to take Catherine to do the shopping that afternoon to allow herself time to rest. When they returned, she joined them in the kitchen to make a supper of roast lamb and potatoes. The lamb had been a gift from one of the parishioners, who occasionally showed their appreciation through practical expressions of food. They always returned the kindness with a call and a bouquet of flowers Lily had cut in their garden.

She was lost in thought when she heard the front door open. Catherine bounded out of her chair and ran to Peter first. Lily followed behind, waiting for him to take off his coat and drop a kiss on the top of their daughter's head. It was lovely to watch. It was the life of which she had always dreamt.

"I need to talk to you," she said lightly a minute later.

He had made eye contact with her but was carrying on an animated conversation with Catherine about what she had done at school that day.

"We wrote stories about our favorite animals, Papa," she said. "I brought mine home to show you."

"Of course," he answered, smiling. He glanced at Lily, aware she was waiting to speak with him. "But let me talk to your mother for a minute first, Princess."

"Ask Mrs. Heaton for a bit of cake," Lily told her. "And a glass of milk."

She led him into the sitting room and took Peter's hand. He smiled, eagerly following after her.

"How was your day?" he asked.

"I have some news."

"You do?" he asked. "What sort of news?"

She couldn't help smiling. "We're going to have a baby."

"What?" he cried. He threw his arms around her, picking her off the floor. "A baby, Lily! We're going to have a baby!"

"Put me down, silly," she said.

Peter obeyed and then kissed her deeply. They stood with their arms wrapped around each other for a minute before he spoke.

"It's been a few years," he said at last. "I suppose I thought it might never happen. Not that I would have minded. I already have the best family in the entire world."

"Are you pleased?" she asked.

"Of course I'm pleased!" he answered. "I can hardly believe it."

She reached up and wiped the lipstick from his cheek. "We should wait a while longer before we tell anyone. I'm only six weeks pregnant, at most."

"What about Gavin?" he asked.

"Well, I think it would be safe to tell Gavin and Susie," she replied, smiling. "I'll call 'round and see Susie tomorrow."

"A baby," he repeated. "When do we tell Catherine?"

"Not for a while, I should think," she answered, considering the matter. "I'll ask Susie for advice about that."

"Do you think it's another girl?"

Lily laughed. "We'll have to wait eight months or so to find out, won't we?"

He led her over to a chair. "I don't care what it is. I just want a healthy baby."

"We will have to tell Mrs. Heaton," she said. "In case I have morning sickness or feel tired."

Peter grinned. "She'll be as excited as we are. She has been over the moon since we brought Catherine to live here."

They went into the kitchen together, and Peter tapped Catherine on the nose. "What do you say we go and read a book together?"

"Yes, Papa," she said. She put down her glass and abandoned her plate, taking him by the hand.

"What's it to be?" he asked. "*The Velveteen Rabbit* or *The House at Pooh Corner*?"

"Pooh tonight, I think."

Lily smiled. Catherine liked it because it was the lengthier of the two books, and she could have his attention for a longer time. After they had gone upstairs, Lily turned to the housekeeper.

"I have some news, Mrs. Heaton," she said, smiling.

As predicted, the housekeeper was as thrilled as they were. Lily was determined to learn to knit in order to make some blankets and cardigans for the newest member of the Ashby household. Mrs. Heaton decided to teach her, and they spent much of the next three months sitting together on the sofa, Lily's feet propped up on a stool, practicing the art of knitting. She was a slow starter at first, showing her early efforts to Peter, who, despite himself, laughed, as did she.

Eventually, however, she produced a beautiful blanket in white and two infant-sized cardigans with ribbons and trim that Mrs. Heaton had brought from her own collection. Showing the result to her husband was one of the more satisfying moments of her life.

Then, everything changed. When she was nearly five and a half months pregnant, Lily began to have cramps the likes of which she had never felt before.

"I think something's wrong," she said to Mrs. Heaton that morning, holding her round, full belly. "I haven't felt the baby move all morning."

"Little ones rest, too," Mrs. Heaton assured her.

But the cramps became worse, and within the hour, she was doubled over in pain, passing blood. Mrs. Heaton called the vicar at the church, and he rushed home to take her to the hospital. It was too late. The baby was stillborn an hour after they arrived.

"I'd like you to stay overnight," the doctor told her.

When he had gone, Peter went over and touched her hand. "I'm staying with you."

"You don't have to do that," she argued.

"Of course I do," he replied. "I'll call Mrs. Heaton and let her know."

Lily turned as he left the room and pulled the blanket over her shoulder, falling into a fitful sleep. She awoke in the middle of the night wondering where she was, and it was a moment before she remembered. Their baby was dead. She was being punished for taking Catherine, and Peter was, too, even though he was guilty of nothing more than loving an unlovable woman who stole other people's children. She wept inconsolably at the pain she'd caused him. Peter believed she was merely grieving the child. She almost confessed, but it would only add to his sorrow. If he were to leave her upon learning the truth, then she risked the loss of everything dear to her.

Lily, miserable and desperate, kept everything to herself. After Peter drove her home, she stayed close to the vicarage for a while, not wishing to interact with people from the village. Susie was the only exception. She brought Alice to play some mornings, careful to leave their younger child at home.

"I appreciate your company," Lily told her, but the truth was, it was difficult not to tell Susie the whole story. If she was honest, she wanted absolution of her sins, though she didn't want anything in her life to change. However, the two desires were mutually exclusive.

A month after the baby was lost, she bent over to pick up one of Catherine's toys and felt a sharp pain in her breast. She straightened up, taking hold of the dresser nearby to steady herself.

She couldn't be pregnant again; they had been careful to let her have time to heal after their loss. The next day, she went back to Dr. Winbourne and told him about it.

"I'll need to do an examination," he said.

He left the room while she took off her blouse and covered herself with a sheet, and he returned a few minutes later.

"Lie down, please," he said.

She reclined on the small medical bed, steeling herself for the touch of his hand. She was still anxious whenever anyone but Peter touched her but forgot her nerves at the discomfort she felt. Dr. Winbourne completed a comprehensive exam, an unreadable expression on his face. When he finished, he told her to get dressed and he would return in a few minutes. Lily did as she was told, her anxiety growing.

When he returned, he motioned for her to take a seat and sat down behind his large wooden desk.

"How long have you had the lump in your breast?" he asked.

She shook her head. "I don't know. I know my breast hurt when I first thought I was pregnant."

"Mrs. Ashby, I'm afraid this is serious. You have breast cancer. I think I've detected lumps in your other breast and your lymph nodes as well. You need to have X-rays at the hospital at once."

"What does that mean?" she asked.

"Cancer is often treatable, but if it has indeed spread throughout your lymphatic system, it may mean that it's quite advanced." He took a deep breath. "I don't mean to alarm you, but I want you and Peter to get out to the hospital as soon as possible today and have some tests made."

Lily clasped her handbag tightly, twisting the handle. "What causes it to occur?"

"We're really not certain what causes cancer or why it strikes people randomly. It's more common in the elderly. Because of your age, it's critical to address the situation at once."

She nodded, standing, and he stood and came around the desk.

"We'll know more as soon as those tests are done," he said. "I'll be with you every step of the way."

She murmured her thanks and found her way out onto the street, heading in the direction of home. Two or three people called out a greeting, and she merely nodded, trying to keep her composure until she made it in the door. When she arrived at the vicarage, she pulled off her hat and went upstairs without saying anything to Mrs. Heaton. Peter burst through the door not five minutes later, barreling up the stairs.

"Lily!" he called.

She was sitting on the edge of the bed, staring into space. She looked up at him as he came through the door.

"Did Dr. Winbourne call you?" she asked.

"Yes," he answered. "Let's get you to the hospital right now."

"We can't go now," she argued. "Catherine will be home from school soon."

"Mrs. Heaton will take care of her," he insisted. "We're going at once."

She didn't argue. She was too stunned to think. She was barely aware of him helping her on with her coat before guiding her down the stairs.

She was struck by a horrible realization: she had known it all along and not been able to admit it to herself. She hadn't wanted to see the signs: the breast pain, the fatigue, the irritability that she had felt more often than usual. It was as though her mind had tried until the last possible moment to protect her from the pain of what was about to happen. If it were true, there was nothing left to live for: no happy marriage, no more precious minutes and hours with her beautiful daughter. No peace left in this life. She knew it was incurable before they even got to the hospital. It was what she deserved.

The machines and tubes and wires all blurred together as she was admitted and began the testing process. Peter was sent to the waiting room for the first couple of hours, and she was, for the first time, glad to be alone. The look on his face had nearly killed her. Worse than having a fatal illness was the harm that it visits on those one loves.

When he finally was allowed to return, she was dressed in a white cotton hospital gown in a bed, intravenous tubes in her arm. He came to stand next to her, taking her hand.

"I love you," he said. "I'm sorry you're going through this today."

"I love you, too," she said. She gripped his hand as tightly as she could. "And I'm frightened."

He brushed back her hair, which she had taken down and allowed to fall about her shoulders. He didn't say anything about being frightened himself, but she could see it clearly from the look on his face.

"I'm here, darling."

"Did you telephone Mrs. Heaton?" she asked.

"I did," he answered. "Catherine is fine. She told her we had some business to take care of, and she didn't mind at all. I think she said they'd be doing some gardening and baking this afternoon."

"God bless Mrs. Heaton," Lily said. "Always there when we need her."

"She'll stay over if we have to spend the night."

It was another hour before a doctor finally came to see them. Peter had fallen asleep in a chair by the window while Lily dozed off and on in the bed. They both stirred and sat up as he approached.

"Reverend and Mrs. Ashby, I'm Dr. Norton," he said. "I want to talk to you about your test results."

Peter stood and went to take Lily's hand.

"I'm afraid your physician's assessment of the situation is correct. You have breast cancer, which has metastasized and invaded the lymphatic system. We can do biopsies and even try surgically removing some of the tumors, but it is very widespread."

Peter gasped.

Lily drew in her breath. "How long do I have?"

The room was silent for a moment.

"We can try to surgically remove some of the tumors, as I said, but then you would have to go through radiation treatments. The outcome is far from certain."

"Shouldn't we try?" Peter asked.

Lily noticed that he said "we" and squeezed his hand.

"Ordinarily, I would say yes, but this is far advanced," Dr. Norton replied. "It may only cause more pain and suffering and merely prolong the outcome by weeks."

"What happens if we don't?" she asked.

Dr. Norton turned to her. "I'm afraid it won't be long. Likely weeks at most."

"But we have a daughter," Lily protested. "She's too young to be left without a mother."

"I'm terribly sorry to deliver such grim news," he replied. "It's especially difficult to give it to one so young."

After he left, she and Peter sat together, not speaking. There wasn't anything to say. Lily could see he was simply trying not to fall apart.

"You need to talk to Gavin," she said.

She didn't say this for herself. Peter and Catherine were all she needed now. But Peter needed his best friend to be there for him during the darkest moments of their lives. A diagnosis of this magnitude was more than any one person could handle, even a clergyman with a solid faith in God.

"I don't want to leave you," he protested.

He was so shaken; it was as though it had happened to him instead of her. She had read about a love that was bigger than one's self, a love that put others first. Peter knew it and lived it every day.

"It's only for a few minutes," she insisted. "We need the support."

She would have to be strong while she could, and that wouldn't last for long.

Her suspicion was correct. She went home from the hospital the following day. Susie and Gavin and Mrs. Heaton were all there for them at various times, but Lily became weaker and more withdrawn. As the pain increased, so did the doses of morphine. Her only comfort was when Peter or Catherine was sitting with her, talking to her. It hardly mattered what they were saying. She couldn't concentrate on the words most of the time. She listened only for the sound of their voices.

Mrs. Heaton was particularly tender, making certain her linens were fresh and helping her change into clean nightgowns every day, or more often if she coughed up blood. She never complained, caring for her like a mother.

Eventually, Lily became afraid that she would lose all lucidity, and she came to a decision. One morning, she refused the morphine. It was time to tell Peter the truth. Mrs. Heaton was bringing in a pitcher of water and pouring her a glass.

"Are you sure you don't want to take your medicine?" she asked, a worried look on her face.

Lily shook her head. "I want to talk to Peter. Is he working?"

Mrs. Heaton nodded. "Yes. He's downstairs in the kitchen with his bible."

He had taken to working from home and rarely went to the church anymore. He didn't want to be far from her side.

"Could you ask him to come up and see me?" she asked.

"Of course, dear. I'll get him."

She left the room as quietly as she had entered. Lily looked at the window, where the curtains had been pulled almost entirely shut. She wanted to go outside and sit on the wooden bench where they had spent warm summer evenings after they were first married. There, they had talked of Catherine and her schooling and how proud they were of what an eager student she was. They shared confidences: he, his imagined failings as a vicar, and she, hers as a wife and mother. He always reassured her that there were no failings of which to speak. She was perfect in his opinion. He had allowed her to sit outside in the sun one day last week, but it had sapped her of her strength so much that she was unable to speak for the rest of the day, and she knew he was unlikely to agree to it again.

"How are you, darling?" he asked as he came into the room.

She reached for his hand, even as the expression on his face broke her heart. He loved her as no one else ever had, and he didn't want to live without her. She didn't want to leave him, either. They had been so close to having it all, even a child of their own. It was going to kill her to break his heart.

"I have to talk to you," she said.

She motioned for him to get the glass of water by the bed and tried to lift her head as he brought it to her lips. It was difficult to move, and some of the water spilled onto the front of her gown. He reached for a cloth to dab at the droplets.

"I'm sorry," he said. "So very sorry."

"You have nothing to be sorry for," she told him.

She reached for his hand again and closed her eyes, appreciating his warmth. Their fingers intertwined, and she looked up at him, so thankful that a man like Peter had been the one to come into her life.

"I need to tell you something that will be difficult for you to hear," she said.

"I don't think you should talk right now," he answered, squeezing her hand. "We can talk later. You need to save your strength."

She shook her head. "It won't wait."

He sat down on the edge of the bed. "What is it, darling?"

Lily sighed. "I don't want to hurt you, but the truth is, I haven't been honest with you, Peter."

He gave her a quizzical look. "We've been married for five years, Lily. I know every single thing about you. And everything I know about you, I love."

"I'm in need of forgiveness."

"We are all forgiven, all who seek forgiveness."

"I want to see our child in heaven," she continued. "And if I go to the grave without telling the truth, I'll be separated from her forever."

"I don't believe God is punitive," he said, looking at her with something near panic. He paused for a moment. It was clear he wasn't prepared for a conversation like this. "He wouldn't keep you separated from the ones you love."

"That's precisely what I need to talk to you about."

She took a breath and rested for a moment. It would be difficult to get the story out in a coherent way, and every sentence was exhausting, though she must persevere.

"I was young when I met you," Lily said. "Young and foolish."

A frown creased his forehead. "Lily, what's troubling you? There's nothing you could possibly say that would cause me or God not to love you. You're my wife. You're the person I love most in the world."

"You love Catherine, too," she said, studying him.

"You know I do," he replied. "She's the daughter I always wanted. The greatest thing that ever happened to me was the day that you and Catherine showed up at my door."

Lily took a deep breath. "I haven't been honest. I haven't told you the truth."

"Tell me, then," he said, "and let me reassure you that everything is all right."

"I didn't come to Cornwall from Kent all those years ago," Lily said, taking a breath. "I came here from Guernsey."

"Guernsey?" he repeated, frowning. He was clearly confused. "In June of 1940?"

"I came over on a cattle barge during the evacuation, after

the English pulled out of the island before the occupation. I was married and trying to get away from a husband who had been violent and abusive."

"Married!" he repeated, stunned. "But…"

"My sister was a teacher at one of the schools, and I went there on evacuation day so that I could go with her to escape my husband and get off the island. In the end, she didn't want to leave, so I took her place."

"You and Catherine."

"No," she answered. "I was alone."

She stopped to look at him, wondering if she could get out the whole story in a way that made sense. He didn't seem to understand what she was saying. He didn't know he was going to hate her in just a matter of minutes.

"At the school, I was put in charge of a nine-year-old boy and a four-year-old girl whom I had never met before, and I looked after them as we went across the Channel together. That evening, we were given tickets and shepherded into groups to board various trains out of Weymouth. I asked someone where our train was headed, and she said Manchester. It felt wrong to me. I couldn't do it, Peter. I couldn't get on that train."

"What happened?" he asked.

She could hear the anxiety in his voice. She couldn't read his expression, but surely he was wondering about the boy.

"I allowed the boy to board a train to Manchester with a

number of other students and teachers, but I stepped back, holding on to Catherine's hand. The two of us walked away from the station and found a hotel. The next day, we set out for Cornwall."

"You took her," he stated. He was shaking his head, as if she could say something to explain everything away.

"I can't tell you why," she replied. "It was an irrational impulse. And yet it felt right. Everything was such chaos. I couldn't leave her to fend for herself. I just couldn't."

"You didn't take her because of the chaos," he said. "You took her because you wanted a child."

She closed her eyes. It was all so much to deal with.

"That's true," she said. "I hadn't been able to have a child of my own."

"What about her parents?" he persisted. "What have they been thinking all these years? That she's safely in the care of the British government and will be returned to them when the war is over? Do you think about them at all?"

Lily shook her head. "I try not to."

He came back toward her and sat down in a chair next to the bed. "I shouldn't tire you out, but I have so many questions."

"I'll answer as many as I can."

He caught her eye for a moment, and they stared at each other, thinking. He wasn't her familiar, safe Peter when he was like this. He might as well be an inspector with the local police department. Of course, that was what she deserved.

"Why did you decide to come to Cornwall?" he asked.

"I knew it from books," she said. "And I knew it would feel more like home, being so close to the sea."

Peter walked over to the window, peering down at the garden below. Lily turned toward him, waiting. He wouldn't understand. How could he? He would never have done something like this, no matter what the circumstance.

"How long until you met me?" he asked.

"We met you on our second day here," she replied. "It was only my third day with Catherine."

He stood and began to pace in the small room. "Let me get this straight. You were married when I met you. And you found a child evacuating without an adult and just took her."

She didn't answer. She had always known if she had to tell him it would be the end of her. She started to tremble.

"Is it really true?" he asked, coming near. "Is it?"

"Yes."

"Do you know who her parents are?" Peter asked, his eyes growing wide.

"No," she answered. "As far as I know, they are simply people who would put a four-year-old on a ship to cross the sea without coming with her."

"And you just left the boy?"

"As I said before, there were other children and teachers with us, and I felt that he could better manage in that environment than a four-year-old without even the ability to speak for herself." She began to cough. When she stopped, she held a handkerchief to her lips. "I couldn't take them both, Peter, and I couldn't let her get on that train with all those strangers. Besides, I felt instantly connected to her in a way I have never felt before. I felt God brought us together, that we belonged to each other. We love each other very much."

"I don't know what to say," he murmured. "I've never heard anything like this in my life."

He ran his hands through his hair, looking older than he had just days before. She had never seen him so distraught.

"Catherine and I became a family," she said, crumpling the handkerchief in her hand. "And for all those years, there was no way to return her to her parents, so I never had to think about it. In some ways, I wanted the war to go on forever if only to keep her here with me."

"But now…" he prompted.

"Now I'm dying," she replied. "And I'm being punished because I loved her and wanted to keep her for myself."

"God doesn't punish people by giving them cancer," he replied. "He doesn't retaliate against his people for the failing of being human."

"That's a nice sentiment, but I'm not so certain you truly believe it."

He turned to face her, crossing his arms, no doubt unaware of how hardened he appeared at that moment. "Would you have still come to Cornwall if you hadn't met her?"

"Yes," she replied.

"And what would you have told me then, if you had come seeking help completely on your own?"

Lily shook her head. "I don't know. I wished him dead, Peter. I might have told you I was a widow."

"He didn't know you were leaving Guernsey?"

"No," she admitted. "I waited until he left the house and then packed a bag and left. He knocked me about, not that it matters now. He made me wish I were dead."

"I can't believe it."

"Well, there's proof if you want to see it."

"What?" he asked.

"Look in my bottom drawer, under my handkerchiefs and scarves."

Peter frowned and then went over and did as he was told. He fished around for a moment before coming up with the faded velvet bag. Turning, he held it up.

"What is this?"

"Open it," she said.

He loosened the drawstrings and opened it, pulling out the contents and setting them on the bed. He ran his hand over the bills.

"There are hundreds of pounds here," he said, incredulous. "What in the world…"

"He was a very rich man," she said. "That was simply money

he had lying around. I discovered it one day and knew it was my means of escape."

"You had this with you when we met?" he said, scooping it up and tucking it back in the bag. He tossed it on the dresser next to her handbag.

Lily nodded. "Yes."

"But you said…"

"I needed help," she replied quietly. "That was true. We needed the shelter and protection of the church and of friends in order to survive."

He scratched his head, unable to look her in the eye.

"I know," she murmured. "This is all unforgivable, isn't it?"

Peter sighed. "God forgives all sins. We have to believe that."

"But people don't," she replied. "You'll hate me for the rest of your life."

He sat down on the bed next to her. "I could never hate you."

Yet he didn't take her hand in that moment or reassure her further. He needed time to try to make sense of the situation, although she feared his reaction once he fully understood what she had done. She had never intended to tell him, but the thought of eternal separation from the child they had created together was too great to risk. Now that Peter knew the truth, she had no idea what he would do, and the ultimate fate of everything—her marriage, her child, her very life—was out of her hands.

# 17

----

*Henry*

In the late spring, Maisie became sick with a terrible cough. The doctor visited regularly to administer medicine and listen to her chest, but she did not improve over the coming days. The whole thing bewildered Henry. Maisie was the strong one. She was the taller, leaner of the two, the clear-eyed one, the one with all the practicality in the family. She was the healthier of the sisters. When she was ill, the whole household was set at naught. Meals weren't served on the usual schedule, and the post and the milk sat on the porch for hours until Henry remembered to get them. He realized that he couldn't go wandering about while Maisie was sick. He had to do his part to help Millie cope, though he was bored, confined to the house and the garden. Sometimes he sat outside with Toby for hours on end, reading or working on his studies. The rest of the time, he did every task he could think of for Millie. He tended the garden, helped in the kitchen, ran errands, made beds. He took meals to Maisie, mostly cold broth, and spoon-fed her when she could barely open her lips.

Henry knew little of lung diseases or what it meant when the doctor said she'd had scarlet fever as a child and couldn't withstand a serious infection. When she passed away ten days after the illness began, Henry was seized by a fear he had never known before. Life would never be the same.

He felt her absence every minute of the day. She had run the household with an iron hand, bringing common sense and structure into their lives. Without her sister, Millie was easily flustered under pressure and had difficulty remembering things, but there was no one in whom Henry could confide his troubles.

The funeral was well attended, the small church packed with villagers paying their respects. The Nicolls sisters, like their parents before them, were well loved here. Neighbors came to the house to bring food, which Henry dutifully accepted. There was a variety of aromas in the kitchen that week: bangers and mash, Yorkshire pudding, cottage pie. None of it, however, tempted Millie, who nearly stopped eating.

She couldn't be still, roaming restlessly through the house in her nightgown looking like an apparition. Henry still didn't stray far, worried what he might find when he came home. He missed Maisie desperately, but Millie's anguish made it all the worse. He was surprised how much he'd come to care for them, Maisie in particular. She had been strong for him through the years when he was young and in need of a roof over his head, and he knew the only way of thanking her was to take care of Millie the best he could.

Two weeks after Maisie's death, he came back from the grocer and smelled smoke as he stepped into the house. He ran into the kitchen, where there was a small fire in a pan on the stove.

"Miss Millie!" he cried.

When she didn't answer, he grabbed flour and threw it on the fire. He wasn't certain how he knew to do it, but he thought his mother might have had a kitchen fire once before. The flour squelched the low flames, and he let out his breath, which he didn't know he had been holding. After he was certain the fire was out, he went in search of Millie, whom he found upstairs in her room, staring at the wall.

"Are you all right?" he asked.

She glanced at him with a curious look on her face. "Yes. Why wouldn't I be?"

"Were you cooking?" he asked.

She frowned at him. "What time is it? Is it time to start supper?"

"I'll take care of it," Henry answered. "You can rest, and I'll call you when it's ready."

He went downstairs and surveyed the damage, opening windows to rid the kitchen of the smell. He'd peeled enough potatoes to know how to start supper, but he wasn't used to doing it alone. He had to talk to someone, if only he could figure out who. Millie wasn't coping with the loss of her sister, and if they weren't careful, she could burn down the house. He prepared the meal and went in search of Millie, but when he stepped 'round the corner, she was coming down the stairs, an old rifle cradled in her arms.

"What's that?" he asked, trying not to look as shocked as he felt. He hadn't known there was a gun in the house.

"It's protection," she said, nodding. "That's what it is. We're out here alone, just the two of us now. I thought I'd get out Father's old rifle."

"Is it loaded?" he asked.

"It's always loaded," she answered.

"I should take it," he said as calmly as possible. "I'm the one who can shoot at wild animals if they come near the house."

Millie frowned. "You're too young."

"I'm fourteen," he argued. He had no intention of using a rifle for any purpose at all, but he was desperate to get it away from her. He didn't trust her not to accidentally set it off, if not something worse. "Fourteen is old enough to handle anything."

Somewhere in the back of his mind, he balked at that statement. A fourteen-year-old was, in fact, still a youth in need of parents and guidance and an education before handling a situation as urgent as an unstable old woman with a gun.

She frowned. "I'm perfectly capable of taking care of it on my own."

Henry sighed and whistled for Toby, walking out the back door. He went part of the way into the village and then back again, unable to decide in whom to confide. There was the vicar, if nothing else happened before Sunday. And there was the butcher, Mr. Bagshaw, who was kind to him. He liked running errands for the old gentleman and trusted his judgment. When he finally returned to the house, the hunting rifle was nowhere in sight. Millie acted as though nothing had happened.

Three days later, when he got home from school, she was sitting stiffly in a chair in the front room, holding a letter. It was obvious she had been crying. He put down his things and went over and sat by her.

"What's wrong?" he asked. "Has something happened?"

"First Maisie," she said, waving the letter in the air. "And now they want to send you home, too."

"Home?" Henry echoed.

How he had longed to hear those words. He was fond of Millie, but he had been waiting impatiently to get the word that his exile was over. *Home*, he thought. It was almost too good to be true.

"When?" he asked.

Millie folded the letter and stuffed it into the envelope. "That remains to be seen."

"What does it say?" Henry asked.

Ordinarily he was careful to use his best manners. After all, he was a guest, no matter how long he had lived there. This, however, was important. In fact, it might just be the most important news of his life.

"I can't talk about it anymore right now," she said.

Henry held his breath and counted to ten. It was the first time he had been angry in a very long time, although he couldn't push her. She was already dealing with a serious loss. Instead, he waited until she went into the kitchen with the letter in hand, and then he gathered the newspapers from the last few days and took them to his bedroom, perching on his bed. In recent weeks, he had taken to scanning the headlines, but now it was time to get serious. He needed to know precisely what was happening and how it might affect him.

Hitler had been bombed out in April, and Henry knew the German resistance was crumbling. Scouring several days' worth of news, he couldn't find many answers to his questions, and certainly none about the evacuees who longed to go home. He decided to ride his bicycle into town and talk to some of the adults he knew who would be far more likely to answer questions. Returning the newspapers to the basket in the sitting room, he went into the kitchen where Millie was staring out the window instead of cooking.

"You should have a lie-down," he said gently. "I think I'll pop 'round the butcher's shop and see if Mr. Bagshaw has any jobs for me to do."

She nodded absently and he didn't dawdle, afraid she would change her mind. For once, he didn't even ask if there was anything he should bring for her. He knew as well as she did the contents of their larder.

There was a hint of rain in the air, so he grabbed his coat from the hook and pulled it on. He took his bicycle from where he had left it propped against the house and took off, pedaling as hard as he could. Normally, he loved the ride into town. When he was younger, he had enjoyed the freedom of setting off on his own, even if it was only for an hour or two, but now, he flew down the roads barely noticing his surroundings. He had one goal and that was to find out when he could go home. But how would he get there? He had saved money from his odd jobs, so he might have train fare and money for food, but he hadn't taken the train since 1940, when he had been unceremoniously banished from the school in Manchester to stay with the Nicollses. He felt a thrill of adventure at the thought of making the trip home.

Henry went into the corner shop and pretended to look at the sweets but instead looked for the maps. He thought he knew the store fairly well, but he had never sought out a map before.

"Can I help you, Henry?" the owner, Mr. Wilkins, asked.

He decided to confess. "I'm looking for a map of England, please."

"Well, well, let me see," the man said, coming from around the counter to stand in front of him. "All the maps are over here, you see."

"Thank you."

The shopkeeper scratched his head. "What does a boy like you need a map for?"

He couldn't very well tell the man that he was plotting his escape. What would he possibly think?

"It's for school," he murmured. "Geography."

"Ah," the man replied. "That means I'll be getting a lot of requests for more of these things."

Henry didn't correct him. Instead, he put his money on the counter and thanked him.

His second stop was the train station, where he wandered inside and looked for a copy of the timetables. Locating one, he put it into his pocket with the map and went outside to retrieve his bicycle.

When he got home, he took out the map and spread it open on the bench in the shed. Even if he had no one to help him, he could retrace his steps. He could take the train from Thirsk to Manchester, and then another from Manchester to Weymouth. That would take him to the port city. He didn't know how much it cost to get on a ferry or boat there, but that was one of the reasons he had always been careful with his money. When the time came for him to leave, he wanted to be able to go on his own, without asking anything of anyone.

Henry decided to broach the subject the next evening after supper. He and Millie were sitting across from one another in the sitting room. She was embroidering a handkerchief, her fingers working at the brisk pace of one who has wielded a needle for a very long time. He missed Maisie being there with them. She probably would have already put him on a train for the coast and possibly even gone with him to make certain he got there all right.

"What will you do when I have to leave?" he asked.

She looked up at him and then lay her sewing in her lap. She looked older than her seventy-one years. Her cropped hair was completely white, and the wrinkles that had been around her eyes when he arrived on their doorstep nearly five years ago now had spread across her face. Henry didn't know what to do. She couldn't manage without him, and he was grateful to her, but he couldn't stay.

"I'll get on just fine, thank you very much," she retorted.

Her answer was so sharp in tone, he couldn't ask anything else. With no idea of what else to do, the following morning, he got onto his bicycle and rode into the village, stopping at Mr. Bagshaw's shop. He went inside to find the butcher, who was parceling out a sliver of meat for a pretty, young customer. He looked up as Henry arrived, nodding his head at the boy.

"Good morning, there," he said. "I'm afraid I don't have any deliveries for you today."

"That's all right," Henry answered. "I came about some other business."

"And what is that, Henry?"

Henry glanced at the customer. "I'll wait my turn, sir, if that's all right."

When the girl had collected her parcel and left the shop, Mr.

Bagshaw washed his hands and came around the counter, drying them on a towel.

"Are you all right, lad?" he asked.

"Yes, sir," Henry replied. "But I have something I need to tell someone."

The whole story came tumbling out. The fire, the hunting rifle, the need to go home. Mr. Bagshaw scratched his head, and then after a moment, he went over to the door and locked it. Then he took off his apron and hung it on a hook.

"Come with me," he said. He led Henry out to his car. "Leave your bicycle there."

"Where are we going?"

"We're going to speak to Mrs. Bagshaw," he said. "She's very good with this sort of thing."

They drove to the Bagshaws' home, a stone house with a large flower garden in front. Mr. Bagshaw led Henry inside and called out to his wife.

Explanations were made once again, then Mrs. Bagshaw gestured toward the chairs.

"Everyone, sit down," she said as though calling a meeting to order. "I have to get the facts straight. It sounds like Miss Nicolls hasn't been herself since her sister died and is a potential danger to herself and others. At the same time, this young lad is ready to return home, which he has every right to do."

Henry nodded.

"She doesn't have any family left, I'm afraid," Mrs. Bagshaw continued. "So I will speak to the vicar and the mayor and see if we can't make some sort of arrangement for her. And first thing on Friday morning, you need to be packed, because you are getting on a train and heading home, young man. Your parents are no doubt desperate to see you."

Relief swept over Henry. That was the end he desired, but at the same time, he didn't want to upset Millie, who had been good to him for such a long time.

"But what about Miss Millie?" he asked.

"I promise she'll be all right," Mrs. Bagshaw said. She looked at her husband and nodded. "It was good to bring him here so we could get this sorted out."

Mr. Bagshaw smiled and looked at Henry. "Didn't I tell you she'd know what to do?"

On Friday morning, Henry did as Mrs. Bagshaw said. He got up as usual, made breakfast for himself and Millie, took Toby out for a quick run, and then went up to his room and packed his bag. He straightened his bed and looked around the room, making certain everything was the same as he had found it all those years ago. Slinging the pack over his shoulder, he took it downstairs and then set it outside the front door. Shortly after, the Bagshaws arrived. Henry answered the door as Millie came up behind him.

"Miss Nicolls?" Mrs. Bagshaw said. "I don't know if you remember me. I'm Carol Bagshaw. I came to talk to you about something this morning." She turned to Henry and smiled. "Why don't you go outside and keep Mr. Bagshaw company?"

The boy and the man stood outside, too nervous to make small talk. Henry found himself emotional about the sudden turn of events.

"Is that your bag?" Mr. Bagshaw asked, breaking the silence.

Henry nodded.

"Well, let's get it loaded, then."

Henry went over and took it and put it in the back of the vehicle. Then the two of them resumed their waiting beneath the shade of the oak tree. Eventually, Mrs. Bagshaw and Millie came out of the house and walked up to them. Henry could see that Millie was emotional, too.

"Henry, you should say your goodbyes," Mrs. Bagshaw said. "You have a train to catch."

He turned to Miss Millie and then threw his arms around her. Neither of them spoke. He could feel her wispy fingers patting him on the arm. He murmured his thanks, and then he let her go and started toward the car.

"Henry!" she called. "Don't leave!"

He turned to look at her.

"I don't want to leave," he said honestly. "You've been so good to me. But I miss my family."

"Wait," she said. "You forgot something."

Mr. Bagshaw looked at Henry and shook his head as they all watched Millie walk back into the house.

Mrs. Bagshaw took a step closer to him. "It will be all right, son. We'll take care of her. She won't have to be alone. Of course you want to go home. That's what's right."

Her husband nodded. "You've been good for both of them. They needed someone to take care of these last few years, but the missus is right."

A minute later, Millie came out of the house, Toby following at her heels. She held nothing in her hands. He'd expected a sandwich or perhaps a flask of water, but she wasn't focused on practical things like that. His brows furrowed, wondering what she was going to tell him.

"What is it?" he finally asked.

"Well, it's Toby, isn't it?" she replied.

"Toby!" he said.

He couldn't believe it. Reaching over, he stroked the dog's head and then went over to Millie, reaching out to kiss her on the cheek. "I'll miss you," he said. "Thank you for everything."

"Go on, then," Millie said, trying to hold in her emotions.

Henry pulled back and nodded.

He whistled for Toby and went over to the car, opening the door so the dog could jump in. Then he sat down next to him and shut the door, leaning out the window.

He waved at Millie. "I'll write."

She waved before walking back toward the house. Mr. Bagshaw got into the car and started the engine. Henry leaned out the window and waved to Millie, who was watching from the doorway. He felt guilty, but this was something he had to do.

To comfort himself, he thought of Maisie. She would understand, he knew it. She would tell him it was time to go.

# 18

---

*Ava*

**The point is, life has to be endured, and lived. But
how to live it is the problem.**

—DAPHNE DU MAURIER, *MY COUSIN RACHEL*

"I'm leaving tomorrow," Becker said one evening.

They had made love hastily in the dark and, after carefully
buttoning buttons and straightening themselves, sat together in
the kitchen where Ava was boiling potatoes. It was always potatoes
these days, but he never complained. Rain was falling outside the
window, and though it wasn't cold, she shivered.

"You didn't tell me," she answered, trying to keep her voice even.

"I just found out this morning."

Ava turned away from the stove and came over to sit across
from him, her heart skipping a beat. The few hours they spent

together each week were the one thing she looked forward to in life. In fact, she had no idea how she would have managed the last year without him. He came at random times and hours, unexpected but always welcomed.

"I don't know what to say," she said, looking up at him.

He looked almost as helpless as she felt, and she would have smiled if her heart hadn't just been broken.

"I know," he replied.

They had been careful to keep their arrangement from being discovered. There were strict rules about fraternizing with the enemy, although attachments had formed across the island. She wouldn't have characterized their relationship as an attachment, perhaps, but as someone to confide in. Becker asked nothing of her. His voice broke the silence of her life.

"You must be glad to go home," she murmured in spite of the fact that losing him, too, after everything else, would break her.

Of course, no one would have understood her relationship with Becker, least of all Joseph. But she needed him. He kept her nerve endings alive. She knew soldiers were heading back to Germany and understood he would leave as well, but somehow, she hadn't expected it to be so soon. But it was not meant to be.

"I haven't seen my wife in years," he continued. "And we have a child. Have I told you that? I left before I could find out if it was a boy or a girl."

"Of course you must go," Ava replied, rising from her chair. She went and stood behind him, wrapping her arms about his neck. "You'll be so happy to see them."

He took her hands into his own and kissed them. He had known her so well. Her life had been an open wound that stubbornly refused to heal. From the first day, he had seen her children's empty rooms, the space she shared with her husband, her fear at finding herself alone during the occupation. Becker was an enigma and would remain so. And yet, she would miss him. Now she realized that he had been trapped just as she was. He deserved to be set free. The war had made them all less selfish, Ava thought. They were grateful simply for their lives.

After he left, the days began to blur into a succession of mindless routines and rituals. Ava woke before dawn after a restless sleep, milked the cow, worked in the garden, prepared food that she barely touched, and repaired and cleaned and toiled and sweat and struggled through a thousand endless tasks, trying to keep their home together, so that one day, Joseph and the children could return and resume their lives, which had been so violently interrupted by war.

But it wasn't enough. She decided to do more for her community with what little time she could spare. On Tuesday and Friday afternoons, she went to Dr. Evans's office, delivering whatever medications he could scrounge for his patients. She had to do something for someone besides herself. Joseph, Henry, and Catherine were all dependent on the mercy of strangers, and if she, too, made time to help others, perhaps God would grant her husband and children back into her care.

For most of her life, Ava had been bargaining with God. She had promised to be more pious and faithful in church attendance if the rain could be more plentiful during the dry seasons; she had offered her vices—primarily in the form of arguing and stubbornness—if Catherine could survive a high fever when she was two; she had given up indulgences like chocolate if God, in his wisdom, would grant her another child. Even now, she would give up eating entirely if it would bring her family home. But none of her bargains were ever accepted by the Almighty. Eventually, the heavens open and rain falls to heal dry fields, fevers pass, and one is either blessed with another pregnancy or not. She was tired of bargaining. She was exhausted from thinking for another minute that she could do anything to influence the world one way or another in the middle of a German occupation during which she had lost everything important. No matter what she did, answers to life's suffering were not forthcoming.

In the days that followed, Ava tried to manage the best she could, marking the days off the calendar, wondering when she would hear some news of Joseph. When she did, it happened as suddenly as Becker's leave-taking, in the form of an insistent knock at the door. Ava heard Dr. Evans call her name. She ran to answer it without even putting down the spoon with which she had been stirring a pot of soup.

"You have to come!" he said when she opened the door. "Get your things."

She looked at him, confused. He had never come to her house before.

"What's wrong?" she asked. She could feel her heart begin to pound. "Has something happened?"

Dr. Evans nodded. "Your husband has been released from the prison camp. My brother works in the government, and he knew you'd been helping me for the last year or so. Evidently, your husband was moved a year ago from Alderney to one of the camps in France. He's sailing over even as we speak."

Ava stared at him, unable to move.

"Come on," he urged, stepping into the house and closing the door behind him. "Take off your apron. And put down that spoon."

She nodded. "I'm sorry, it's just so unexpected. Is it true?"

"It's absolutely true," he answered, smiling. "I've come to drive you down to the port so you can be there when he gets off the boat."

She dropped the spoon onto a table and removed her apron, laying it over a chair.

"I'll get my things."

She grabbed her handbag and settled a hat on her head, one she hadn't worn during the entire war. Glancing in the mirror, she gazed at her reflection. She was only thirty-four years old, but she felt twice that. What would Joseph think when he saw her? They hadn't seen one another in fifteen months. What would he think of her sunburnt skin and limp hair and calloused hands? Hurrying down the stairs, she turned to the doctor.

He led her out to his car, opening the door for her.

"I'm nervous," she admitted.

"He'll be so happy to see you, it will erase all your fears."

She turned to look at him. "What if he's changed?"

"War changes everyone. Be patient and give him time to recover from his ordeal."

"I'm sure it's been terrible," she answered.

"He may need medical attention," Evans said. "If you need anything, be sure to come and see me."

When they arrived at the edge of the town, he drove down to the dock and parked the car.

"I'd better let you out here," he said.

Ava nodded, touching his arm. "I can't thank you enough."

He patted her hand. "No thanks are necessary, Mrs. Simon. Would you like me to wait with you?"

"No, thank you," she replied. "This is something I have to face alone."

After she closed the door behind her, he turned and pulled away. She waited until he had gone before she found a bench where she could wait. The ferry hadn't arrived yet, giving her time to collect her thoughts.

It had been two long years. She wasn't even the same person anymore, a mere shell of her old self. The Joseph she knew had changed after the children left. He'd been morose throughout the beginning of the occupation and then angry, as had she. Their lives had been upended by a power-hungry despot nearly a thousand miles away who wanted to rule the world, thinking nothing of what it cost those who stood in his path. She would know the face of her husband, but would she recognize the man he had been? Had she changed too much to be recognizable herself?

She waited an hour and twenty minutes, sitting rigidly on the wooden bench. Nearly a hundred people crowded onto the dock, waiting anxiously. She was grateful that Dr. Evans had warned her of Joseph's arrival. It would have been too much of a shock to find him suddenly standing at her door.

A cry went up from the crowd when the ferry was spotted in the distance. Ava rose to her feet, shielding her eyes as she watched its slow progression toward the harbor. As it grew closer, she could see dozens of men standing at the railing, eager for their first look at their homeland. Some waved, others cheered, wondering if their loved ones would be there to greet them or if they would have to find their way home without a penny in their pocket.

Ava moved closer to get a better look. As the ferry docked, she scanned the crowd. They were a ragtag group. She walked down the dock, trying to find Joseph. She finally spied him near the back of the ferry. He had lost so much weight he was almost unrecognizable. He had a long, unkempt beard, as did most of the men. When he disembarked, she could see his trousers were held up with a length of rope. Nothing he had at home would fit him until he had gained back some of his former weight.

But his face was the dear face she had always loved. She smiled and waved at him, her heart surging with love. He pushed his way through the crowd and walked up to her.

"Oh, Ave," he said, taking her in his arms.

"You're home," she murmured, gripping him tightly. "Home for good."

She had forgotten how broad his shoulders were, how deep and comforting his voice. He was brittle, however, half-starved with hollows under his eyes from deprivation and torture. She could see it in his eyes.

"We have to get you home," she said, taking his arm.

"Did you bring the car?" he asked.

Ava shook her head. "I can't start the engine. We'll get a taxi. Some of them are running again."

She rounded up a driver and helped Joseph into the car, holding his hand on the way back to their house. When they got inside, she turned to him, touching his face.

"You should take a hot bath."

He nodded, weary from the hours spent traveling. In their room, he turned away and lifted his shirt. She saw whip marks across his back, scars that he would carry for the rest of his life.

"What about the children?" he asked, turning. "Has there been any news?"

"No," she said, shaking her head. "I haven't heard anything."

"Have any others begun to make it home?"

"The newspapers say that some of them are starting to come back," she answered. "It should only be a matter of time."

She didn't tell him about the rumors she had been hearing about children and their reaction to the war, some happy to be home, some angry to leave the people who raised them during the past five years. The thought was as foreign to her as the concept of war. How could one not be desperate to arrive home after such a long separation? But she did not reveal her fears to her husband.

"When I'm strong enough, I'll get work, and we'll go to England and track them down," Joseph said.

Ava took his hand. "First, we have to take care of you."

She was struck by how gaunt he was, his cheeks hollow from lack of food and his shoulders slumped in a way she had never seen before.

"In the meantime," she said, "I will write letters."

Every day for weeks, she put pen to paper. First, to the bailiff of Guernsey and to the lieutenant governor, asking each of them to make enquiries on their family's behalf. They weren't certain if the children were together or not. Over the next few weeks, she received polite if uninformed replies.

"They kept poor records," she said, frustrated at yet another letter encouraging her to be patient. It would take a long time to get several thousand Guernsey children collected and shipped back to the island from which they had come.

"We've gotten this far," Joseph answered. "We can make it just a while longer."

One day, a letter arrived, written in a hand she did not recognize. Ava took a knife and slit it open carefully so as not to damage its contents. Turning to the last page, she saw that it was from Henry.

"Joseph!" she shouted.

She ran up the stairs two at a time and went into their bedroom where he lay and sat down next to him.

"There's a letter from Henry."

He sat up, reaching out to touch her shoulder.

"What does it say? Read it to me."

Ava held the letter up to the light and read it aloud.

*Dear Mum and Dad,*

*I am so happy that the war is over. I'm writing to tell you that I am coming home. I was staying in Middleham with two sisters, Miss Millie and Miss Maisie, who have taken care of me during the war. A friend is putting me on a train to Weymouth on Friday and I will take the first boat I can to Guernsey when I arrive. I believe I will be home on Saturday.*

*I hope you have heard from Catherine. We were separated on the day we arrived in England and I have been so worried about her. When I get home, I will tell you everything. I miss you very much.*

*Your son,*

*Henry*

The letter fell onto Ava's lap, and she looked at Joseph, unable to speak. The best thing that could possibly happen and the worst had all occurred in a single minute. Henry was coming home. But Catherine, her baby, had been lost for the entire war. She put her head on Joseph's shoulder and wept.

After the tears passed, she wiped her face and watched as Joseph wiped his own.

"We'll get her back, Ave," he said. "This is one miracle. Maybe there will be another miracle, too."

But in their heart of hearts, neither of them believed it.

The following day, they drove down to Saint Peter Port in their own vehicle for the first time since 1940. The engine coughed and sputtered at first, but as they drove, it began to settle down. Ava had tailored a pair of Joseph's trousers and one of his shirts to fit his slender body in order to make him as presentable as possible.

He'd shaved off his beard and looked more like the young man she had married fifteen years ago than the man who had been arrested in 1943. She worried that his appearance would startle Henry, but her thoughts were forgotten the minute their son bounded off the ferry and came running up to them, a dog following at his heels. He was so tall and thin and looked so much like his father that Ava's heart swelled.

"Henry, my boy," Joseph said, pulling into a deep embrace. He held him like that for a couple of minutes as Ava tried not to cry. When Henry stepped back, Joseph smiled. "Look at you! You're nearly as tall as I am."

"I can't believe I'm home," Henry said. His voice was deeper than it had been. He was becoming a young man. "I missed you so much, every single day."

Ava stood back, taking it in.

Henry stepped back and looked at his father. "You're skinny, Dad."

"He's been in a camp in France," Ava replied.

"A camp?" Henry exclaimed. "Are you all right?"

"I'm fine now," Joseph answered.

Ava put her arms around her son. "You don't know how good it is to see your face. It's been so awful not knowing what happened to you."

"I'll tell you all about it, but I wrote you letters over the past few years," he replied. "I brought them with me. You can read them if you'd like."

"My darling boy," she answered. "Of course I'll read them. I want to know everything."

"Yes, we do," Joseph said, concurring.

"And who is this?" Ava asked, nodding at the dog who had waited patiently next to his young master.

"This is Toby," Henry replied. He bent down and scratched the dog behind the ears. "He's a really good boy. He took care of me while I was gone. I hope you don't mind that I brought him home with me."

Ava bent down and gave the dog a pat. "He's beautiful. And I'm sure he would have been lost without you when you'd gone."

Henry nodded sadly. "Like Miss Millie."

"Come on," Ava said, taking his arm. "I want to hear all about everything. Every last thing."

Henry whistled to Toby, who trotted next to him as they made their way to the car. When they arrived home, it was as if he'd never left. He asked for a snack, he read in his room, he helped his father with the chores. The only difference was the presence of the dog, to whom they all quickly became attached, in no small part because it was a fourth heartbeat in the room. They were four again in spirit until Catherine returned home.

"Can you tell us what happened?" Ava asked Henry that evening at supper. "When was the last time you saw your sister?"

Henry had taken a big gulp of the soup and put down the spoon as he swallowed. "We were at the school with you and Miss Matthews. A strange lady came up—"

"Your teacher's sister," Ava interrupted.

"She looked after us on the boat to England, and it was that first night, after we had been checked by doctors and hundreds of us were standing in the train station to get on different trains to different places." He looked at his father and sighed. "We were in line, and I saw someone give her the tickets. I was standing in front of them, and I remember she patted me on the back and said something nice when it was my turn to board the train. I got on and took about five steps, but when I turned around, she and Catherine were gone. Completely vanished, Mum. And suddenly, the train was moving, and I couldn't find them anywhere. I never did find out what happened."

Ava drummed her fingers on the table. "She was with Helen Matthews's sister. That means I have to visit the Matthewses in the morning to find out what they know. Perhaps they've heard from her. She and Catherine might even be on the way here now."

Joseph raised a brow but said nothing. She knew he wanted to tell her not to get her hopes up, but it was impossible.

The next morning, Ava went about her chores more quickly than usual. Then she got out her bicycle, tossing her handbag in the basket. Joseph came out of the house and stood next to her. He had only been home a few days but was starting to get color in his face again. She was certain it had more to do with getting Henry back than her cooking.

"Are you off to see Mr. and Mrs. Matthews?" Joseph asked.

Ava nodded. "I need to know if they've heard from their other daughter."

*The one who took Catherine*, she almost said. Instead, she held her tongue.

"Shall I drive you?" he asked.

"I'll be fine," she answered. "You stay and talk to Henry."

The Matthews family lived six miles away, on the northern side of the island. Ava paced herself so she wouldn't be out of breath when she arrived. She tensed as she passed the former checkpoints where so many times she had been accosted and interrogated. She would probably never pass that way again without having a reaction to it. Trying to put it out of her mind, she concentrated on the ruts and grooves in the road until she reached the Matthewses' home. It had been five long years since she had spoken to Henry's teacher. Ava walked her bicycle to the front of the house and knocked on the door. Helen Matthews herself opened the door, looking shocked when she saw Ava.

"May I help you, Mrs. Simon?" she asked.

"I need to talk to you about your sister," Ava replied.

Helen looked at her for a moment. "Come in," she said. "Please, have a seat."

Ava decided not to waste a moment of her time. "Have you heard from Lily? Has she managed to contact you from England?"

Helen shook her head. "I'm afraid not. We haven't heard a word from her since the day she left."

"She has my daughter," Ava stated. "At least, she had my daughter when she was separated from my son."

Helen sank into a chair, and Ava sat down across from her.

"I don't understand," Helen said.

Ava softened her tone. "Please tell me everything you know about that day."

"I was at the school, as you know, speaking with you when she simply walked up," Helen replied. "Lily said she wanted to go to England with the evacuees, and it was decided she would take my place."

"I remember you said she was escaping a troubled marriage. But did she tell you specifically why she suddenly wanted to go in your place?" Ava asked, frowning. "Did she have a destination in mind when she got there?"

"I don't know," Helen admitted. She looked down at her hands. "I've wondered myself a million times."

Ava decided to ask the question she had been wondering about for five years. "Why did you stay behind?"

"I should have gone with her," Helen said. "But I wanted to take care of my parents. I didn't know where we would end up if I went or how long we would be gone. I didn't want to leave, and Lily did. So there you are."

"My children were separated on the very first day," Ava explained. "They were taken to a train station by your sister, and she let my son board the train and left with my daughter. I have no idea how to find her. Are you certain you don't know where she might have gone?"

"I would tell you if I knew, I promise. I'm longing to hear from her myself."

"Would you please contact me if you find out anything?" Ava asked. "Anything at all?"

"Of course." Helen tucked her hair behind her ear and looked up. "I'm very sorry, you know. I've felt terrible ever since the evacuation. I made you a promise, and I didn't keep it."

Ava looked at the woman, perhaps seeing her for the first time. She was so young and inexperienced. Of course she was hesitant to leave the only home she'd ever known and the parents she loved so deeply.

"We can't know how things would have worked out if we'd done things differently," Ava said at last. "You might have gotten lost or let go of one of their hands yourself. Someone in charge might have taken them away from you, to be honest. You were terribly young, after all. It's not your fault. I blame myself for not going with them."

"Thank you, Mrs. Simon," Helen replied. "I'll let you know if I hear anything at all."

As Ava left, she wondered what to do next. How did one find a lost child after the war? Was there anyone who could help her? Was there anyone left to write? However, no matter what she tried, there was no clear answer. Sometimes it felt as if Catherine had never existed at all.

Fall arrived on the island, bringing with it the harvest of the crops, apples ripe for picking, and cooler nights with breezes coming in from the sea. The three of them had fallen into a comfortable routine of household chores and gardening, treating one another with special care. Joseph was still healing, gaining back part, though not all, of the weight he had lost. Henry was dealing with guilt from leaving the woman who cared for him, although fortunately, the dog was comforting him in his loss. Ava's emotions were still a jumble of fears and recriminations that she kept to herself. No one else was strong enough to hear them.

The churches were being restored little by little, and the Simons began attending services once again. One day, the vicar had an announcement that took them all by surprise.

"There has been so much loss and sadness over the last few years," he said. David Allen was a good vicar, and she hadn't realized how much she had missed the ritual of going to church and having a place to lay her burdens every week.

"I want to have a service for those who are lost," he continued, looking about at the small congregation. "For those we wish were with us but for whatever reason cannot be here now."

Ava froze, listening.

"On Friday afternoon, we will lay wreaths for our missing loved ones after a brief service. Perhaps for you, it was a soldier killed at war or someone who died during the occupation. Whatever the reason for the grief, I think it important that we come together and acknowledge it as a community."

That afternoon, Ava set to work gathering twigs and small

branches, working outside in the barn through the afternoon to fashion a wreath. It was rustic and simple, a perfect expression of the uncontrollable longing she felt for her lost daughter.

Joseph came up beside her and watched as she twined the small branches together, intent on her task.

"Do you really think we should go?" he asked. "She might come back, Ave. I feel as though attending this service means we're consigning Catherine to be lost forever."

"It's something I have to do," she answered.

"We have to have hope."

"She's never coming back, Joseph," she replied, laying the wreath on the table in front of her. "Henry's been home for months. We have to face facts. And we have to honor our daughter's memory."

He didn't argue. He didn't have the strength.

She'd held out hope for as long as she could. It was time to let go, Ava knew, no matter how difficult a proposition that would be.

The service was set for Friday afternoon at two o'clock. It was held outside on the church grounds, between the building and the small graveyard where so many of them had parents and grandparents who had been laid to rest. A crowd of thirty or forty people gathered in the cold autumn air to pay their respects. Joseph and Henry were with her, although she had determined that even if they didn't come, she would go alone.

Joseph turned toward her, looking like a broken man. He blamed himself, she knew. After all, it was at his insistence that they sent Catherine away. On the other side of him, Henry looked troubled as well. She would have to help them heal. Losing Catherine wasn't anyone's fault. She didn't blame either of them anymore. All one can do is make the best decision they can in the moment and hope that things work out for the best. Joseph wanted the children to be off the island during an occupation, and it would have been terrible for them if they had stayed. Henry didn't mean to let an adult take his sister's hand, but he was just a young boy. Naturally he trusted the adults around them. That was what children were supposed to do.

"I'd like to share some verses from Psalm 85," the vicar said, opening his copy of the Book of Common Prayer. "Let us receive comfort from the Almighty together."

They bowed their heads to listen.

"'O, how amiable are thy dwellings, thou Lord of Hosts,'" he began. "'My soul has a longing and a desire to enter into the courts of the Lord: my heart and my flesh rejoice in the living God. Yea, the sparrow has found her a house, and the swallow a nest where she may lay her young. Blessed are they that dwell in thy house: they will be always praising thee. Blessed is the man whose strength is in thee: in whose heart are thy ways. For the Lord God is a light and a defense: the Lord will give grace and worship: and no good thing will he withhold from them who walk uprightly.'"

Catherine was a sparrow, Ava realized suddenly, a small bird defenseless against the forces of fate that took her away. Wherever she was, wherever her nest may be, Ava thought, may she have found a house that brings her safety and peace.

The vicar closed his small, leather-bound book and took out a slip of paper. "One of our parishioners wrote a poem to mark this occasion. I'd like to take a moment to read it to you."

The crowd was silent, waiting for the words to wash over them, to try to mend their broken hearts. His voice rang out in the still of the evening, the breeze ruffling hems and hats, reminding them they were alive.

*"FOR THOSE WHO ARE LOST*

*a poem*

*There are, in this world, those of us who linger*
*And those of us who are lost;*
*Where time intersects and twines 'round the moments*
*We yearn for, now and for always, taken from us,*
    *perhaps forever.*
*The winter of our years comes far too soon for some*
*And for others, it never comes at all*
*But we remember to the grave and beyond*
*The splendid, heart-wrenching grace of loving*
*And of being loved.*
*Christ opened the tomb to defeat the hand of Death*

*And promised eternal life;*

*Yet the glimpse of heaven afar,*

*That vision of cloudless skies and meadows, ever*

   *verdant,*

*Sheltering the ones we have surrendered against our will*

*Is beyond our reach*

*And seems, at times, so far away as to not exist at all.*

*We cannot penetrate the veil between life and that*

   *which comes after.*

*Therefore memory—the sounds, the sweetest kiss, the*

   *brief moments shared—*

*Are buried in our hearts forever.*

*Let us not forget to summon the good,*

*Putting away sadness and loss in exchange for those*

   *moments that held meaning,*

*And keep love alive and burning in our souls.*

*For without love,*

*We are nothing.*

*Do not forget those who brought you joy;*

*Hide them in your heart to keep it beating."*

"Amen," he murmured.

"Amen," the mourners echoed.

For they were all mourners, Ava knew, whether they had a body to bury in the graveyard behind the church or not. Some, like the

Simons, grieved without knowing what had become of the child they loved. Some days, she told herself, it still wasn't too late to be reunited with Catherine, but in her heart, she knew differently. Nothing would ever be the same again.

One by one, families came forward to lay a wreath at the small memorial that read *For Those Who Are Lost*. An elderly couple walked over and lay the first wreath.

"Lieutenant Ralph Taylor, our son," the man said. "Lost in France in 1944. Age twenty-nine."

"Cecil Baxter," said another. "Taken to a prison camp in 1940 where he died. Age forty."

A younger couple came forward. "May Richards," the husband said. "Age nine. Killed in the bombing of Saint Peter Port."

"Jean-Marc Dubuc," murmured an old woman. "Sent to the prison camps in 1942. Age thirty-eight."

Several others stepped forward, and then Joseph squeezed Ava's hand. She nodded at Henry, and they walked up to the marker together.

"Catherine Elizabeth Simon," Ava said. "Lost on the twentieth of June, 1940, at age four during the evacuation."

After laying the wreath, she stepped aside and stood until everyone else had laid their own and every name was reverently spoken. Then, without a word, she took Joseph's and Henry's hands, holding them tightly as they left the churchyard, trying to hold what was left of her family together.

# 19

---

*Peter*

Peter stood in the cemetery, staring at Lily's grave. In his hands, he held a bouquet of lilies swathed in tissue paper. He had never asked her favorite flower—wartime and rationing prevented thoughts of things like favorite flowers—but he would associate her with lilies now and forever. After a few moments' contemplation, he leaned over and placed them on the grave. Ordinarily he would say a prayer, but his spirit was so grieved he couldn't form the words.

A breeze blew in from the sea, and he was glad he had persuaded Catherine to wear a coat.

She walked over to a bench and sat, lost in her own thoughts. At nine, she was even more beautiful than she had been as the bashful four-year-old he'd met five years earlier. She was tall for her age and thin, refined in her manner and appearance. Lily had done a wonderful job raising her, which made everything all the more perplexing. Catherine wasn't her child by birth but by abduction, and he was the only one who knew the truth.

He had known the truth about Catherine for three months, but he still couldn't get his mind around the fact, no matter how hard he tried. Everything about Lily had been so good and decent, so much at odds with the facts she had delivered to him shortly before her death. She hadn't seemed the sort of person who could take a child who didn't belong to her, yet somehow, she had. He hadn't confided in anyone yet, though he thought several times of talking to Gavin and Susie. But confiding in someone involved risk. If anyone found out that Catherine had another family somewhere, he would be forced to give her up. And giving her up wasn't an option. She was all he had left. That was the one thing that helped him understand his wife. Now that Catherine had been his daughter for five years, she wasn't easy to give away at all. Lily knew it even after a moment.

"Come on, Princess," he said. "Let's go have lunch."

She nodded and stood, following him to the car. She was his daughter as far as he was concerned. For five years, he had protected and cared for her, grateful to have such a perfect child in his life. And from what he could determine by careful probing, she seemed to have little or no memory of her life before the war.

"Where do you want to go, Papa?" she asked.

*To the ends of the earth*, he thought. Just the two of them. Away from the world with its confusing, heartbreaking realities. He wanted to forget everything Lily had told him so he could get back to the business of living. Trying to do that without his wife would be difficult enough without losing Catherine, too.

"Let's go 'round to the hotel and have a proper meal," he suggested. "We haven't done that in long while."

"I'd like that," she replied.

It was Sunday, and he vowed to take her every Sunday. A new tradition for the two of them, while they learned to cope without her mother. She fell in step beside him, and he looked down on her crown of lovely blond locks. When she sensed he was looking at her, she glanced up and took his hand.

"I miss Mama," she said.

"We always will, won't we?" he replied, clearing his throat. It was suddenly difficult to swallow.

He'd been so determined to be a bachelor for most of his life, but Lily had changed everything. Her beauty had never left her, even in her finals days, when she had lost so much weight and her face was gaunt and pale. Still, she was the most beautiful woman he'd ever known, and in spite of everything, she was a good person. He wished he could have her back so he could tell her he understood. He'd tried at the end, but she hadn't believed him. The guilt was piercing.

They drove to the hotel on the outskirts of town and sat at a table where the three of them had once had tea. He'd hoped it would cheer up Catherine, but his daughter was uncharacteristically silent, preoccupied with her own thoughts. They were served plates of sandwiches and cups of tea, and they ate occasionally nodding at the other, no energy left to make conversation. The tearoom had a balcony overlooking the sea, and after they were finished, they went to look at the water lapping onto the shore. Some of the barricades erected to keep out the Germans were being taken down, and he wondered how long it would be until life seemed normal again.

"Would you like to stop by and see Alice?" he asked.

"Yes, please," she answered.

She hugged him in her enthusiasm, and he realized he was going to have to stop moping about, if only for her sake. Children couldn't be expected to grieve as adults do. She had her moments of tears and frustration, but she was comforted by him and Mrs. Heaton and the routine that Lily had set in place so well.

They drove down the lane to the Brookses' house. It was September, and Peter couldn't help thinking if Lily hadn't lost the baby and been diagnosed with cancer, they would be expecting their child within the month. He still had the cradle he'd found in the attic of the vicarage and painted for her, where she had placed the white blanket and the cardigans she had knitted. He'd closed the door to that room but hadn't had the heart to move anything. It had represented so much hope and longing that to remove them would have felt a betrayal of the highest order.

"Papa!" Catherine cried, breaking into his thoughts.

He jerked himself back to the present and hit the brakes before he ran through an intersection, not paying any attention to what he was doing. That was the problem with losing a spouse—it was harder to hang on to reality and stay in the present. His mind drifted constantly these days into the realm of hopelessness and despair.

"I'm sorry," he said, idling the engine at the curb.

She said nothing but put her hand on his arm. It was as if Lily were there with him. He pulled himself together and turned the car in the direction of the Brookses'.

Gavin answered his knock when they arrived and welcomed them in. Catherine slipped past them and went to find Alice while Peter sat down with his friend.

"Are you all right?" Gavin asked. "To be honest with you, you look like hell."

"I feel like hell," Peter admitted.

"What did you do today?"

Peter sighed. "We went to the cemetery."

"Again?" Gavin asked.

Peter shrugged. "There was so much I didn't get to say."

Gavin raised a brow. "Well, it's fine to get it off your chest, my friend. But you probably ought to do some of this without the little one there to see your suffering."

"I know," Peter said, putting his head in his hands. "But I can't seem to pull myself together."

Susie came in and sat down next to him. "Of course you can't. It's only been a few weeks. What can we do for you to make things easier?"

"How could anything make things easier?" he retorted, regretting the outburst immediately. It wasn't her fault. It wasn't anyone's fault. Things like this happened. They were a part of life. How glib he'd been counseling others who had suffered, as if one could be expected to snap out of it and get on with the business of living. If it weren't for Catherine, he wasn't certain he could.

"I'm sorry, Susie," he said. "I'm not myself."

"Would you like us to take Catherine for a few days?" she asked. "You know we'd love to have her."

"No," he said quickly. "I can manage."

He understood how Lily must have felt. Catherine belonged to them. He didn't want to share her, even with his closest friends. Peter looked up into their sympathetic faces. He wanted nothing more than to tell them what had happened, but if he did, he couldn't stand behind the pulpit again. He wasn't ready to be forced into making any sort of ethical decision. First things first, he thought: deal with the suffocating grief. Make certain Catherine survives the latest blow in a life that, he now knew, contained many.

"I'd tell you I understand how you feel, but I don't," Gavin remarked. "I can't even imagine losing Susie. She's the thing that makes this world worth living."

"I can't believe I'll never see her again," Peter answered. "I'll never look into those blue eyes or hold her hand. And I don't think Catherine really understands, either."

"She's just a child," his friend replied. "They can only handle a little dollop of grief at a time. I'm glad you brought her over. She'll need a fair bit of distraction in the coming weeks."

"We took lilies out to the grave this morning."

"You know, she came along when we least expected it, didn't she?" Susie remarked. "Everyone in the parish had been trying to introduce you to someone, and I thought you were perhaps immune to them all. Then your lovely Lily dropped right into our lives, and none of us were ever the same."

"I was thinking the same thing myself today," he answered. "She came into my life so unexpectedly."

"At least you have Catherine," Gavin said. "She'll bring you comfort through this trial."

"Are you hungry?" Susie asked. "Can I get you something to eat?"

"No, we stopped for tea on the way back from the cemetery."

She touched his arm. "Well, I'll put on the kettle anyway. I think I could use a cup myself."

He managed to keep his secret to himself, but even in the company of his greatest friends, he could find little in the way of comfort.

Eventually, with help from Mrs. Heaton, they began to adjust to life without Lily. He still had not gone back to work, even though it was beginning to raise some eyebrows. It wasn't merely the grief; he was wrestling with a spiritual dilemma now. Could he remain in his position if he were to keep Catherine and try to move on after her mother's death? If he did, could he live with himself?

The answer changed from day to day, but his curiosity about Catherine's real parents grew over the next few weeks, even as he resolved to stop thinking about it entirely. One morning, the jar of stones Catherine had collected caught his eye. Lily had been careful to save them, although she had never explained why. Suddenly, a memory jolted his brain, and he picked up the jar of stones, now nearly full, and walked to Catherine's door, knocking softly.

"Come in."

"Can I talk to you for a minute, please?" he asked, opening the door a fraction of the way. She was sitting at the table, drawing.

"Yes, Papa," she answered.

The term of endearment tore at his heart, but he plunged ahead anyway.

"We haven't been to the beach in a while," he began, holding up the jar. The stones made a clinking noise against the glass. "You haven't had the chance to collect more of these stones since last summer at least. Perhaps longer."

She shrugged, looking at the jar for a moment and then turning her attention back to the paper, where she was drawing a picture of their cat on a low stone wall. She drew a great deal, and she was very good at it. He watched for a moment, wondering where she had gotten her talent.

Peter tried to smile. "Do you remember who you were collecting these stones for?"

Catherine looked back at the jar and frowned, shaking her head.

"Does the name Henry ring a bell?" he asked.

He had no idea who Henry was, but he remembered it from their first trip to the beach all those years ago.

"Henry?" she repeated.

She went still, resting her pencil on the pad of paper. He could almost see the cogs turning in her brain. Suddenly, the color drained from her face, and he was stricken with guilt that he'd caused her to dredge through all manner of confusing and painful memories. Perhaps he should have let it alone. But he couldn't. He had to know.

When she finally spoke, her voice was a whisper. "Henry is my brother."

Catherine began to cry. Peter put the jar on the table and took her in his arms. She wept for the brother she couldn't remember and for the mother she'd so recently lost. After a while, he realized he was crying, too.

"What does it mean?" she asked, wiping her tears with a handkerchief embroidered by her mother. She looked up at him, searching for answers. "If I have a brother, where is he? What happened to him?"

"I'm not sure," he said, realizing he couldn't tell her about Lily's deathbed confession. It occurred to him that perhaps Lily had been delirious and the story she related hadn't been the whole truth. Of course, he didn't really believe that. She had been lucid in those moments. "You were only four when you came into my life. I only know as much for certain as you do about the past."

"Did Mama give him away?" she asked. "But that doesn't make sense. Why would she let one of us go?"

"We don't know the answers yet," he replied. "But I will try to find out, for both of us."

"If we find him, can we bring him here to be with us?" she asked.

He drew in his breath. "A lot of years have passed, Catherine. We don't know what happened yet. But whatever we do, we'll decide together. All right?"

She nodded, looking more frightened than he could ever remember.

"Try not to worry about it," he said gently.

Peter walked out of the room and waited a couple of minutes before going downstairs. He put the jar back on the shelf where it had sat since Lily and Catherine had moved in with him, impulsively reaching in and selecting one of the smaller stones. He slipped it into his pocket, a reminder of the decision he had before him. He couldn't help feeling relieved that trying to find a boy named Henry who had been separated from his sister in the chaos of 1940 would be an exceedingly difficult proposition.

A few weeks later, he went back to the pulpit, choosing his sermons carefully. He preached for a month on the substance of faith, trying to be the encourager that he believed he was meant to be. It was healing to be among his flock and comforting to slip back into his old routines. Catherine had returned to school, and things were beginning to feel somewhat normal.

He'd started following newspaper accounts of the Guernsey evacuees with great interest. There was the occasional article on a child being reunited with their parents and accounts of Guernsey citizens trying to rebuild their homes, businesses, and lives after the Germans had left the island. There was no concrete information, however, not of the sort that he wanted. Eventually, he decided to take a gamble. He wrote the Home Office in London, the official government agency for domestic issues, and asked if they had information about two children named Henry and Catherine who had evacuated from Guernsey on the twentieth of June 1940. From what he could tell, there may have been few records if any kept of the children, since the evacuation was done in such haste. Islanders had been given less than twenty-four hours to decide if they were sending their children off that day, and more than five thousand had been taken from Guernsey alone on various vessels, from ships to fishing boats to barges. When they arrived in England, they were scattered from one end of the country to the other. Peter had read that many still hadn't been reunited with their families after all these months, and some never expected to see their children again.

He tried to imagine how he would feel to lose Catherine like that. The thought alone filled him with dread. She belonged to him, he reasoned. He raised her; she knew no other parent in the world. Yet the complexities of the situation nagged at him with a ferocity he didn't understand.

Weeks passed, and there was no reply. He began to breathe easily again. And then one day in early January, he got a letter from the Home Office. Mrs. Heaton walked from the vicarage to the church to bring it to him, she was so concerned.

"I thought you might need to see this, sir," she said, handing him the letter.

As he took the letter, his heart sank. It might contain information that would force him to make a difficult choice, or it might not. He wasn't certain, but either way, it wouldn't be an easy letter to read.

"Thank you, Mrs. Heaton," he said, trying to keep his tone normal. "It was good of you to bring it all the way here."

"No trouble at all, sir," she said.

She lingered for a few moments, but he set it aside as if he had more important things to do. Eventually, she bid him goodbye and went back to the house. He sat back in his chair, thinking. He didn't actually have to read it, he decided. He hadn't given any personal information about himself or Catherine; he merely expressed interest as if he were aiding a local resident with a difficult case. He slid the letter from his desk and then dropped it into the bin and walked to the pub.

The Queens Head was quiet at two o'clock in the afternoon.

Only one other customer was at the bar, and he was snoring over his pint and an open newspaper. Peter put his money on the counter and took his beer to a table in the corner. He sat down, pressing his thumbs against the sockets of his eyes. Sighing, he sat back and drank his beer, feeling the warmth of it calming him.

Perhaps the letter he had tossed in the bin would say there was no record of the evacuees for that day. Perhaps it would tell him there was no Catherine or Henry listed on any official document. Then he would have nothing to worry about at all.

But something else troubled him. What was the best thing for Catherine? To never know the people to whom she belonged, who birthed her and raised her and loved her, the people who had made the heart-wrenching decision to send her away from her home to spare her from the inevitable invasion of the Germans? Peter wondered where Henry had lived during the war and if he had safely returned to Guernsey after Hitler was dead. If he hadn't, then Catherine's parents would have lost two of their children. He couldn't even begin to imagine how terrible their grief must be.

Peter finished his beer and then walked quickly back to Holy Trinity and went into his office, shutting the door behind him. He retrieved the envelope from the bin and smoothed it out with his fingers. Then taking a letter opener, he slit open the envelope and extracted a single sheet of paper.

He read the letter quickly and then once again more slowly. And there it was: *Henry Simon, nine years old, and Catherine Simon, four years old, son and daughter of Mrs. Simon, Saint Peter Port, Bailiwick of Guernsey.*

Lily had told him the truth. She escaped a violent, abusive husband on the day of the Guernsey evacuation and met Henry and his sister, perhaps on the boat crossing the channel. Then she had taken Catherine, arriving with the girl in Cornwall just days later. He could remember the first time he'd seen her. She had been so compelling the day she had come to the vicarage asking for help. She'd been an irresistible force, and he'd been blinded by his feelings. For a second, he remembered the day of their wedding, when she had not had a death certificate for her husband. She couldn't produce one because it did not exist.

That evening, he barely touched his meal. Mrs. Heaton lingered before leaving, waiting to clean up and to help Catherine get ready for bed. He listened to the quiet murmur of their conversation and then stepped outside into the cool evening air. Walking over to the bench where he and Lily had sat so many times, he buried his face in his hands. Somewhere out there, a woman was waiting to hear about her daughter who had been lost for five long years. A child wasn't like a favorite strand of pearls or a diamond ring; it would sting to lose either of them, but eventually one could replace it. However, there was no replacing a child. Nothing could ever dim the loss. He understood how dark the world must seem to endure such suffering.

However, a problem still remained. He couldn't give away his only child. Lily's dilemma, however harshly he had judged her for it, was now his own. No matter what he might think, no matter the morals of the situation, after losing Lily, he couldn't stand the thought of losing Catherine, too.

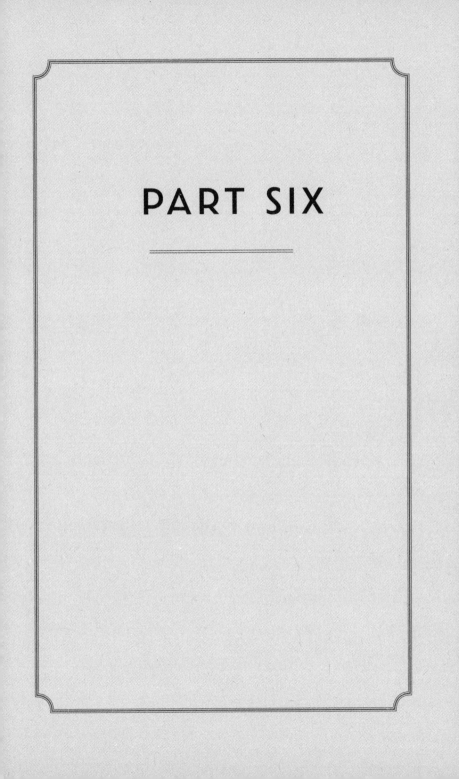

# PART SIX

# 20

JUNE 20, 1972

*Catherine*

I've always been afraid to tell my story because it has the element of the fantastical to it. So many children suffered greatly during the war. They were ill fed, terrified, and lonely; some hidden away in unfit shelters or concentration camps without the benefit of human kindness and love. Others, like my brother, Henry, found themselves in a better situation yet still an unsatisfying one, living a life apart from his own, away from every family member and friend.

There are many stories about the children who were evacuated from the Channel Islands during World War II, each as different as the people who tell them. And there were many different outcomes from that enforced separation that tore families in two. Henry's life went one way and mine another, but both contain important truths that have changed us forever. He was nine years old on June 20, 1940, old enough to remember his life and past and also to cope with the strain of war with hope and suffering. He suffered not from a lack of physical or emotional care but from the guilt of losing me. He's never gotten over the pain of it, and I doubt he ever will. He cared very much for the elderly sisters who looked after him in the Yorkshire Dales for five long years, who spoiled him and sheltered him and encouraged him to remember his past. He also deeply loved our parents who had sent us away, trying to spare us from the horrors of war. Henry is a good man all these years later, one I am proud to call my brother, and I have much to learn from him.

My story is different, with many twists and turns. It is the story of a girl who was loved too much. I am the daughter of two different mothers. And I am the daughter of two fathers as well. It is only now, at the age of thirty-six, that I can begin to express what my life has come to mean for me and, in fact, for all of us.

My earliest memory takes place on the island of Guernsey. I am playing with my older brother. We are wrestling and chasing one another on a grassy hill. Our parents are there, I know, but they are not clearly defined in my mind. They exist as an idea, a safeguard against worry or pain, not as the people they were. Henry and I are laughing and tumbling about, then he takes my hand and we walk down a long, winding path to the shore below. There is a rocky beach and I am glad for shoes, for somehow I recall the rocks have hurt my feet at some unspecified point in the past.

The waves crash loudly against the rocks, and I strain to hear Henry speak. For a while, we cup our hands and reach into the rushing waves, splashing one another with the frigid water, soaking our hair and our clothes. And then, after a time, we grow bored and begin to explore. I remember being fascinated with every detail of the scene: the way the dry sand is pale, almost cocoa colored, and the wet sand, a deep, rich brown. The rowboat with peeling blue paint that bobs against the shore reminds us that adventure lies ahead. We fill our pockets with tiny stones, gray and white, that we found along with sodden seaweed and shells. Henry digs for crabs and holds them too close to me, making me squeal. His face is beautiful as he leans near, laughing and splendidly happy, the sun glinting in his eyes. Freckles are scattered upon his nose, and his hair is sticking up in all the wrong places. It was then, and remains, the best moment of my life.

My second memory is taking a train trip with my mother some indeterminate time later. I was still young, only four, I understand, and it was not a happy day. I was frightened and confused and felt I didn't know or trust her well. But she was kind and gentle, and I eventually began to relax in her care.

We lived in the village of Saint Austell, Cornwall, the most beautiful place in the world. I know now that she brought me there the day after our evacuation from Guernsey in 1940 and we lived in a small house—which I do not recall—for a short time before she married my father. Peter Ashby, the vicar at Holy Trinity in Saint Austell, was the only father I knew, and I can't remember much of anything before he came into my life. We were happy together, the three of us, our home full of laughter and teasing. I remember my parents kissing when I wasn't looking and then taking me into their embrace when I caught them. They lived a life of ministry to others, one that I grew to love as well. We took food to the hungry and flowers to the sick, mindful of the needs of others, always aware that our joy was meant to be shared.

It was at the age of nine, after losing my mother, that my father showed me the jar of stones we had collected through the years, the jar that brought back an unbidden memory of Henry. After that day, we didn't speak of it again for months. I somehow managed to suppress the conversation entirely. I didn't know then that he was making inquiries into my past life, the life I had forgotten.

A few months after my mother passed away, my father was still not himself. Mrs. Heaton, our housekeeper, struggled with her loss as well, but his was all-encompassing. He even took leave from the pulpit, something he didn't want to do. But when one is an empty vessel, how can one fill others? Some people believe that too much grieving is wrong and judge how long and how immersed one is in sorrow. However, I believe that grief is normal, and one must allow oneself to take whatever time one needs to refill one's spirit. My mother, Lily, was beautiful and lovely and a shining light for us all, and it hurt us to lose her so young. My father most of all.

He was a shell of himself for a while. What I didn't understand at the tender age of nine was that he was grappling with a decision that would change his life forever. He had lost the woman he loved and, in doing so, would also be forced to lose me. He told me the story a few years later about his shock at the news she gave him on her deathbed. He'd been furious to learn she was already married when she came to Saint Austell, that she stole a child being evacuated from a war zone, that she lied to everyone. I remember the first time I heard this story as a teen, how angry I was at her that we should be so deceived. But at nine, I was simply a young girl who had lost the only mother I had ever known. And then one day, my father decided to take me on a journey to a small, unfamiliar island in the middle of the English Channel.

I remember the day I met my parents. It was February, eight months after my mother passed away. The day was cold, and I was unusually fearful and uncooperative on the ferry. My father later said he believed my reticence was due to my having been traumatized by being shipped off to England with a barge full of strangers five years earlier. We had a great deal of luggage with us, which didn't concern me at the time. I wasn't aware then that he had packed nearly every single thing I owned in order to leave the daughter he loved with a family who were perfect strangers to me.

We took a room in a hotel in Saint Peter Port, in a beautiful old stone building with blue shutters. Our room had two beds and a dresser and just enough space for us to squeeze in all our luggage.

"We're going to visit some friends tomorrow," he said, opening one of suitcases. "This is the island where your mother was born, and there are a lot of nice people here to meet."

"I don't want to meet people, Papa," I argued, suddenly suspicious. "Couldn't we stay and explore the village instead?"

"Sit down, Princess," he replied. Once I was seated on the bed across from him, I realized that he wasn't merely sad. He was afraid.

"What's the matter?" I asked.

Terror struck my heart. I couldn't imagine what it could be. The worst had already happened. At least the worst that I could possibly imagine. We had lost my mother. I didn't know something terrible was yet to come.

He folded his hands in his lap. "I want to talk to you about Henry, Catherine."

My eyes grew wide at the name. We had discussed it only once before, when he showed me the jar of stones that I had collected with him and my mother at the beach over the last few years.

"Henry," I whispered. "My brother, Henry?"

"Yes, Catherine," he answered. "Your brother, Henry. He lives here on Guernsey."

"With who?" I asked. My heart quickened, waiting for the answer.

"With your mother and father," he said quietly.

"You're my father," I replied.

"Yes, I am," he answered. "I am your adopted papa, and I love you with all my heart. But you have parents you were born to who haven't seen you in a very long time."

I could see the emotion on his face. "Do we have to stay long?"

"As long as you would like."

I had to stop and think about it all. I wanted to see Henry, but I didn't know what to think about his parents. Of course, I couldn't think of them as mine.

The following morning was Saturday, and we ate our breakfast downstairs in the small dining room and then bundled up warmly for the weather. My father arranged for a taxi, and when it arrived, we got inside and he gave the driver the address. I know the two of them spoke, but I was too nervous to pay attention. Instead, I pressed my nose against the window of the car and absorbed the landscape of the island, trying to remember something. Anything. Yet nothing seemed familiar at all.

When we neared our destination, my father asked the driver to stop and paid him.

"We'll get out here, please," he said.

We watched the taxi turn around in the middle of the road and head back to town, and then my father held out his hand to me and I took it. We squeezed our fingers tightly together. He took a step, and I fell in beside him, walking up a short hill. There was a house at the top, and I froze when I saw it. An indefinable feeling came over me as I gazed at the tall, white house overlooking the sea. In spite of the cold, a woman was hanging the wash on a line. It took a few moments for her to notice us, and when she did, she stepped toward us, frowning.

She shaded her eyes against the sun. "Can I help you?"

"I'm Peter Ashby," my father replied. "I'd like to speak to Ava and Joseph Simon."

"I'm Ava Simon," she said with a puzzled look still on her face. "I—"

Her voice broke off as she caught sight of me, and she grabbed her throat. We both thought she was going to collapse. She went completely still, and we approached her slowly, our hands still clasped together. Instinctively, I pulled closer to my father, trying to hide behind him.

"Won't you come in?" she said when she recovered her voice. She was a small woman, blond, like me, with a thin coat over a dress and apron. The tails of the apron fluttered below the edge of her coat.

"We'd like that, wouldn't we?" my father said in a gentle tone.

We followed her into the house. It wasn't like the vicarage, with its generous-sized rooms and cheery songs on the phonograph. It was a darker house, everything faded and worn and nothing in its place, not like the neat and tidy home where I had lived for so long. The woman began gathering newspapers and cardigans and placed them in baskets before stopping once again to look at me.

"Let me get my family," she said.

She went up the stairs, and the two of us, not knowing what to do, walked over to the fireplace where a fire was burning bright. We warmed ourselves, huddling close together.

"Can we go?" I whispered.

I didn't want to stay in this place. It was too difficult to look that woman in the eye, and I knew I must, for my mother had taught me good manners.

"Let's give them a chance, shall we?" he murmured in reply.

A moment later, the woman descended the steps with two people behind her—a boy of about fifteen and a man. They all wore the same shocked look upon their faces.

"Won't you sit down?" the woman said. She turned to the boy. "Henry, put on the kettle for tea."

My stomach tightened as we sat on a long sofa and she sat in a chair across from us. I didn't know what to make of any of it. Henry was a teen now, not the boy I remembered. The man who had followed her down the stairs still stood somewhat off to the side of the room, unable to account for what his eyes told him he was seeing.

"I'm Peter Ashby," my father said again. "I'm the vicar at Holy Trinity Church in Saint Austell, Cornwall. In June of 1940, I met a woman named Lily Carré who was newly arrived in England. She came with her daughter, Catherine, to ask for help in finding some accommodations."

He paused in the story to allow them to absorb what he was saying. The man crept over and sat in a chair near the woman, and Henry came out of the kitchen and leaned against the doorframe so that he could hear better. A border collie settled at his feet, gray mingling with the black in his fur.

"Mrs. Carré was a kind and gentle person," he continued. "She told me she was a widow. We grew to care for one another and married a few months after we met."

"Was?" Ava Simon asked.

My father nodded. "She recently died of cancer. Just before she passed, she confided in me that she had been on a ferry on the Guernsey evacuation day with two children, Henry and Catherine, and after they arrived in England, they were set to board a train to Manchester. She put the boy on the train with a ten-pound note and took Catherine with her. She found her way to Cornwall instead."

The kettle suddenly whistled, startling us all. Henry went to turn it off, and Ava rose to get cups and saucers. We waited patiently while she brought the tea in on a tray and poured everyone a cup, even me. She put milk and sugar in mine, and I took it and held it in my hands for warmth. For some reason, I was shaking. I leaned so close to my father that our arms touched.

"I remember the ten-pound note," Henry said, still leaning against the doorframe.

Everyone was deathly quiet, as if Papa and I were deer and the slightest movement would startle us away.

"You do?" asked his mother, turning to look at him.

Henry nodded.

My father cleared his throat. "I thought perhaps we could all get to know one another."

I took a sip of the tea and put it back on the tray. Every eye in the room was on me. I took hold of my father's arm so no one would get the wrong impression. I couldn't help noticing my shiny patent leather shoes and snow-white stockings were in stark contrast to the plain clothes of these farm people. I didn't want to talk to them. They seemed sad and broken. Everyone except Henry, that is.

"I have something for you," Henry said to me suddenly. "I bought it for you a couple of years ago when I was in Yorkshire. I'll be right back."

A minute later, he came down the stairs with a book in his hand. Handing it to me, he smiled. It was a copy of *The Wind in the Willows*.

"This was my favorite book when I was your age," he said. "I saw it in a shop and bought it to give you the next time we met. I knew we'd see you again. I knew it."

I took it solemnly, looking at the cover, and then glancing back at him. "I love books," I said.

Everyone in the room nodded.

Ava even smiled. "Yes, you do," she said, putting down her cup. "You always did, even when you were a baby."

"She was always pulling them out of Henry's hands," her husband said, almost to himself.

"She wanted me to read to her," Henry replied, nodding to his father.

"Tell us about yourself, Catherine," Ava continued. "Do you like school?"

I nodded. "I like school very much."

My captive audience waited for me to continue, but I was tongue-tied in the face of such pressure. At one point, the only sound was the fire crackling in the grate.

"I remember playing with Henry on the beach," I said, breaking the silence. Everyone turned to look at me, even my father. "It's the only thing I remember from when I was small."

"It's just outside," Henry said. "Would you like to see it?"

"Yes," I answered.

I looked at my father, who nodded. I followed Henry to the door, where he took a coat from a hook. The rest of them stood, uncertain what to do, and eventually decided to join us. Henry led the way into the garden, where Ava had been hanging clothes on the line when we arrived. There was a path that led down a trail toward the beach, and Henry reached out his hand to me.

"You have to watch out for the rocks," he said.

I took his hand, tentatively at first, and then more naturally. He was safe, I thought. He was Henry.

"How old are you?" I asked.

"Fourteen."

"I'm nine."

"I remember."

We made our way down to the beach. For winter, it was a sunny day, though cold. We listened to the crashing waves beat against the shore. He let go of my hand and wandered toward the water's edge. I saw him bend down and run his hand along the wet sand, his fingers closing around a stone. Absently, he rubbed the sand against the leg of his trousers and put it in his pocket. Something like joy surged in my chest. It was us, together again on the beach, gathering stones. But it wasn't the same as before. I was in a place I didn't know that was still somehow familiar. Henry's parents—my parents—were so full of emotion I could hardly look at them. I waited a few minutes longer and then turned to go back. My father stood with Ava and Joseph a short distance away, unable to take their eyes off us.

They followed Henry and me back to the house, and we all went back to our polite formation in the sitting room, no one willing to be the first to speak. There was so much to say and no idea of how to say it. Later, however, my father said we all were thinking the same thing, the one thing that couldn't be said.

I sat there nervously, twisting my fingers together, not daring to make eye contact with anyone. "May I ask a question, please?"

"Of course," Ava said. "Ask us anything."

"When is my birthday?"

Ava and Joseph gasped, and my father made a strangled sound in his throat. All three of them were shocked by my bluntness. My mother had celebrated my birthday on September 20 every year, but I realized that if she met me when I was four, she may not have known when it really was.

"I'm sorry," I said, contrite. I knew they were all miserable and because of me. "I just wanted to know."

"November twelfth," Joseph said.

"November twelfth at seven o'clock in the evening," Ava added. "You were born on a cold and rainy night."

I looked at my father. "That means we can't celebrate on the twentieth of September anymore."

Everyone went silent. After a moment, Ava stood and we all looked up, wondering what she would say. I moved closer to my father and took his arm.

"I think that's a long enough visit for today," she said.

It may have been my imagination, but I believe I heard more than one audible sigh of relief. Someone called a taxi for us, and all the adults shook hands, even Henry. As we left, no one knew what would happen next or if we would ever see each other again.

We stayed on the island for a week, visiting the farm every day. Ava was kind but distant, aware that if she allowed herself to get too close to me, it would be a brutal parting when we went away. Joseph did not allow himself to show any emotion at all. He watched the week unfold without any remark.

I often wonder what they thought in those days. Did they hate Peter Ashby for not delivering me to their doorstep and walking away? For allowing a nine-year-old to make the choice herself? But he couldn't have left me like that. It was obvious to all that a child newly grieving her mother's loss wasn't ready to lose her father, too.

Henry held us all together. He laughed at my father's attempts at jokes and conversation. He comforted his mother and put a strong hand on his father's shoulder when it seemed he could stand no more. He befriended me without asking anything of me. It seems remarkable now that a boy of fourteen could be so strong.

An unspoken thought hung in the air: how much longer could we do all this, pretending that we weren't leaving Guernsey soon, perhaps forever? We had made little headway in the business of transferring Catherine Carré Ashby back to Catherine Simon, releasing me to my prior owners. Or perhaps that is simply how it felt at the time. Finally, my father put an end to our suffering. We were seated in the Simons' house, making awkward conversation.

"Well, I hate to say it, but I must head back to Saint Austell tomorrow," my father announced. He sat back and let us take it all in, his usual patient self.

"*You* are," Joseph said, putting the emphasis on *you*.

Everyone looked at me, and I suddenly had trouble breathing.

"What do you say, Catherine?" my father asked. "Your parents care for you very much and would like you to come and live with them and Henry."

I glanced at Ava and Joseph, studying them. Ava was as thin as a rail and without a doubt the saddest-looking woman I had ever seen. Joseph was hardly different. He sat in a deep chair in the corner, taking everything in. Neither had any fight left in them. They could see the bond between my father and me, and to me, they were strangers. I didn't have the ability to see them for the people they were or for what I had meant in their lives.

"May I show you something?" Ava asked.

I nodded.

She stood and held out her hand. "It's upstairs."

I gripped my father's arm tighter.

"Come with me," I whispered to him.

Reluctantly, he stood, the tension palpable in the room. I was terrified to be left with them. My father was frightened of losing his only remaining family member. My Guernsey parents had suffered intolerably during the years I was gone and were afraid of losing me the very moment they had me back in their life.

We all followed Ava up the dark, narrow staircase and into a small bedroom. I knew it at once.

"This is my room," I murmured.

"That's right," she replied.

The color drained from my father's face. What had seemed abstract to him before that moment was now a vivid, glaring truth none of us could escape. I released his hand and walked around, looking at everything. A pink dress hanging on a hook. Tiny pearl white combs on the dresser. A doll in a toy baby carriage that had been much loved. A small carved bed painted gray that was the prettiest thing in the house. I was their treasure, I realized. I was the thing they loved the most.

Ava clasped her hands together and took a deep breath. "We're so glad you came to Guernsey to visit us, Catherine," she said.

We all looked at her in surprise, even Joseph. Something about her caught my eye then. It was a spark of something beautiful, something that had been hidden through years of sorrow and pain.

"How would you feel about us coming to visit you in Saint Austell this summer?"

I looked at my father and saw him smile. "We'd like that very much, wouldn't we, Catherine?"

"Can Henry come, too?" I asked, a wave of relief washing over me.

For some reason, everyone laughed.

"Of course I'll come," he answered in his normal, good-natured way. "I want to see where my sister lives."

"Then, yes, please," I said.

A surge of affection rose in my chest, and I went over to wrap my arms around Ava. For some reason, the men all turned away and began to walk downstairs. She didn't let go for at least a minute, and when she did, she took my hand and we followed them without uttering a single word.

I was his longer than I was theirs. Perhaps they all knew that I couldn't lose another parent so soon, but one thing is certain: they all put my feelings above their own. I didn't understand it for many years.

And so began our joint family holidays. Joseph, Ava, and Henry came to see us in Saint Austell in August, and we went back to Guernsey for Christmas. It became our routine, blending our families two or three times a year for the rest of my childhood. I became fond of Ava and Joseph as one would a distant aunt and uncle that one begins to get to know. They never felt like my parents, but I came to care for them anyway. My father welcomed them into our lives in Cornwall without reservation, and I was pleased to see how much they liked him, too. A true friendship developed between them. I began to relax and enjoy our trips to Guernsey, learning about the island, which I found to be beautiful, and even looked forward to seeing my second family when too much time had passed between visits.

Four years later, Henry turned eighteen and went to university. We still saw him at Christmas every year, but he wasn't able to join his parents to meet us in the summer. However, he did manage to get away once each spring, taking the train from Oxford to Saint Austell to stay with my father and me.

Years later, I met Henry in London during my second year of medical school. We had never gotten together on our own before, but I like to think our relationship was precisely what it would have been had we never been separated. Like my father, he had gone to Oxford. He graduated with honors and took a position as a barrister in Guernsey. He's quite talented. Ava sends me clippings from the newspaper every time he wins a case. He could have had a brilliant career in London, but he didn't want to be far from our parents. In fact, he married a Guernsey girl named Pippa, and they were expecting their first child.

"I've done some digging," he said one evening over a pint at the Jamaica Wine House in Cornhill.

It's the oldest coffeehouse in London, though we always go for the beer. We ordered a couple of Guinness, along with an enormous plate of chips. In college, I lived on the things.

"What sort of digging?" I asked, dunking my chip into ketchup like an American instead of malt vinegar like my brother. I'd picked up the habit when I met my first college flatmate, who was from Philadelphia.

"On the island," he said, raising a brow as if I was to know what that meant. "I wasn't sure if you wanted to know or not."

"About my mother," I replied.

He nodded. I don't think he ever thought of her as my mother, but he never contradicted me when I said it.

"Is this about her previous life?"

"I don't have to tell you, Cat, if it's too upsetting."

I loved when he called me Cat. It was his own personal nickname for me when we met again at nine and fourteen. I was crazy about kittens and cats, as I had been from the first moment I set eyes on the neighbor's cat in Saint Austell.

"It's not upsetting," I stated. I wouldn't let it be. "I know about her parents, George and Edith. They passed away a few years after the war. And she had a sister, Helen, who was your teacher the year we evacuated. She's the one who let Lily take her place."

"Helen is married now and living in France with her husband. The memories were too painful, from what I understand. But no, I wasn't thinking of the Matthewses."

I put down my pint glass, peering at him carefully. "Are you talking about her husband?"

My brother sat back in his seat. "His name was Ian Carré. He and Lily lived in a fabulous, huge house on the west side of the island. I looked up some of their old help and found a housekeeper who worked for them for more than three years."

"And?" I prompted. "I know some of her backstory from what she told my father. They had marital issues."

"That's putting it mildly," he said. "She was being beaten pretty regularly. They had trouble getting pregnant, and he blamed her. He felt his political ambitions were being affected by their childlessness, as though it made him less of a man. He was cruel. She really had no choice but to leave him."

"What happened to him after the war?" I asked, curious.

"He died before it ended, in a confrontation with a soldier over something nebulous like disrespect. The officer who shot him was put in prison." He pushed back his glass. "They had an awful time of it, those who were left behind."

"I know," I said, nodding. "It's easier to understand it now than it was when I was only nine."

"Do you?" he asked. "Do you really understand what it was like for Mum and Dad?"

They had expended so much energy trying to make me happy through the years that they didn't talk about what they had personally gone through. I knew that Joseph had been sent to a prison camp and suffered tremendously but little of what Ava had gone through apart from losing Henry and me.

"How did you come out of the war unscathed?" I asked him.

His personality was always sanguine. I had never seen him put out or angry or unhappy. Henry is always Henry: calm, reasonable, kind.

"No one came out of the war unscathed," he answered. For a moment, he fiddled with his napkin. "I've done some reading about the psychological effects of the war as it pertains to the child evacuees. They came out of the war in three categories, really. The first was the group who desperately missed their homes and couldn't wait to get back."

"That's your group," I noted, sprinkling salt on the chips.

"Yes," he replied. "The second is a group of older children who came of age during the war and then found they didn't want to go back to a small island afterward. They had begun to find jobs and husbands and wives, setting down roots. Many different scenarios played out with their parents back home after 1945."

"And the third group?" I asked.

"Ah," he said, lifting his glass and taking a gulp of his stout. "The third group is the most unfortunate."

I cocked my head at him. "I'm listening."

"That's the group of children who forgot their homes and their families and bonded with the people who had been raising them. It was especially difficult for people like you who were so young, and it was traumatic for them when they were returned to parents they couldn't really remember."

"Peter tried to bring me back," I said, musing on the subject.

"Can you imagine how hard that must have been for him, finding out the truth?" Henry asked. "I've thought it one of the most astonishing things I've ever heard. Many people wouldn't have done it."

"He's a pretty wonderful person," I replied. After a moment, I looked up at my brother. "I should ask Ava to tell me about everything that happened during the war the next time I see her. She's never really talked about it with me."

"I think you should," he said, nodding.

"I suddenly feel like I've disappointed you."

"Of course not," Henry answered, shaking his head. "Everyone knows how young you were when it happened. No one blames you for anything. And it was devastating for you to lose Lily like that. But if you ever want one, there's another mother who has been waiting for a long time to be there for you. She loves you, Cat."

I nodded, though I couldn't answer. My feelings on the subject have always been complicated. Our lives were like roads that intersect. I was headed in one direction, she in another. That was never more apparent than when I graduated from medical school with a degree in pediatrics.

"Have you thought about working in Guernsey?" she asked at my graduation.

"I love Guernsey, you know that," I said. "But I'm thinking about a different sort of career."

Ever the diplomat, she didn't pry. She always let me tell her what I wished and no more, but I knew she was disappointed.

In 1971, I heard of a new organization called Doctors Without Borders, an international humanitarian group that brought medical care to countries ravaged by war, conflicts, and disease.

I grew interested in their work in Africa, where in addition to providing medical care, they provided food and water for starving families. I applied and was accepted not long after, surprising all my relatives, who had grown used to our routines, traveling back and forth between Cornwall and Guernsey. But for once, I needed a life of my own. Not one defined by my birthright or the repercussions of the actions of a woman who took a child who wasn't hers. I didn't do it to punish anyone or to separate myself from them, but because I loved the work. I had been raised to understand what it meant to do for others, and this was the way that I wanted to do it.

I decided to do it for another reason as well: it meant I wasn't choosing my father over Ava and Joseph. I was grown and able to make decisions for myself, and it allowed me some space to think about what my childhood had meant in the grander scheme. I corresponded with all of them regularly, promising to go to Guernsey to see everyone for Christmas. But in the spring of this year, something unexpected happened.

She came to Africa: Ava, my Guernsey mother. The idea had formed in our frequent and searching letters. I talked of Kenya in mine, of the difficulties of learning Swahili, dealing with the heat and the mosquitoes, the adjustments of living in more primitive conditions. Certainly, after medical school and a brief stint in London, it was a major life change. I had been there almost a year when she said she wanted to join me and volunteer for a few weeks.

Although I had known her since I was nine years old, I had never seen her without the buffering influence of my father or Joseph or Henry, so I wasn't certain what to expect. She could appear stern at times, though perhaps she was merely circumspect, rarely wishing to insert herself too much into my life. I came to realize that of all of us, she had lost the most. I never shook the feeling of guilt that I had wanted to go home with my father to Saint Austell when he was trying to return me to them all those years ago, nor forgotten the look on her face when she told us that we had to go home. It was wrenching for everyone, but Ava the most. Even though we had a cordial relationship, it was never one I could call close. Now this woman who had given birth to me was going to see me away from all the emotional ties and on neutral territory. Would I like her? I wondered. Would we have anything in common? I was almost afraid to find out.

A young Swahili man, Jafari, and his wife, Nia, had become an unofficial part of the Doctors Without Borders camp, and I had grown particularly fond of them because of their good natures and their desire to help in any way possible. Jafari ran errands, usually taking the mail and picking up deliveries for us, and Nia liked to work with me, helping me hold infants when I was giving vaccinations and testing for whooping cough and diphtheria. I had grown so used to them, I thought of them as an integral part of the team, but after Ava arrived at the camp, I saw them anew from her eyes. I noticed how she took in my relationship with Jafari and Nia, realizing they were perhaps the first Africans she had ever known. Though obviously taken aback at first, she was soon chatting with them and learning from them as well. Their English was better than most. Before Doctors Without Borders had come to Kenya, they had attached themselves to a missionary team from Alabama who did similar work to ours, without all the medications and surgeries. Ava was fascinated with them. Her desire to learn was strong and her desire to know me even stronger. She took the time to get to know them, which I had never expected her to do. I realized then that I might be underestimating her. She was truly interested in my work, wanting to know everything: what I did all day, what the conditions were like, whom I talked to. She followed me around the camp, observing my life with a keen eye.

One day, she was sitting with me as I spoke with a teenaged Swahili mother and her toddler son. I examined his eyes and ears and mouth and then took his temperature as he began to cry. When I reached with one hand for my clipboard to record his vitals, Ava came over and picked him up. She's a small woman, barely taller than the child's mother. But her hands were capable and firm as she lifted him and began to speak to him in a tender tone of voice, and suddenly, I was taken back a thousand years to when that voice had soothed Henry and me. The jolt of memory was so strong, I had a physical reaction.

That evening, when we went back to my room, I wanted to tell her, but I didn't know how. I had given her my bed and was sleeping on a thin mattress on the floor. We'd eaten a dinner of black beans and rice, something she had never tried before, but of which I had become fond after my American boyfriend, Devin, had introduced it to me. After we ate, we sat on my bed and talked about Henry, always our favorite subject. I loved the way her face lit up whenever he was mentioned.

"So the baby is due in a few weeks," I said, rinsing out the bowls. "Henry and Pippa must be so excited."

"They are," Ava said. "They've wanted a child for such a long time."

"He's going to be the most amazing dad."

"He's pretty good at everything," she said, smiling. "And so are you. You two have turned out to be such lovely, capable people."

"I'm so glad you're here," I confessed. "It's grand to share this all with you and let you see how it works."

"I'm glad I came," she replied, looking up. "I never thought I'd go to Africa one day. And when I think of all the good you are doing, well, it's just wonderful. Lily would be so proud of you."

I looked up, startled at the comment, but it was delivered sincerely, with no self-pity in her tone.

"Do you think about her much?" I asked.

She lowered her eyes and sighed. "I'm sorry. Perhaps I shouldn't have said that. The hardest part of all this is that I simply can't hate her. She was good to you. And to be loved by someone like Peter, well, she had to be a wonderful person."

"Tell me about that day," I murmured. "You've never talked about it to me before."

"The day you left?"

"Yes."

"It was gut-wrenching," she answered, sighing. "The government gave us twenty-four hours' notice about the evacuation. We found out one evening and had to send the two of you off the next morning. Neither of us slept a wink that whole night. Joseph thought we should send you because we believed you would stay with Henry's teacher until we could join you a few days or weeks later. I argued against it, wanting to keep you both with us. Of course, he won by painting a vivid picture of what life would look like if the Germans occupied Guernsey. We decided we couldn't let that happen to you, too."

"How long did you go without news?" I asked.

"I knew within days when I saw Henry's teacher in Saint Peter Port. I saw her walking down the street just days after you left. I was completely horrified. As long as she wasn't with you, you could be anywhere." Ava gazed at me solemnly. "And as it turned out, you were."

I reached out to touch her hand. "I am so sorry. You must have been so scared."

She gave a slight smile. "I was, although over time, you just become numb. There were so many changes, so much pain and suffering among those we knew."

"Do you think about it much?" I asked.

Ava nodded. "I think about it a great deal. It's the guilt. You were only four at the time. You weren't supposed to go without a mother. I was angry with your father for a long time for not letting me go, too."

We stopped talking for a moment, lost in our own thoughts. I tried to see her point of view, to imagine how I would have felt if I were in her shoes. Or, for that matter, how she felt now.

"Tell me about Lily," she ventured.

"She's been gone for such a long time now," I replied. I wasn't sure how I felt about talking about her with Ava. The woman was responsible for destroying her life.

"It's all right," she answered. "You don't have to talk about it if you don't want to."

"I've gone over it a million times since I met you," I said. "I think children simply bond with the people they're with if they're kind. And she was certainly kind. She wasn't like my father, so funny and outgoing and interesting. She was quiet, very ladylike and proper, very respectable and nice. She made a good vicar's wife. They adored each other, and she would have done anything for him."

"I think about her life sometimes," Ava said. "Imagine living in such a fine house and having a husband who is on his way up the political ladder and then giving it all up. On the outside, she seemed to have everything."

"Except a child," I murmured. "Can you imagine how desperate someone must be to steal one like that? Someone who was respected in society who will go against all their core beliefs and take a child by the hand and leave with her?"

"Who knows what any of us would have done in her shoes?" Ava said.

"That's a generous comment," I remarked, standing to stretch my legs. I walked over to the window and flicked the curtain. We could hear howling in the far distance. There had been packs of wild dogs recently coming near after the cover of darkness was upon the camp. "My father has tried to explain that she didn't plan to kidnap someone that day. It was a terrible combination of circumstances. She wanted to escape her life, and a child was left alone with her in a vulnerable position. She acted on impulse, believing she saved me from a fate far worse."

I remembered the day he told me what my mother had done. I was fifteen at the time, too old to be considered a child and too young to be an adult. We sat together on the beach, and I knew he was going to tell me something important, although I had no idea how life-changing it would be. I had asked him a few times through the years how I had gotten separated from Henry during the evacuation, and he had always been vague about the answer.

"Your mother met you and Henry on the day of the Guernsey evacuation," he said, folding his hands in his lap. "She brought you both safely to England on a barge. She intended to remain with the evacuees and look after you both, but when it came down to it, her courage failed her."

"What do you mean, her courage failed her?" I asked, fiddling with her charm bracelet, which he had given me the Christmas before. I loved that bracelet. I remembered her wearing it often.

"You have to understand how difficult that day was," he continued. "And what chaos there was in Guernsey when they realized the Germans were coming. She evacuated with the teachers and children who were trying desperately to reach English soil. Later that evening, when it came time to board the train to a distant, unfamiliar English city, your mother found she couldn't do it. She put Henry on the train and decided not to let you go with him."

I was shocked. "How could she let Henry travel so far away on his own? He was only nine."

"She was young and inexperienced," he answered. "She'd never had children. At the time, she thought Henry would be safe with the teachers and other boys his age, but she was afraid to let you go. You were only four after all."

"So we weren't separated by accident," I said. For the first time in my life, I was angry with her. Lily Carré had made a conscious decision to abandon one child and take another. "I don't understand how she could have done such a thing."

He had no answer for me. Furious, I removed the bracelet and tossed it onto the sand. He reached over and took it, placing it in his pocket.

"Catherine, your mother was a good person. I'm sure she did what she thought best at the time."

"You're wrong," I said, eyes flashing. "She did what was best for her."

It was a long time before I forgave her, or at least made peace with what had happened. I never forgot that if it hadn't been for Lily Carré, I wouldn't have lost Henry or my real parents. But looking at Ava now, I knew I couldn't explain it to her. Too much time had passed.

"We didn't think we'd ever see you again," Ava said, interrupting my thoughts. "We thought you were lost forever."

"In some ways, perhaps I still am," I answered honestly. "You never got your daughter back. You had to share her with an adopted father who lived across the sea."

"I've tried to be philosophical about everything," she said. "Knowing you were alive was the most important thing. And while we want to believe our life plans will work out in the best possible way, sometimes they don't. Sometimes things go terribly wrong. Not every mother is loved by the children she gave birth to. I had to accept that in order to be in your life."

I turned back from the window. "If it matters, Lily was in a terrible marriage before the war. He was cruel and abusive. That clouds the issue for me, though. I'm glad she escaped a horrible life, but it's still wrong to do what she did. In fact, most would say it was unforgivable. It changed the relationship between the two of us forever."

"What about Peter?" she asked. "He must have been so hurt to find out the truth. He doesn't often speak of it."

"He was hurt," I answered. "And then he thought he had to lose me, too."

Ava took a breath. "We felt the two of you needed one another," she said simply. "Neither of you could have stood to lose the only family you had left."

"Literally no one else would make that decision," I replied. "But being his daughter was the only thing I knew."

"As long as you understand that we let you go because we loved you, not because we didn't."

"I could never think that."

She gave a slight smile. "I think I should get some sleep. It'll be another long, hot day tomorrow."

I nodded and went over to the mattress on the floor, pulling a blanket over my shoulders. She turned out the light, and within minutes, I could hear her rhythmic breathing. However, I couldn't sleep. She'd lost everything and gotten so little in return, yet she couldn't even bring herself to hate the woman who was responsible for it all.

She'd been expected to have the wisdom of Solomon before she was thirty, hoping against hope that everything would turn out all right. And yet for some of us, life doesn't work out that way. I wondered if I could have chosen someone's happiness over my own the way she had done for me. It's a difficult question without a ready answer. And possibly because that answer might be a resounding no. This woman had chosen better than any of us, and we respected her for it. Of course, even I knew respect wasn't enough.

Devin arrived back in camp from Lebanon that week. As one of our senior members, he was occasionally asked to travel to other Doctors Without Borders locations to teach and instruct newer recruits. We'd been dating for several months. My friend Marina had suggested that he might propose one day soon, but I knew neither of us were ready. We cared for each other, but our first love was our jobs.

I was proud to introduce him to Ava, who sized him up in that way of hers that I had come to know so well.

"This is Devin Sanders," I said, introducing him. "He's one of the doctors here."

"The boyfriend," he supplied, shaking Ava's hand. "When she has time for me."

I saw a smile crease her face. He was handsome, charming, and talented, quite a package for a single human being.

"Devin," I said. "This is my mother."

It was out of my mouth before I even thought, and I felt her glance at me and then quickly look away before I could catch her eye. But it was a moment neither of us would ever forget. I had never called her my mother before.

Joseph's sixtieth birthday was a couple of months later, and we all met in Guernsey for a long weekend to celebrate. Peter had taken the ferry from Weymouth, and I had flown from Nairobi to Paris and taken a series of small, rickety French trains to Saint Malo, where I boarded the ferry to Saint Peter Port to meet them all.

Henry and Pippa introduced me to my new nephew, Finn, a beautiful, dimpled, fat baby with a constant smile. I imagine he takes after his father. I hugged everyone, Ava the longest, and listened to the conversation as my father asked Ava to tell them about her experiences in Africa. Everyone was interested except for Joseph, who had heard it all before. As usual, he was lost in his own thoughts, and I went up to him, smiling.

"Feel like a walk?" I asked.

He nodded, surprised. The two of us slipped from the room and through the kitchen, going out the back door. The day was cool, but fortunately, there wasn't a lot of wind.

"I wish you could have come to see me, too," I said, taking his arm.

"I've never been so far from home."

"It's scary at first," I replied. "But then you get used to it."

"I can't imagine you afraid of anything," he answered with a laugh. "You and your brother both—so brave, so intelligent."

"We're your children," I said lightly. "As far as I'm concerned, we got all our good qualities from the two of you."

We stopped for a moment and looked out at the sea. I could only imagine what he must feel every time he looked in the direction of France, where he had been held at a prison camp during the war. He had never spoken to me about it, but I knew some of the story from Henry and from reading I'd done in the university library. The conditions had been atrocious. Food was scarce, and what little they had was of poor quality. They lived in leaky cabins that let in the rain and the cold. There was no sanitation or plumbing; in fact, discarded animal troughs were used as rudimentary toilets. Prisoners slept not on beds but on sacks of straw. I couldn't imagine how he had suffered, this gentle man who, even after all these years, held his feelings inside. You wouldn't let an animal exist in those conditions, let alone a human being. It angered me every time I thought of it.

We walked for a while under the apple trees, arm in arm. Making our way to the edge of the cliff, I was struck anew by how beautiful Guernsey was and how fortunate they were to have their house by the sea. It would have been a wonderful place to grow up. I shivered, thinking about it.

"Are you cold?" he asked. "We can go back."

I nodded and then took his hand. "It's time to celebrate your birthday anyway, Dad."

We walked back to the house to celebrate his sixtieth birthday, to blow out candles and cut the cake with our big, beautiful, unlikely family.

My father says this is a story of forgiveness. He had to forgive my mother, Lily, for lying to him and hiding the truth during their five-year marriage, placing him in the worst position imaginable for a man dealing with grief. Henry has to learn to forgive himself for losing me, something I hope will happen over time, as he sees that sometimes, things turn out as they are meant to be. Ava had to forgive Joseph for sending away their daughter, who was much too young to evacuate without a parent, and even perhaps God, whose ways are not our ways and who gave her a life that was at times unbearable. And today, on the thirty-second anniversary of the day that I was lost, I, too, have a great deal to forgive and of which to be forgiven. My life was a long series of twists and turns, none of which were supposed to be. But in the end, we do forgive, don't we? Because that is the way we get to love.

# AUTHOR'S NOTE

*For Those Who Are Lost* began with the germ of an idea I found while reading one day. My favorite subject at the time was World War II, and I had immersed myself in both fiction and nonfiction books about the effects of the war across the world.

One day, as I was doing some research, a single fact stood out to me: five thousand children from the island of Guernsey had been evacuated to the southern coast of England with their teachers in June 1940. As a teacher myself, I found the idea shocking, and it piqued my curiosity. Further study showed that the government of Guernsey, a self-ruled British crown dependency, had given the islanders a mere twenty-four hour notice of the evacuation, disrupting everyone's lives.

I couldn't imagine thousands of men and women across the island having a single day to make a decision of whether or not to send their child to England for the duration of the war. When France fell to the Nazis, it was clear that the Channel Islands, which lie between England and France, would be the next target of the German army. Guernsey and Jersey would soon be occupied; it was only a matter of time. As it happened, a mere ten days after the evacuation, the Germans made landfall on the Guernsey shore.

Every detail of this novel was carefully researched, from the strict curfews to the collaborators, who aided the Germans during the occupation to make their own lives easier. Not only did the Channel Islanders have to suffer the same wartime fears and hardships as England and allies across Europe, difficult restrictions altered their daily lives. Meetings of more than three people at a time were forbidden on the island. Churches were closed and ransacked, radios and cars were banned. Bus service on the island ceased, and fortifications were built on the coast to prevent England from making any attempt at rescue.

I studied books, articles, and films, including firsthand accounts of those affected by the evacuation and the war, which lasted from June 20, 1940 to May 9, 1945, in order to add as much realism as possible to the book.

Using the backdrop of history enabled me to highlight the difficult decisions made by the two main characters of my story. As we all know, some major life decisions are made in a day, others in the blink of an eye.

*For Those Who Are Lost* is a story of love, loss, and courage, exploring the choices we make in a moment and the reverberations that echo long after those choices are made.

# READING GROUP GUIDE

1. The children's evacuation from Guernsey really happened. If you were one of the Guernsey parents given such short notice, would you have sent your children off the island with their teacher or kept them at home?

2. Throughout the book, Lily changes her mind several times about why she decided to take Catherine with her. Which motivation do you think was most powerful for her in that moment?

3. Compare Ava's and Joseph's methods of dealing with their children's absence and the occupation generally. How do their needs compete?

4. Why do you think the Walkers' deaths were included in Ava's story? Discuss the necessity of imports for people living in isolated areas like Guernsey.

5. Describe the development of Ava's relationship with Becker. Do you think she would have had an affair under any other circumstances?

6. Why do you think Peter decided against enlisting? How do community and ritual help us cope with times of enormous stress?

7. When Lily finally tells him the truth on her deathbed, Peter is left with a very complicated situation to figure out. How do you think he handled it? Do you think the reveal changed the way he grieved for Lily?

8. How would you characterize Henry and Catherine's relationship? What role does Henry play in the eventual reunion of his family?

9. What did you think of the arrangement Ava, Joseph, and Peter made regarding Catherine's care? If you were in Ava's or Joseph's position, could you allow someone else to raise your child? If you were in Peter's position, could you leave your daughter with people she hardly knows?

10. How does Lily's past shape her relationships in Saint Austell? Is she able to make any decisions without the interference of her secrecy and shame? In the end, would you consider Lily a good person?

# A CONVERSATION
# WITH THE AUTHOR

**What inspired you to write *For Those Who Are Lost*? How do you approach writing a new book?**

In the summer of 2019, I attended the Yale Writers' Workshop, and the experience made me think about writing in an entirely new way. I realized it's more important to write something that takes hold of your imagination rather than to try to conform to a notion of what sells or others' expectations of you and your work. If you do the former, you'll have written something you truly love. A couple of months later, when reading about World War II, I came upon information about Guernsey in June 1940, when five thousand students and their teachers were evacuated off the island in a single day. Less than a week later, German troops invaded and would keep these families apart for five long years. I couldn't stop thinking about the heart-wrenching decisions those parents had to make. It felt like the perfect starting place for a story.

**On the surface, Lily's decision to take Catherine is amoral and wrong. Was it challenging to write through that and still present Lily as a sympathetic character?**

For me, Lily began as a sympathetic character, trapped in a terrible marriage with no possibility of escape. When she is presented with an unexpected opportunity to leave the island, she has no idea that she's about to make a terrible, life-altering decision. When forced to choose between going with the evacuees to Manchester or setting off on her own in a new land, she tells herself that she can't abandon the four-year-old in her care, but neither can she take the girl's nine-year-old brother. Later, she struggles with the ramifications of what she has done and explores the hidden motives and consequences of her actions. In the chaos of war, she felt like she was saving a child but soon realizes she has stolen from her daughter the family and future she was meant to have.

**The information about the Guernsey occupation—rationing, surveillance, and limited imports of medicine—is equal parts fascinating and horrifying. How did you research these hardships?**

Research is one of my favorite parts of writing! For this novel, I studied books on the war, devoured articles, talked to World War II veterans, and watched films made both during and after the war to get the feel of the time period. However, the most important source of information was reading firsthand accounts of Guernsey's evacuation and occupation. It gave me a sense of the panic and anxiety that took hold of the island residents. I was also able to find videotaped interviews with people who had either been evacuated or were left behind, witnessing the horrors of war. Watching them retell their stories sixty or seventy years later, you could see that they had never forgotten a single detail of that terrible time and how it had changed them to go through it.

**Why did you decide to keep Catherine with Peter after being reintroduced to her birth family? In your research, did you find any examples of real-life families who made a similar decision?**

There were a wide variety of endings for the evacuated children after the war. Many of the older teens stayed in England with their adopted families to finish school and begin their adult lives. While some children were happy to return to their homes in Guernsey, others suffered a second round of trauma, distressed at being forced to leave their new families and their lives in England. A fraction were never accounted for at the end of the war, leaving their families to cope with a permanent loss.

I think Peter's reluctance to give up Catherine is a beautiful picture of what it must have been like for Lily, and perhaps it helps him come to forgive her. He overcame his own fear of losing his daughter and chose to let the truth come out. However, the truest love in the book is Ava's sacrificial love for her child. When she discovers that Catherine is still alive, she refuses to allow her to go through any more turmoil. Taking her from Peter would cut her off from any parent she had ever known, and Ava couldn't bring herself to do that after everything Catherine had already been through. Joseph was still struggling after being released from a French prison camp, and

Henry was just fourteen, so this was a decision Ava had to make on her own, another split-second call that changed everyone's lives.

**Although guilt plays an obvious role in the book, the characters ultimately choose forgiveness. Why was this important for you to include?**

Life can be messy and complex because we are imperfect human beings. We all need forgiveness at times as well as the ability to forgive in order to have healthy relationships. It's an integral part of happiness.

**Do you relate to any of the book's characters in particular? Who would you most want to befriend?**

I had an equal love for Lily and Ava, two women who have to cope the best they can during the hardships of war. Lily is the more flawed character, but Ava also proves we're only human. We make mistakes and do the best we can with the life we're given. The character I would most like to befriend is Henry. Even as a child, he had such resilience and strength. In the end, he's the glue that holds everyone together.

**What drew you to historical fiction as a writer?**

When I decided to write a novel, I pulled out my five favorite books and spread them out to look at them. The common denominator was that they were all historical. I realized then my love of history and research were perfectly suited to writing historical fiction.

# ACKNOWLEDGMENTS

There are so many people to thank for their help and encouragement in making this book come to life.

First, I'd like to thank my wonderful agent, Victoria Skurnick, for her expertise, guidance, and sense of humor. It keeps me going. Also, special thanks to my editor, Shana Drehs, and the incredible team of professionals at Sourcebooks who have worked tirelessly on my behalf. I have so enjoyed the opportunity to work with each one of you on this book.

In the summer of 2019, I had the pleasure of attending the Yale Writers' Workshop, where I worked to refine my craft under the guidance of director Jotham Burrello and my writing instructor, author Sergio Troncoso. Sergio, you taught us to look at our writing in a whole new way, and I will always be grateful. Thanks also to my fellow writing students, particularly Russell, Suzanne, and Eva. I'm a better writer because of you.

As always, I'd like to express my appreciation to those who encourage me during the process: Lori Naufel, Connie Miller, and Leslie Purcell, along with my sister, Sherry, to whom this book is dedicated.

The book was written during the lockdown of 2020, and my

family was instrumental in helping in so many ways. Thank you to Caitlin for reading rough drafts, to Heather for helping me with technical issues and providing inspiration, and to David for cheering me on. And of course, no acknowledgment would be complete without thanking my husband, author Will Thomas. No one could have been more encouraging during this process than you. Thank you for your love, guidance, and support.

Finally, I'd like to express appreciation to the people of Guernsey who lived through the occupation and who have shared their experiences with us. My life was changed because of you, and I am grateful.